I0598803

This book is a work of fiction. Names, characters, businesses, organizations, places, events and incidents are either a product of the author's imagination or are used fictitiously. Any resemblance to actual persons, living or dead, or locales is entirely coincidental.

Published by Griffyn Ink

www.griffynink.com

Copyright © 2021 Griffyn Ink

For ordering information or special discounts for bulk purchases, please contact Griffyn Ink at Mail@GriffynInk.com.

SAVANNAH KADE

WILDFIRE
HEARTS

UP IN
Smoke

WILDFIRE HEARTS #4

CHAPTER ONE

His breath was heavy in his ears, the sound rattling inside his face shield and through his SCBA gear. Luke moved by feel alone, unable to see through the heavy smoke, but he moved quickly. It was more than just his firefighter training that led him along the path.

He *knew* this house. And the guilt of it weighed heavier on him than the oxygen tank and all the gear.

Oily black smoke rolled down the hallway and was pouring out the windows when the trucks had pulled up. It was obvious the burn was bad at first glance. From inside, it was worse.

Visibility was zero.

Behind him, Jo Huston followed along, staying in constant contact through their comms. He answered her questions by rote, his brain staying focused on what he knew he would find. His heavily gloved hand hit the bump of a doorframe. It had taken far longer to walk the few short steps down the hallway than he'd expected.

Luke could only hope Ivy was still alive.

He quickly issued instructions to Jo to cross the hallway and clear the room opposite this one. It was a single bedroom, normally situated, he knew. Turning back to his own task, he found the doorknob and twisted it. As he entered, the smoke followed him in. That was maybe a good sign that the fire hadn't yet begun to eat this room. Maybe Ivy could be here and be safe …

There was no *safe* inside a burning house, but he prayed she would survive.

The fire wasn't in here. The question was, *was Ivy?* If she was smart, this was where she would come. And Ivy was smart.

He quickly traced the edge of the room, bumping into shelves and desks. It hadn't been his home for years. The furniture was hers. He didn't know where it was or where it would stop him, and he couldn't see a damn thing now that the room had filled with the smoke he'd allowed in.

Locating the closet, and hoping that Ivy would be inside, he swung the door open and reached in almost completely blindly. The place where he'd hung his clothes as a kid and piled his stinky laundry in a heap on the floor was now completely built in with shelves.

As he waved his heavily covered hands through the space, he thought that it wasn't fair that he was protected from the fire and Ivy might not be. But he continued through the check. He'd begged the chief to let him do the search but hadn't said more.

His hands collided with all manner of things. Unidentified items fell off the shelves and tumbled to the floor as he bumbled his way through what seemed like boxes, maybe pens. He hunkered down, wondering if maybe she was curled in a ball, cowering at the bottom of the closet. When people got caught in house fires they hid and they often passed out, unable to call out to firefighters to aid in their own rescue. But the shelving went all the way to the floor. Large boxes were stuffed into place, and there was no room for Ivy Dean.

Quickly abandoning this search, he stood abruptly and returned to tracing the edges of the room. There was another door here. This is why he had chosen to come in here. At some point before even he had lived here, this once midsized second bedroom had been cut in half in an attempt to make two smaller rooms. In the worst possible design—a bedroom off of a bedroom—and Luke was willing to bet it had been someone's home job that wasn't up to code.

He hadn't known it as a kid, and he hadn't been back in this house since then, but even from his memory it had been a shoddy build. His hands touched the wall and sure enough, it still existed. With the heat and pressure, he could almost feel the cheap materials flex under his touch. If the fire touched it, it would burn fast and furious.

He had to find Ivy.

It was the only way to redeem himself.

In recent years, the neighborhood was just starting to gentrify. The local librarian had definitely taken a chance buying this place. Luke continued to feel along the wall, whispering prayers in his native tongue as he went.

As he finally felt the door and grabbed for the doorknob, he would have let out a sigh of relief if he weren't so well trained. It was the only thing keeping him upright now. He pushed open the door and wandered into the space as the voice came through his comm system.

Jo Huston declared her room clear. There wasn't much more to do. He directed her to check the bathroom. Maybe Ivy was cowering in a cool tile tub. He could only hope.

Actually, he hoped the neighbors were wrong and Ivy wasn't really home for this nightmare, despite the fact that all signs indicated she was. If she was, she was here somewhere and he couldn't live with himself if someone didn't find her and save her.

Jo Huston probably shouldn't have been in here, looking for her best friend. But small towns were like that: It was nearly impossible to never run a rescue on someone you didn't already know … or maybe love. He'd seen it before and it was brutal.

The smoke followed him, black and oily, it supplanted the thin gray film that had already found its way in here. But maybe it had been safer to be in this room for a while. Luke felt his way around.

If Ivy were here, she would probably be low to the ground. The librarian was savvy and would have done everything correctly to save herself. But would it be enough?

A preliminary check showed no broken windows. She hadn't escaped from this room. *Shit.*

He ran into a piece of furniture, and then another. Luke circled the room, alternately swearing and praying to a god he wasn't sure he believed in. Then something bumped his leg.

CHAPTER TWO

I vy jolted awake at her first gulp of fresh air. She was jostled about, unable to control her movements. She could only hold on for dear life, but even that seemed to be beyond her.

She was held tightly in the arms of a firefighter running across her front lawn. Her brain swam with the sudden intake of usable oxygen and her thoughts circled like a choir singing too many songs at once as she worked to orient herself.

Reaching up, she looped her arms around the firefighter's neck and held on for dear life. He turned his head, and only as he looked at her square on, was she able to see through the clear face covering.

Luke Hernandez was quiet but competent on the job. Around town, he had a reputation for being a bit of a wild card. He didn't grin at her now the way he did when he came into the library. Now there was no charm, only a disturbingly relieved expression that she was awake and looking at him.

Had she almost died?

Though his bold good looks and his disturbingly disarming smiles had always made her stomach twist, Ivy knew better than to read it as anything more than the slimmest of flatteries. Luke did that with every woman he met. She'd been there when he slid his laminated card across the desk with a grin as though he were gifting her diamonds … only to turn and offer an even sexier smile and a sweeter compliment to Mrs. Diamond—a widower who was eighty if she was a day.

Ivy turned away from Luke's obvious but confusing relief and looked down the street at the neighbors watching her rescue. They were cheering as she felt her face crack into a smile … or maybe almost-sobs. By force of will, she held it together.

She'd built this new life for herself from scratch. She hadn't lost it today. Taking another deep gulp of fresh night air, she realized none of that mattered if it was all burning up behind her.

"Ivy? Ivy?"

He was not … no, he wasn't. Luke Hernandez wasn't asking her out. He was simply doing his job.

"I'm going to put you down now. You're a safe distance from the fire."

The fire. Not *your house.*

He set her onto the cold grass, peeled his face mask, and began an assessment. Still far too serious to offer her that Hernandez charm that he and all his brothers possessed in spades and spread like ones at a strip club.

She was pushing his hands away, about to tell him that she was fine, when two other firefighters showed up. Ronan Kelly had his kit in hand, and his father Patrick—also on the crew— was hastily strapping an oxygen mask on her face, preventing her from saying anything.

"You're not fine, Ivy," Luke told her. "You were just in a serious house fire. You have smoke inhalation and probably burns. I'm just so grateful that you were in that back room."

The other two looked at him oddly as though they, too, felt

his heartfelt declaration was a little over the top. *The guy was just doing his job, right?*

Luke explained, "She was smart and put multiple doors between her and the origin point."

He talked over her head as if she wasn't even there.

She pulled the mask down again to say, "I'm fine," when she remembered her manners. "Thank you."

She sighed. "I wish I was as smart as you're giving me credit for. I was just working in the back office and fell asleep." She didn't mention why she'd been in her office so late and hoped her computer had turned the screen off before he got there.

A hand fell on her shoulder, jolting her thoughts.

"Damn, Ivy. I'd hug you, but I'm filthy."

Ivy jumped up and hugged her best friend Jo anyway. She was already a mess and despite being blond and small and always dressed like a librarian, she didn't care about dirt. Over Jo's shoulder, she looked back to see smoke billowing out from every window of her home. Firefighters with hoses turned on to it and some aimed for the neighbor's houses, wetting them down so that her burn didn't turn into theirs.

As she watched it all get eaten by flames, Ivy felt like she was going to vomit. That was everything. *Everything.* There was no backup plan.

She'd bought the house at the higher end of her ability, thinking she only had to make it three or four years with no major disasters. She hadn't made it one year.

The only good thing was that she'd absolutely forbidden herself from buying a house she couldn't afford to lose. She never invested in anything she couldn't afford to lose. But this came close, so painfully close. Fixing this would hurt hard and take every bit of the cushion she had. She'd be back at zero and zero had been a shitty place.

She had no family to stay with and only her own savings as a cushion. This was definitely going to be a hard fall.

She held on to Jo far too tightly until Jo had to extract herself explaining, "I'm so sorry Ivy. I've got to go finish the job."

Jo was trying to save her house. But Ivy could see it was a lost cause along with everything in it. Black inky smoke billowed out, stealing everything. Orange flames licked at her new living room furniture, taunting her as they ate her prized possessions.

Grasping for something, for anything that made sense, she said, "I don't think I left anything on. Did something short circuit?"

She'd had the house thoroughly inspected before she bought it—exactly so that she wouldn't have a disaster in the first few years. Had her inspector not been competent?

She was chasing these odd thoughts to keep from going crazy as Luke crowded her, his bare fingers now pressing softly on her wrist. For whatever reason she hadn't felt them before, but now the human contact jolted through her.

On her left Ronan Kelly still examined her, probably checking for burns and scrapes. She looked first to Luke, but his mouth was pressed into a thin line. Whatever this was, he didn't like it.

Ivy turned to Ronan, her eyes asking the same question.

He shook his head at her. "It wasn't your fault. This was arson."

CHAPTER THREE

"Oh, I couldn't," Ivy protested. The words automatically came out of her mouth, though Jo was offering her exactly what she needed.

"Yes, you can." Jo didn't push so far as to say, "And you *will,*" but it seemed implied.

Ivy's automatic protests continued even if she knew it wasn't what she wanted. The refusal was ingrained. "I can't afford half your rent. Certainly not after my house—"

"Your house burned down," Jo interrupted smoothly. "Which is exactly why you need to be my guest."

Ivy was still shaking her head. There was something about the offer that put her father's voice right back into her head. *We don't owe anyone.*

Always refuse offers. Never be indebted.

But her old life didn't work. And her old life wasn't here in Redemption, the place where she'd landed after she'd worked so hard to shed her past. It was impressive how often the old ways still reared their head. So many times she realized she was wearing the old mantel and she had to once again take it off, though she had no idea when it had been put back on. It was simply always appearing.

"There's no rent included," Jo told her as her friend moved her head back and forth, trying to catch Ivy's gaze. "I've been paying the rent on this place by myself for some time, so I don't need the help. I do have a trust fund."

Jo grinned at the last one, though Ivy had no idea what that kind of safety net would feel like. Still, she opened her mouth one more time, the protests trying to come through.

Ivy was up to her neck in trouble. Her homeowners insurance would take her deductible, and that would chunk part of her savings. And the insurance wouldn't cover everything. Though it should cover a place for her to stay in the meantime, there were still so many other expenses—food, clothes, and transportation sprang to mind. And she was confident that others would continue to surprise her randomly.

Her brain faltered. *Her car! How was her car?* It had been in the garage and she hadn't even thought to ask about it. Latching onto one idea, she told herself that if her car was okay, she could survive this hit.

So her brain churned and her mouth opened to ask, to cling to one hope. She wasn't crying yet, but she would be. She was just still in shock right now.

Jo waved a hand in front of her face, palm open, as if to say, *just stop.* What Jo actually said was, "If this were me and my home had burned down, you would have offered me a place to stay. Wouldn't you?"

Ivy nodded. She knew where this was going, and she was already caught in the trap.

"And you wouldn't have charged me rent, would you?" Jo pointed out.

Ivy shook her head. She wouldn't have. Trying to think rationally, she walked through the reverse option. Had she given Jo a place to stay rent free, she never would have considered that Jo would owe her in return. So this time, when she opened her mouth. She forced herself to say the words. "Thank you. It means everything."

The relief on her friend's face at having won the argument was clear. But Jo was always about moving forward. "Can you get one of your neighbors to bring you to the station?"

Now that the decision was made, Ivy's best friend was all tactical logistics. Ivy looked around and found herself nodding. She could make that happen. She had trained herself to accept small favors, like a ride here or there, a paid-for lunch, a present. Birthday presents had been the hardest to accept, but she'd done it.

In the early days, she wouldn't have been able to take the offer. Staying at Jo's apartment just seemed like such a big ask. But she hadn't asked, Jo had simply volunteered, and Ivy needed to learn to accept help.

The firefighters would be leaving on their trucks once all the cleanup was done. Jo was still on shift until eight in the morning. Maybe they'd let Ivy sleep at the station for a while. Maybe she could get into the library and stay there. Did she even have her keys?

With a massive sigh, she realized she didn't. They were all on a hook hanging just inside the kitchen. So neat, so organized ... so inaccessible.

Also, she smelled awful and desperately needed a shower. Her head almost fell back as she realized she didn't have any clean clothes. Everything was inside the house, since that was a normal place to store clothing, and everything in the house was possibly damaged beyond repair. At best, it was going to take several days to get in and anything salvageable would need serious cleaning.

A hand fell on her shoulder, heavily padded by thick gloves. Jo grabbed on and rattled her a little bit. "I got you covered for everything. You can borrow anything in my closet, too. Please, don't worry about this."

The last line indicated that Jo knew there was no way Ivy wouldn't worry. So she was only telling her not to worry about a place to stay and clothing to wear. For a moment Ivy imagined herself heading into the library the next morning in Jo's clothing—as if she could show up in leggings and a sports bra, probably in a bright pink or orange. Would Jo's running shoes fit her? She almost laughed hysterically.

But Jo's voice was calm and reassuring. "Come to the station. We'll get you set."

Ivy nodded, looking around. "My car?"

Jo shook her head, and Ivy felt her heart fall as though this were the straw that would break her. But Jo's words were at least a little better than she expected.

"We won't know about it until the last of the fire is out and we do a final inspection. We'll open the garage and see."

That was better than the car simply being gone.

"The keys are on the hook, just inside the kitchen," Ivy told her as though they might find her car was drivable and that Jo might deliver it.

High hopes.

When Jo turned back to the work, Ivy tried to step toward the house to get a better view of the damage. She had to know what was wrong before she could fix it.

"You can't go in." Luke Hernandez held his arm in front of her, the touch jolting even through all his padding.

Still, she tried to move her way past his bulk. "I'm not going to go inside."

Was her voice really that raspy? Did her breath hurt just a little or was she making it all up because she was traumatized? Ivy also tried to snap the words out, though she wasn't sure she'd really achieved it.

She knew better than that. "I just wanted to get close and—"

"But you can't." He cut her off. "It's too dangerous."

But she *needed* to check. She needed to count what was salvageable and what wasn't. She couldn't plan and prepare if she didn't know. And she believed that if she could just get a handle on it, she could save herself from the overwhelming feeling that the fire had been cosmic.

Luke had found her in the back room and praised her for getting to the safest place, but she hadn't done any such thing.

She'd turned the odd little back room into her office because it had more windows, even though it moved through another room first. She'd been back there into the late hours and had fallen asleep at her little desk. Not because she was escaping the fire, but because it was her anniversary.

Every year on her anniversary, she allowed herself to search for anything she could find. The rest of the year, she let them not even exist to her. Last night, she'd found a new baby and a wedding.

They weren't easy to find, and she'd eventually fallen asleep across her open laptop. The firefighters had saved her from that room. There was at least smoke damage and maybe more. Maybe her computer was burned, but maybe when the firefighters went in today to inspect the damage, they would see what she'd been looking at.

And how would she survive if they knew?

CHAPTER FOUR

"Did Ivy seem off to you?" Luke asked to the open room and anyone who would listen.

It was Ronan who answered. "Dude, her house just went up in flames. Any one of us would be off and we're firefighters. She's not."

"No." Luke shook his head. "It was more than that."

But Ronan dismissed him, once again suggesting that barely getting saved from a house fire was more than enough to account for it.

Maybe he was wrong, Luke thought. He'd possibly just misread the whole thing. Lord knew, he was more than a little "off" right now himself. Maybe he was trying to drag everyone's attention away from the fire, simply by stoking the conversation with something new.

It was five a.m. before the last truck had left the street where Ivy lived. Yellow tape had been cordoned around the yard and a police officer had been stationed to keep any lookie-loos from getting too close and to keep teenagers from killing themselves thinking they were being brave. And to keep anyone—maybe even the arsonist—from tampering with the evidence that would need to wait until it had cooled off and until there was daylight to see it.

Technically it wasn't his problem anymore, but Luke knew it was. And it was going to be his problem for quite some time. Chief Taggart and Sebastian Kane would head back after the sun was up and do a thorough arson inspection. Though even in the dark of night and through the roiling black smoke, all the firefighters agreed, it looked like an accelerant had been used.

The whole place had gone up in flames, looking like the fire had started at the base of the foundation. He might not be a trained investigator, but Luke had been able to see clearly that the area around the house had been doused.

Aside from going in to rescue the librarian, they'd mostly been concerned with staying safe and making sure no one was caught in a flashover or under a falling beam. It seemed the good news was they caught the fire early enough to stop it. A neighbor had been smart enough to call it in at the first sign of odd smoke. But the flames had spread quickly before the time the trucks had arrived.

Even now his heart clenched at the sheer luck that Ivy had been lucky to be in that back room. And for that Luke was grateful. Live saves were rare. He wasn't sure if this one counted. *Hell, if anyone else knew what he knew, it wouldn't count at all.*

If they knew what he knew, he would be getting carted off to prison.

When they'd returned, he'd entered the station, feet dragging as he waved the others into the showers first. They had it down to a science so all the firefighters could go through in two quick rotations. Tonight, he'd been more than willing to be in the second round.

So far, no one had put him in handcuffs and dragged him away. So he was counting that as a win.

The fact that he was still standing here a free man, made him suspect the others didn't have the information that he did. Thus, he would hold out a little bit longer, see if he could figure out what was happening with a minimum of damage to himself and those he loved.

"Hernandez!"

The voice came from over his shoulder and, lightning quick, all of his blood froze. *He hadn't fooled anyone, had he?*

Trying to act normal, and wishing he could remember what normal looked like, Luke turned to see the chief waving him into his office.

Fuck.

So much for not being hauled away.

The chief was a wonderful boss, and he was likely letting Luke know that the officers would be here at any moment to arrest him.

Trying not to let any of his thoughts show, Luke headed in. The chief didn't make him close the door, which either meant the news wasn't that bad or else Luke was simply the last to find out.

Looking at his boss, Luke tried to keep his face neutral and hoped that any odd responses would simply be chalked up to the crazy evening and the fact that everyone was exhausted.

"Why'd you trade out for Kelly?" The question was somehow both blunt and pointed.

Luke lied through his teeth. "One of my friends lived there growing up and I know the layout. I knew it was weird."

"What do you mean weird?" Taggart asked, tapping his pencil on the desk. He'd leaned back in the way that they all knew meant he was thinking things through but hadn't reached a conclusion yet. The good thing was the chief was easy to read.

"The room where I found Ivy— I mean Miss Dean—" he corrected himself, "—was a room off of a room." He hoped all of this made some semblance of sense. He hoped it passed for the truth.

16

"The family that lived there—" *true*, he thought, though not *the truth*, "—had several kids. I don't know if that family did the work or not, but they divided the one bedroom into two with a flimsy wall, and between the rooms they still only had the one hallway door. The other bedroom came off from the first one."

He was motioning with his hands, but Taggert was still frowning at him. Luke quickly grabbed a pencil from an old tin can and a scrap of paper, sketching out the odd shape of the room.

"So it was evenly divided?" Taggart asked.

"Right. But if you look at the layout, I don't think there was any way to connect this room into the hallway." He pointed to each space, showing how the odd little room was tucked too far into the corner of the footprint. "And it wasn't a very good job, either. The wall was flimsy, and I don't know the materials it was made of. And I'm sure it wasn't on the blueprint. But, because I knew the house, I volunteered to go in."

After a few more moments of explanation, Taggart was nodding at him, "Good call."

The praise fell heavily onto his shoulders. It was entirely unearned and Luke only nodded and headed out as soon as he was dismissed.

He hit the showers, as though he could wash away the lies. Then he waited out the few remaining hours until the shift was over. His body ached for him to go home, crawl into bed and sleep for the next day, the way he was relatively certain the rest of A-shift was going to do. But he couldn't.

Instead, he climbed in his car and made his usual right hand turn out of the station, so as not to tip anyone off. But very quickly he doubled back, hoping he knew where to find his prey.

CHAPTER FIVE

Luke groaned and lifted his head as his phone buzzed loudly at him a second time. *Not* okay.

Then again, he thought, none of it had been okay. He hadn't found what he'd been looking for despite the fact that Redemption was plenty small and he shouldn't have had to try so hard.

He'd fought the urge to follow a path that would take him past the old arson sites. It wouldn't do to be seen there, especially if Kane and chief Taggart had caught on to the pattern. He could almost feel his heart breaking, thinking about watching his beloved childhood memories burn, one after another.

How many more would it take before someone else saw where the path led?

There were only a few options for how this could play out, and none of them were good. None of them were safe for Luke. He would either rot in prison or go down in flames himself ... Unless he could get ahead of it.

Today hadn't helped though. He'd certainly tried but, eventually, he'd given up, come home, and tumbled face first into bed. While everyone else had been asleep since maybe eight-thirty or nine, he'd now barely had a few hours.

So as his phone buzzed at him with another text from Ronan, Luke cursed it and tried to decide what to do.

Though Luke was only able to read it through fuzzy eyes, he made out the message.

—At Snafu. Where you at?

He blinked but his eyes only got fuzzier. Luckily, the message was pretty standard between them and he was able to make it out by the shapes of the words. It was a command invitation to head out and join the crowd.

What if he said no?

The problem was that he'd already fucked up in the middle of the night with the fire by telling his chief that he needed to be the one to go into the house. Then he'd screwed up further by lying to Taggart. If the chief figured out the connection, that would only look worse. But Luke hadn't been able to figure out any other way to save everyone. And he wasn't going to let Ivy Dean burn because of his own bad decisions.

If he didn't show up tonight, it would look odd and he couldn't afford any more abnormalities to his behavior. So he sat on the side of the bed, holding the phone between two hands, and forced himself to tap out a message.

—On my way.

He needed a shower. He'd fallen straight into the bed without one. At least he'd had one at the station last night, but he needed another after the hard sleep he'd just powered through. Running the water cold, he tried to think through what he needed to do just to be normal.

Normal was everything right now. It was his only cover. He needed to have two beers—probably enough to look reasonable and hopefully not enough to knock him out tonight. He needed to flirt with Tierney or Amy or whoever was waiting on his table. He always flirted and it never went any further. His reputation was entirely unwarranted.

As an adult, he could look back and see how he'd wound up here. Hindsight made it clear that flirting had been the only way to not be an asshole in his family. It wasn't rude, and it wouldn't get him mercilessly teased by his older brother or his father. After his father died, his mother had been her same giving, kind self, but then she'd worked two or three jobs to support her four sons. She'd never been home. Though the boys had been fed and housed, they had raised themselves.

Luke was sad to report that he was the most stable of the lot. He'd gone into firefighting because four-year college hadn't been an option. Sadly, with his record and his family ties, neither had police work. Firefighting was respectable work and luckily, he loved it.

He had a lot to live down, much of it inherited, but much of it of his own making, too. And now was not the time to make waves.

Just when he'd begun to think he could inch his way forward, the fires had started. He was torn between feeling angry and sad and worried that the universe was actively and constantly working against him.

Stepping out of the shower, he ran a towel over his head. Awake enough to play out the evening, he put on jeans and a T shirt and shoved his feet into sneakers because his brothers wore boots and he wasn't them.

In a handful of minutes, he was walking in the door at Snafu, the large circular booth in the corner already occupied by his buddies from A-shift, only tonight, Jo had brought along her new roommate, Ivy Dean.

Luke was surprised by the jolt in the center of his chest as he laid eyes on her.

She wore jeans and a bright pink sweater with enough holes to see the black tank underneath. She didn't look like Jo, whose closet Luke suspected she'd been shopping in, but she didn't quite look like the prim librarian, either. Scooting over, she patted the seat next to her as everyone shuffled to make room for him.

"Hi Ivy," he said softly. "I hope you're doing okay."

"I'm barely holding it together!" She said it far too jovially for the stark admission the words offered. And she raised a huge mug in her slim fingers as she saluted him. "But thank you."

The last words were soft and somewhat scared and only for his ears.

The booth was packed with him in it. His thigh laid alongside hers, his shoulder touching the soft yarn of the sweater and Ivy turned to him, a small smile on her lips.

She might be alive today because of him.

Was the smile one of gratitude or was it maybe something more?

CHAPTER SIX

Ivy was watching everyone. With everything that had happened, her concerns about her clothing were superfluous and stupid. But she held on to them tightly.

Maybe it was easier to think about clothes because she could do something about it. Everyone had commented on what she wore—all of it kind and complimentary. She'd showed up in Jo's tight jeans and bright pink sweater, not her usual colors.

Had she been in Redemption long enough that this wouldn't change what they thought of her? Had she established herself as smart, but not interested? As hard working, but not a party girl?

This clothing wasn't as unfamiliar to her as they might think it was. In fact, she'd pushed decency much further, many, many times. And she'd been so used to the skimpy clothing and the tight, short skirts speaking for her that she wondered what this was saying now. So far, it hadn't caused a problem.

What was causing a problem was Luke Hernandez. Why was her heart skipping a beat? And why was she drawn to him when he wasn't even flirting with her?

That had to be the worst. He couldn't find a cute or casually praising thing to say to her when he always had a ready compliment for everyone. He did it so much that the phrases and the sweet nothings rolled off of his lips like honey. But now, when he looked at her in full sincerity, and inquired about how she was doing, she lost it.

For the first time, his smile worked on her—the shy one, not the overly charming one. The simple movements, where he grabbed for her beer right before she would have knocked it over, lifted it up, and handed it back spoke of attention. He'd carefully set it in front of her, his fingers lightly brushing hers as she reached to steady herself.

"Sorry," she said, scrambling to say something to somber Luke.

"Too much to drink?"

She pointed to the glass. "This is my first beer." And it was quite obvious that it was barely halfway gone. It shouldn't have been enough to make her drunk.

"Are you okay?" There it was again. The concern in his voice grabbed at her. And that was stupid—just stupid. It was worse than being charmed by his flirting. The concern wasn't even plausibly personal: It was his *job*.

So she told herself to stuff it down. "I don't know. How long was I without oxygen last night?"

She smiled as she said it, but Luke shook his head at her. "That's not funny."

Perfect, she thought. She'd been chastised by the man who was charming to every single person in town, apparently everyone except her.

"I was worried about you."

Oh, hell. He shouldn't say that. She wasn't dealing with anything well enough to handle the onslaught that was a truly concerned-looking Luke Hernandez.

She told herself he *shouldn't* have been worried. His job was to detach himself from the fires and the victims. At least that's what Jo told her. Jo had the advantage of still being relatively new in town. The guys, especially some of the ones who'd grown up around here—like the Hernandez boys—apparently knew pretty much every address.

Dispatch had sometimes received calls that said, "Ted's house over on the East End had a fire in the garage." And that had apparently been enough for the Redemption 911 operator to be able to send units to the right place. She and Jo had laughed about it. So she told herself that Luke knew everyone and he knew he wasn't supposed to get personally involved in the cases.

Interestingly enough—though Ivy had grown up in a small, tight-knit community—even use of the fire department would have been considered an obligation to pay back.

"I'm fine," she told Luke, having a sudden moment where everything in her rebelled at the concern in his voice. She bit off the words, *I can take care of myself, and make my own decisions.* But it was almost as though he heard them anyway, despite the fact that they had not come out of her mouth ... not for some time.

She'd quit saying it, and started doing it, years ago, and it had cost her *everything.*

That had all been her doing though. When she and Lily had gone out that last night, she'd known what it could set in motion. And though they'd rolled the dice before, and always come up lucky, that night they hadn't. She hadn't been prepared for the betrayal, though.

But at least when she left that place, she had been her own person.

Now her house burning felt like karma—Karma that she wasn't sure if she deserved or not. Karma that she wasn't sure why it had come at her.

Leaning closer to Luke, she ignored the way the scent of him made her breath catch. Surely, that was just leftover smoke inhalation, right?

"Was it arson?"

Maybe she'd caught him unprepared for that question. Hell, she'd leaned in and whispered, maybe he'd expected the kind of come on that he must surely get plenty of, the way he flirted.

He nodded and took another sip of his beer. He wasn't really drinking it, she noticed, and filed that thought away for later.

"Why my place? What did I do?"

"It wasn't you." The words came too quickly and too easily to be anything but the truth. She wondered how he could know that.

"Do I need to worry about bringing something to Jo's?"

Even though he told her it wasn't her fault, that didn't change anything. It didn't matter whether it was or wasn't. If something was after her, it was after her.

He hesitated before he answered, and that spoke volumes.

CHAPTER SEVEN

"*A*re you ready?"

Ivy took a deep breath, but she didn't move and neither did Luke. They stood on the front porch where she'd stopped, unable to take another step. Maybe she was close enough.

To either side of her she could see the black streaks that climbed the outside walls of the house. No bit of her cheap vinyl siding had been left unscathed. It would all have to be replaced. But in most places the walls had held.

Through the window, she could see the charred and black interior—furniture crumbled, curtains missing, rough edges lined with soot. What had once been her home was now ruined.

Maybe they'd been right. The old thoughts about 'they' entered her head, unbidden but still there. Maybe she *had* been too prideful of what she'd accomplished.

But when she'd walked away, she told herself that she didn't believe that anymore. And if she didn't believe it, she had to not believe it. *This wasn't a punishment.*

"Are you ready?" Luke asked again. There was no change in

his tone, just the repetition as though he hadn't even said it the first time.

"Yes." She offered the one word with conviction, though it was conviction in tone only. She didn't feel it.

It had been three days since the fire, and she still wasn't prepared to look at the damage. Luke had volunteered on his day off to walk her safely through, so she could make a plan. So that B-shift wouldn't have to lose a firefighter to help her.

As he opened the door, she looked at the hollowed out black shell. Large patches of drywall were missing and the studs she could now see were blackened and cracked. The ceiling was soot from corner to corner, and the smell was overwhelming. It must already be starting to mold.

Luke's arms came around her before she even realized she was crumpling to the dirty floor and crying.

There was nothing left. No way this could be salvaged.

"It's okay," he told her. "It's okay."

But it wasn't. Forcing her legs underneath her, Ivy stood of her own accord. With her voice having returned, she simultaneously thanked Luke and pushed him away.

"May I?" She pointed toward the center of the room and waited until he nodded.

"That's why we had to wait so long to get you let in. But it's all been cleared. The floor is safe."

She nodded resolutely, not looking at him as she stepped inside. She was being crushed. She couldn't breathe. And when she did, she inhaled the after-effects of smoke, flame retardant, water, and a hint of something volatile.

Stepping gingerly into the room, Ivy made her way past the wooden frames and shriveled synthetic tufts that had once been her prized chairs. Comfortable and fluffy, they'd looked like the ones she'd always wanted when she was a kid and snuck the magazines out of the mail. Another loss.

She moved quickly past the carcasses and into the kitchen.

She didn't have much. She'd been brought up in a simple life and once she was on her own, the small number of things she had still seemed a bit excessive to her. It wasn't that she was trying to make her life small, it was simply that she'd realized she didn't need all of the extras. So it hurt even more to lose what she had decided to keep.

The kitchen was an odd mosh of death and life. Some of the cabinets retained their shiny, glossy coating, while others were blackened. One charred door hung by the lower hinge, hinting that it would clatter to the floor at any moment. Turning away from what she couldn't bear to look at, she hoped Luke couldn't see her tears as she headed down the hallway.

There was black around the doorframes, but she turned the handle to the odd little pair of rooms that she had cobbled into both a storage and an office space. But as she stepped inside, she gasped.

"Amazing, isn't it?" Luke's voice startled her. He must be right behind her, but she'd been lost in her own grief.

She stumbled back into the hard wall that was his chest. His hands came up to grab her shoulders and steady her, but in a moment she was back on her feet and walking across the carpet.

The room was practically pristine.

"We opened the windows and let it air out." He was following her inside, explaining despite the fact that she wasn't absorbing any of it. "You'll need to air it a little bit more. But a good carpet cleaner can take care of it."

She almost laughed. Why should she get a good carpet cleaner service for what had never been a good carpet? It was old and beaten. When she'd bought the place, it was already faded. The combination of the little house being all that she could afford and it already having a personality of its own was enough for her. Ivy had promised herself she'd upgrade as she went along, but now she was going to have to fight just to get back to the status quo.

Heading into the second room, she was stunned to find it much the same—pristine and almost clean. Her laptop still sat on the desk under the window. It was easy to see where she'd sat looking into the small backyard. When she looked out, she saw her hibiscus was still in bloom.

Small wonders.

But it wasn't, she reminded herself. The fire couldn't be a punishment for pride or how would her garden still be so lovely?

She almost laughed. It had likely gotten watered to hell and back the other night. Hitting a key on her computer, Ivy watched as the screen came to life. Nothing was missing in here, even the tech seemed intact. As the system filled in every icon and opened her documents a huge sigh of relief fell out of her. Then her internet browser restored all the information she'd been searching when she'd fallen asleep in here.

While she was glad her router hadn't burned, she wondered how many people had been through here and seen what she was searching? Her history was probably now part of the investigation.

Turning around and ignoring those possible ramifications, she pushed past Luke and practically ran into the bedroom. Aside from the hallway, this whole part of the house was mostly intact.

"You closed your doors," Luke told her by way of explanation. "It's dramatic. It prevents the spread of fire."

"But the outside ...?" She'd seen the blackened streaks on every wall. So how could what was inside have survived?

"Someone put accelerant all around the outside of the house in a ring, right at the base—in the flower beds and everything. So the siding is a mess. But accelerant burns faster than other materials, which means it burns first. So the damage didn't come through the walls. On this half of the house, just the outside needs work."

She could live with this, Ivy thought. Maybe she could even live in this end of the house while it was repaired.

But Luke seemed to see what she was thinking. "You can't, you can't stay here. The living room and the kitchen, they all need to be repaired before it's livable. It's not safe with the odors and the mold. How's your homeowners insurance?"

At least that was okay. "It's good. The deductible is pretty high."

"We can help."

His offer made her shake her head. "I've got it."

"Unless you went really high end ..." he trailed off, letting her know that he didn't expect anyone in this neighborhood to have top notch insurance. "It won't cover everything. But I'll help."

For a moment, she stared at him, wondering at the sincerity of the offer and hating again the impulse to just say no. That she would need to do all of it herself.

"I don't know." Ivy was proud of herself for finding at least a middle ground. "How would I ever repay you?"

But Luke Hernandez only shook his head. "You don't need to repay me. You won't owe me anything. I need to help you fix this place up because I owe you."

CHAPTER EIGHT

Oh, wow. He managed to hold in the comment that wanted to roll off his tongue. Luke had not been prepared for the woman who walked toward him. In jeans and a T shirt, Ivy Dean strode across her own lawn wearing sneakers and a tool belt strapped expertly around her hips.

It matched his own, only hers was brand spanking new. He wanted to ask, *do you know how to use that thing?* as he was always worried when someone showed up with a shiny hammer and a tape measure that had never been pulled before. But he'd learned better than to ask that question. No one liked to be told they were out of their league.

Her head tilted to the side as she spotted the setup in the driveway. "What's this?"

"The guys dropped their tools off so we can get started." He was proud of that. The A-shift crew all loved Ivy. Hell, Sebastian and Kalan owed her a debt that they might never be able to repay. Now, Luke did, too. He tried to cover his guilt with words. "We'll need to lock them all in the garage before we leave."

The garage had been spared, though the siding would need a

total replacement. But the interior of the garage—and even Ivy's car—had survived fine thanks to the cinderblock construction.

"Do you guys just collect woodworking tools?"

He shrugged. "Pretty much. The job requires that we're familiar with a variety of kinds of construction. If we don't know how it was built, we don't know how it comes down." She was nodding along and Luke had always enjoyed watching people absorb that aspect of his work. "Also, carpentry is an easy gig to pick up on the side."

"I'll pay you," she offered, once again hopping on any kind of mention of his work. But again, he refused.

This was his fault. He had come close to telling her so when they'd done the walk through. But even though he'd like to admit it, he couldn't. He didn't even know what he'd be admitting to. And that was the problem: if he threw someone under the bus, he needed to know that it was the right person.

If he told the world his suspicions and he was wrong, he would ruin a life. If he didn't tell, and this got pinned on him, he'd spend the rest of his life in prison unless he could prove his way out of it.

His heart beat harder these days. It had ratcheted up a little with the first fire. And then the second arson had torched the home where his family had lived when he was four. A third fire had eaten a small, abandoned store at the edge of town where he and Tiago had once held jobs—a job that he'd loved because the owner had taken good care of him and treated him like family.

The recent spate of arson fires in Redemption traced the path of Luke's childhood. He might have figured it out before anyone else, but very quickly, someone else would too. He had no idea how much time he had to save his own ass.

Hell, even he would have suspected himself. Had he gotten blackout drunk and lost hours, he would have believed he was doing it. Because who else could it be? But he had his suspicions, and they only made him feel worse.

"What do you think we should tackle first?" Ivy asked when she turned away from admiring the sawhorses and makeshift tables that held compound miter saws, sanders, and even a tile cutter.

"I think we have to go through the main rooms where the walls are exposed and check every stud and replace every one that doesn't pass muster. The inspection showed the roof is fine, though."

"Well, that's a relief." Ivy opened the front door and left it standing wide.

Luke followed her in, but moved quickly through the house opening windows to let it air out again. It was cold, but they'd be working and since they could monitor the building, now was a good time to freshen as much as they could without worrying about looting. Ivy followed him from room to room, and once all the doors and windows were open, she stepped back into the living room.

Moving into one corner, Luke got to work. He pulled out his flashlight and peered behind what drywall remained. It looked okay, he thought, but he'd need a better view. He started reaching for his crowbar when a sound came from behind him.

The cracking of plaster had him turning and he was surprised to see that Ivy already had her own crowbar out and was making short work of what few pieces remained on the wall in front of her. She'd clearly had the same thought as him, but Luke held his tongue.

In a few moments, they'd littered the middle of the floor with pieces of drywall until all the studs were bare.

"Where did the furniture go?" he asked.

"Jo and I rented a little trailer and hauled it to the dump." She sighed again. "Then I had to spend money on these clothes because Jo's jeans cost more than my weekly salary."

He almost laughed but understood about Jo. His fellow firefighter didn't need the paycheck, but she'd proven herself time and time again.

Ivy was still talking, and he found himself paying rapt attention. "The good news though is the hall closet was closed. So, while I need to wash every piece of linen in there, it all survived. I have to wash every piece of fabric. Jo's laundry is getting a workout."

Luke smiled. No one had quite known what to make of Jo Huston when she'd first arrived on A-shift. The brusque, straightforward firefighter with the trust fund had seemed a highly unlikely friend for the prim and proper town librarian, but the two had seemed inseparable since the day Jo arrived. Now, Luke was glad that Ivy had a warm home and a welcoming friend with room to spare.

As he cataloged all the ways he could help Ivy, she turned away and began testing the studs in the walls. In the corner, they were sturdy, still yellow wood, protected by the drywall that had remained, but the fourth was blackened, the fire having alligatored the surface. Ivy deemed it unsuitable.

With a steady gloved hand, she went after it until she had it expertly removed. Then she proceeded to pull out the next three.

Just as Luke was reaching out to stop her, she turned away. Lifting the wood pieces she'd been chucking onto the ruined flooring, she hefted them against her hip and carted them into the front yard, where she unceremoniously dropped them.

He was almost too stunned to do anything. But he quickly got himself together and grabbed the remainders of what had been heaped on the floor and followed her out.

Just as he was getting ready to open his mouth, she pulled a two by six from the palette of lumber she'd had delivered for the job. Hefting it up, she sighted it to check it was straight before carrying it to the small workshop they'd set up.

Moving into place, she quickly measured it with her too-new tape, and flipped the switch on the saw. He'd managed to hold off judgment until that moment, but Ivy Dean, sweater twinset wearing librarian, was handling lumber like she'd done more than just read about it. She'd known not to remove too many studs in one location, and that she should replace them as she went. He watched as she handled a vice clamp, expertly creating a jig that would make all the boards a uniform length.

"You know what you're doing, don't you?"

With her safety glasses in place, her hands cleanly away from the moving blade, she turned the noisy saw off and looked up at him. "Did you think I wouldn't?"

He shrugged, not wanting to admit he'd not expected it at all. "I didn't think the librarian would have mad carpentry skills."

She only laughed and said, "You have no idea how many barns I've raised."

It was such an odd phrase. One that he wouldn't use, despite the fact that he'd replaced countless numbers of walls and built far too many decks to remember.

"When were you raising barns?" And why did no one know about this?

But she brushed him off as though she hadn't even said that. "Help me line this first one up?"

Luke followed her back inside, her expertise and easy handling of the lumber told him this wasn't her first wall. *So why wouldn't she talk about it?*

CHAPTER NINE

"Mama, where's Tiago?" Luke watched as the ash on her cigarette grew to a horrifying length. When he'd been a kid, her ability to grow ash and never drop it was a skill he admired. Now it petrified him.

Whoever was following his childhood path and lighting it on fire wouldn't need to set his mother's home ablaze. She would do it herself, eventually. Taking another drag on the cigarette, she eyeballed him as if to say that was the stupidest question she'd ever heard. "I don't know where Tiago is. He's an adult."

Luke fought the urge to throw his head back and laugh. Tiago had never been an adult. He was merely older these days. "Is he in prison, Mama?"

"I don't think so."

Didn't that just say it all? His mother loved her four sons. She'd shown it by working herself to the bone and making sure they had what they needed. But what she'd missed was being there for them. Not her fault, Luke knew, but it had manifested in different ways in all four of them.

Most of those ways had not been good. Though Luke was

confident she still loved them all, she was tired, so tired that she didn't even know if her oldest was in prison or not.

"All right," he said. "Thank you, Mama."

He leaned over and kissed her on her forehead. That at least made her smile. It was the least he could do for all she had given them—even if it hadn't been enough.

"You have to get back to that fancy job of yours?" she asked, finally flicking the long ash into the old brown glass tray next to her. Both it and she looked like relics.

Again, he wanted to laugh—as if being a firefighter was a *big fancy job*. But seeing his mother and seeing where his brothers had ended up, he could also see where she would believe that. "I do."

As he turned to leave, he had another almost more horrifying thought. "What about Mario?"

"What about him?" She shrugged as though she also had no idea about her third child.

"Is he in rehab?"

"Why would he be in rehab? He's doing great." She took another drag and Luke's heart broke for her lungs and all the damage her smoking had already done. Again, though, he knew she was a victim of her circumstances. She'd given the boys enough to get out and make things better even if she hadn't been able to do it for herself. Luke and Carlos had actually taken advantage of the possibilities.

Luke didn't even know what she meant that Mario was "doing great." For a brother who'd already been through rehab twice and had insisted all the way up until the moment he entered the facility each time that he was clean and had stayed sober, there was no trusting what he reported. Luke couldn't trust his mother either. He'd have to see it for himself.

Another thought hit. "What about J-ho? You see him anymore?"

His mother looked at him like he'd gone off his rocker. "Why are you asking about J-ho? And why would I even see him?"

J-ho and Tiago had been inseparable as kids and that was the problem. Lupe Hernandez had never hidden the fact that she wasn't home. It wasn't unusual in their neighborhoods. So the neighbors had relied on each other to watch the kids because they'd all worked their fingers to the bone and none of the parents could afford real childcare.

Luke realized now that meant the possible suspect pool of arsonists who could have followed Luke from home to home was larger than he might imagine. Tiago had done time. If Luke told the chief to look into his oldest brother, Tiago would likely go back in whether he'd done it or not.

His mother would plausibly disown him for turning his brother in, no matter what the evidence showed. What if Luke turned the suspicion on Tiago and he was wrong? What if it was Mario?

Mario concerned him. He hadn't seen his youngest brother in some time, and the last time he had seen him, Mario had been in one of those jovial good moods, where everything was right. With the third Hernandez brother that was suspicious. But with nothing to act on, Luke had asked his few pointed questions and was now forced to let it lie if he didn't want to turn in his family members on a horrid suspicion that he couldn't back up.

Though at one point he'd wanted to be a police officer, Luke was now grateful that his own criminal record had made certain that it didn't work out. At the time, he had been furious with Mario for getting him caught and then trying to blame it on Carlos. But now the thought of being in a job where he consistently had to put his own brothers up on the suspect list was something he was grateful he didn't have to do.

This was hard enough.

But if he didn't find out who the arsonist was soon enough, someone was going to die. Previously, the homes their firebug had set ablaze had been abandoned. It didn't pass Luke's notice that two of the places he had lived in had been in such bad repair that they'd been left to rot. The store where he'd worked might not have quite been rotting, but it had been sitting empty.

Ivy's house, however, was an entirely different story. Not only was the home lived in, she'd been in it at the time and, according to the neighbors, it had been obvious she was home. That was going to go down as an attempted murder.

The game had just become deadly.

If he couldn't figure out who knew his own personal history and was lighting it on fire, those deaths would fall on Luke. It didn't matter if he set the fires himself or simply hadn't stopped it.

Tiago would be arrested as soon as they could find him if Luke even hinted at the possibility. People in this town knew the Hernandez boys, knew what kinds of trouble they could cause. Luke had worked so hard to distance himself from a family that he couldn't untangle himself from. But, as he thought about how to go about his investigation, an idea began to form.

He wondered just how much he trusted her.

CHAPTER TEN

"What do you mean?" Ivy stopped, the paint roller still in her hands as she turned to look at Luke.

"Nothing." He covered too quickly.

She was going to have to fire him. Could she fire someone she wasn't paying? "That was super cryptic. And I *don't* keep secrets."

She turned back to the wall, applying the paint, but stopped when his voice came again.

"What do you mean you don't keep secrets? You're one big secret."

She was about to break into a sweat and not because she was getting a workout despite all the windows being open to the winter air. This was a cold sweat. She'd meant she didn't keep secrets *now*. But everything before she'd arrived in Redemption was not up for discussion. She would show people her degree for a job interview and that was the only thing she would say about it.

She couldn't have people picking at her past. She'd worked too hard to get away from it. So she shifted the topic, hard. "You keep asking things that sound like you know more about my fire than you're letting on."

"I'm a firefighter." He took the bait. Or so she hoped. "I know a lot about a lot of fires. It doesn't mean anything."

But why would he say that last phrase if it didn't actually mean something? Before he could ask her something else, she tried again. "You know, in a lot of cases, it's a firefighter who's the arsonist."

That seemed to shut him up, but she was still so irritated. She'd come to Redemption to escape everything in her past— the things she didn't want to remember, the heartaches, and the lies that she wanted to leave behind. The first life she'd lived was not on her own terms, then she'd had a second life that she'd screwed up to hell and back. This one was her third life, and it was holding together just fine except for a house fire. To have Luke start picking at it was more than she could handle.

She was also dealing with the fact that Luke had changed since he'd carried her out of her burning building. He had stopped flirting with her. And, lo and behold, Ivy Dean was such a dumbass that she'd decided to fall for him *now*.

She told herself she wasn't seeing the real Luke Hernandez. That it was just her heart over-writing some stupid tripe about a good looking man. Just because he was treating her differently now didn't mean *he* had feelings for *her*.

She wondered if this was something other women learned in middle school. She'd been homeschooled and therefore not been exposed to these things. Why on earth would she like this man better when he *wasn't* flattering her and saying nice things than when he was?

Ivy had prided herself for a long, long time on not letting her heart get involved. Somehow that one thing had followed her through all three lives she'd lived. Even at a young age, she'd known she wouldn't fall prey to becoming some man's wife, like her mother and older sisters had. She couldn't believe in a God that had given her this brain and this ambition and wanted her to do nothing with it besides bake pies and homeschool her fourteen children.

She had gotten an advanced degree in library science, maybe in part because she'd so loved having access to all the knowledge she'd been denied as a woman. Now, there was nothing she couldn't look up—no textbook she couldn't borrow or research paper she couldn't find.

So she told herself that she should be able to find out who'd set her home on fire. She had access to city records and more. But she had also told herself she had plenty to do and that the investigators would figure it out and she didn't have to.

"So why are you investigating this?" she asked Luke. Why didn't he have the same idea that she did: that there was already a team assigned who would take care of it? She obviously had a personal stake in the whole thing, but why did he? What was making him ask these odd questions?

Her roller stopped moving as she realized something stunning. Turning, she looked at him, though he didn't look at her. His back was strong. He was sturdy and well-trained. Her only advantage was that he might not see her coming. "You knew my house."

"What?" He paused *so still* that she knew she'd hit the mark.

"They told me you were the one who found me. Ronan said it was amazing—that you had told the chief to put you on the search. And then you walked right in and found me and carried me out. Which means—" she pointed to the back rooms. "—you knew that room was divided. You've been in my home. And since you weren't here after I moved in, you were here before."

His body had stiffened; he stood rigid, still holding the roller.

She would have worried about it dripping on the floor if she hadn't needed to still replace the flooring. If she wasn't more worried about the man in her house with her.

Could she trust him or not?

He was helping her. Help that she'd had to admit that she needed. The homeowners insurance had covered the basic rebuild, but it wasn't enough to replace her missing blender, her microwave, or the fridge. Hell, she'd seen the itemized list—she couldn't buy a used fridge from a want ad for what they'd paid out for the old beast of an appliance.

So she decided to pay herself to do some of the work and Luke had volunteered to help with much of that. She'd hired professionals to do the drywall, but she and Luke had rebuilt the walls first. Now that the walls were back in place, she and Luke were painting, knocking out another bill and leaving her with more cash to put the place back together.

Turning back to the wall, she dipped the roller and tried to act normal.

She was planning to lay the flooring herself. Though she'd had the cabinets professionally installed, she'd saved still more cash by staining them and finding the hardware on her own. That was how she was going to be able to afford a new blender and eventually replace the big fluffy chairs that she loved so much.

But why was Luke helping her? This wasn't one of those cases where the whole team showed up and pitched in for the community. This was just Luke. Each day, he showed up as though he were paying off a debt. But what was the debt?

Maybe she'd missed all the important clues because she'd been so worried about organizing her rebuild and replacing the furniture. Luke Hernandez had been asking disturbingly pointed questions all along.

With her roller still in her hand, Ivy turned again slowly swinging it wide. She positioned it between her and him as though it would protect her.

He was charming. But weren't they all? "Charming" hid a multitude of sins. She knew that.

Maybe that was why she'd never fallen for the flirtatious and overly forward Luke. Maybe that was why her heart had shivered and jumped when he'd begun speaking to her as though she were an equal. Maybe it was that he'd simply figured out what made her tick.

Because he was a firefighter, and he had asked to come into her home and he'd positioned himself as her brave rescuer. Now, he was here alone with her.

With the long-handled paint roller positioned in between them, she waited for him to turn around. Then she looked him dead in the eyes and planned an escape route.

"Was it you?"

CHAPTER ELEVEN

Ivy followed the old blue Chevy down the long road leading out of town. Redemption was not the place to try and tail someone.

The town population was small enough that even she could identify someone else's car on sight a lot of the time. Someone who'd grown up around here—like Luke—would notice sooner rather than later that she was behind him.

This time, she'd left Shannon covering at the library. She hated leaving the library in someone else's hands. It was her baby. Running a library, even a small one like this, had been her dream. But she'd had to take time off because of the house. It was a lesson in letting go, Ivy supposed. At least with all her recent absences, this wouldn't look unusual. And she trusted Shannon implicitly. It was the universe Ivy had trouble trusting in.

"Where are you going?" she asked into the silent space of the car as she tried to stay back but keep up.

When she'd asked Luke point blank if it was him, he denied being the arsonist. For a moment, she'd caught a glimpse of the old Luke Hernandez—the charming smile, the dimple, the cheeky shrug. He'd said, "Why would I even do it?"

But that wasn't an answer and Ivy wasn't about to let it slide. "That's great. And I don't know why you would. But you sound guilty as hell right now. You can talk your way around it, but if you're going to lie, you'll have to do it straight to my face."

She'd been so mad. Her house was uninhabitable. It was costing her so much money and she had very little safety net and he was grinning and shrugging at her? This was why she'd had no time for Charming Luke.

But it had all faded away when he'd seen how she felt. Luke had looked her in the eyes and plainly and clearly said, "No, Ivy. It wasn't me."

Even as she breathed out relief, not questioning that she believed him, she'd been hit with an idea. *There was something about the way he said it.* She didn't move the paint roller, still bracing it between them as though holding him at the point of a sword, she pressed. "But you know who did."

"No! I don't."

Though she had believed the words, she didn't quite believe *him.* There was too much at stake. She could have died in that fire, and who would they even have notified?

Ivy had learned by age fourteen that she'd believed in some truly ridiculous and stupid things in her life. Her family believed those things, so she believed them. The minister denied the crimes he was accused of, and they all wanted to believe such a nice man wouldn't do that, so they chose to believe him. How her sisters had ever found forgiveness was beyond her. Ivy still hadn't.

So she was more than aware of her attraction to Luke, and how it could make her believe truly ridiculous things. Without that stupid desire, her gut instinct was quite solid. But now, she followed Luke Hernandez down Paper Mill Road and out of the city, toward the old, abandoned factory.

He'd led her on a bizarre trek around town to say the least. He'd stopped at an old house, an apartment complex on the edge of town—a nice shiny new one. Then he'd checked an older home with the siding sagging. It made her place look like the Taj Mahal ... even before it was getting put back to rights.

That one he'd gone inside and stayed for a short while. Who would live there? She'd sat outside and waited and didn't get answers. When he left, a much older woman had come to the door, cigarette in one hand that she waved as she gestured. She looked so much like Luke that she had to be a relative, maybe even his mother, maybe his grandmother.

Ivy had jotted down the address. She could look up a lot of this on her phone, but she'd most likely need to make use of the city records. Then he'd turned down this road and headed out of town. If he was going the other way, she might have followed him into Lincoln, but he was aiming west into open fields.

Trying to stay inconspicuous, she slowed as he parked at the side of the road in a pullout that looked like it had been created by cars stopping there before. Ivy wasn't familiar with this area. Whatever little shops had been out this way had closed long ago. The houses were farmsteads, few and far between. She passed old barns, rotting and falling down in the spaces between the properties. Ivy feared for the kids who might play there and hoped their parents were keeping them out of harm's way.

She tried to keep an even speed and look as though she belonged here. She didn't. She'd turned her head to look the other direction, as though Luke might not recognize her car and not get a good look at her either. On a regular day, she would have waved at him and maybe stopped and said hello. People out here did that kind of thing—it was the sense of community she'd loved about her childhood without the terror of it.

But not today. Turning her head away was maybe the dumbest thing she'd done. Luke had gone into her home when it was on fire, he'd saved her. He'd consoled her about not knowing if her car could be driven ever again, or if that too was something she might not have quite enough insurance money to cover.

In the end, it had been Luke who'd had the joyous news of telling her the car had survived. He'd even talked her through how to take it into Lincoln, and which place could detail it well enough to get the smoke scent out.

So, though she might have been looking the other way, her blonde hair and a ponytail would have been obvious. Her shell pink sweater set would have given her away on a good day. But, even if he didn't see the person at all, Luke Hernandez likely recognized the car he'd spent three days calming her down about.

A mile later, she turned around and told herself she'd drive past the parked car, go back into town, and mind her own damn business. But as she passed the spot, she saw the old blue Chevy was still there and that Luke was nowhere to be found.

Ivy found herself saying that following Luke *was* her business. The fire had destroyed most of her home. And this man was spending an inordinate amount of time with her these days under the guise of owing her a debt that he wouldn't name. She had a right to know.

Turning again and tucking her car into another pull off just a little further down, she hopped out and followed the little foot path that became more obvious as she stepped into the grass. Soon she found herself amongst the trees and heard voices.

"Give it to me! I paid for it."

"It doesn't matter if you paid for it. You're not supposed to have it. You'll get arrested!"

The two voices sounded so much alike that Ivy frowned. Was Luke having a psychotic episode and arguing with himself?

But as she approached, she realized there were two men, standing in a small clearing, carrying on like teenagers. They stood over small, charred remains of a campfire in what looked like a bad spot for flames. Luke ignored it and stayed focused on the other man. He held something away, like a game, but the anger in the voices was real.

Ivy stepped closer, and as she did, she snapped a twig, making her freeze with fear. What would they do if they saw her?

At least one of them was Luke, and she didn't think he would hurt her, but she had no idea what she was witnessing—only that she shouldn't be witnessing it. When the two continued arguing and didn't seem to hear her, Ivy let out her breath and began creeping forward again. This time she stepped more carefully as their voices rose and they almost came to blows.

As she got a good look at the second face, she saw it was clearly not Luke. He'd sounded like Luke, and he was built the same, but shorter. He lacked the charming grin and happy light to his eyes. It was just the voice that sounded the same.

Luke held his arm extended away from the other man, and she caught a flash of what could only be a small baggie of drugs.

She was not supposed to be here.

Ivy gasped, and she could see from the way his shoulders jerked that he heard her.

CHAPTER TWELVE

L uke threw the small bag of drugs back at Mario, not surprised when it bounced off his brother's chest and fell into the leaves nearby.

Shit. It would have been better had Mario caught it and gotten the hell out of here. If his brother was startled at his sudden change in attitude, he didn't complain. After all, he'd gotten his drugs back. And Luke guessed he'd gotten his answer.

"You don't know!" Mario yelled.

"Know *what?*"

"Carlos—"

"This is about *you,* Mario. Only about you!" Not again. He'd wanted his mother to be right, but now he felt the pressure at the back of his eyes from what he'd just learned. It was anger and sorrow and frustration to the point that he wanted to hit something—most likely his brother.

It had cost them everything they had to get Mario into rehab the last time. Mario made shitty decisions and they all paid for it. His brother stole from his mother and she let him, and Luke had no idea what he was going to do this time. He knew it was a disease, and it wasn't truly Mario's fault ... but it wasn't *his* either.

He sighed. He didn't have much time for a moral dilemma. Mario leaned over and swiped the drugs from the ground. Thank God, because if he hadn't been able to find them, and they'd had to search for Mario's stupid blue pills that contained God-knew-what Luke wasn't sure how he would have handled it. He had to get Mario out of here before his brother spotted Ivy.

Putting his hand out to his side, he kept his palm facing backwards, in a motion for Ivy to stay back, and he could only hope she heeded him.

Lord knew what she was doing out here following him. When his brother was finally gone, Luke turned around, not surprised to see that she was no longer hidden but standing in the middle of the path. One hip was cocked, her arms crossed, and a glare graced her beautiful face. She was so mad, and she had no right to follow him, but every right to be upset about what she'd just seen.

"What the hell are you even doing?" she asked, but before he could answer, she shook her head. "No, I don't care. I don't want to know. Don't come back to my house."

She turned to walk away, and he didn't know why he did it. There was simply something so harsh about her telling him not to come back. Was it because he felt a deep need to pay off his debt to her and this would stop him? The debt she didn't know that he owed, but he did.

Was it simply because he wouldn't be able to see her again? There was something about Ivy Dean that drew him like a magnet, that hit him hard in the solar plexus.

Everything was jumbled, and he had no idea why. But he reached out and grabbed her arm. "Wait a minute."

Her eyes flared wide—in fear or anger, he couldn't tell. With an expert move, she twisted his hand until he let go. He was smart enough to release his grip before she got hurt. Ivy Dean was not going to be held on to.

"Ivy, we have to talk."

"I don't know that we do." She turned away again.

Out of habit or sheer need, he reached to grab her once more. But the sharp look she gave him told him that she would likely press charges for kidnapping if he even tried it.

"Please?" It was the only thing he could think of.

She spun to face him but still managed to give no quarter. "You're dealing drugs now, too?"

She wasn't agreeing to talk, but he would have to if he didn't want to be on her bad side. For some reason, that felt even worse than what he'd just learned about Mario. So he decided to tell her what he could. "No, that was my brother."

As the words left his lips and he saw the reflection of his own pain in her eyes, he realized there was nothing to do but come clean. Whatever Ivy would imagine—like he'd suddenly become the local dealer—would be infinitely worse than the truth. As bad as the truth was, it was his best option.

"He's been in rehab twice. It costs my mother and me and my youngest brother Carlos everything to put him in."

Her expression softened for just a moment but hardened again, quickly. "So he's using again and you're ... *What?* meeting him in the woods to discuss it?"

"No," Luke shook his head, his hand reaching up to cover his face. This got worse and worse. How could he untangle what she'd seen and what had happened and what he'd actually been intending to do when he drove out here? "How long did you follow me? All the way through town?"

"Why? You answer me first. What the hell are you doing in the middle of the woods trading drugs with your brother?" Her tone was sharp enough to cut him deeply. Far deeper than she should have the power to do.

Luke was breaking one of his cardinal rules: don't get involved. He didn't have the room in his life. His family was too fucked up to bring anyone decent into the fold. Ivy didn't deserve his feelings.

"We weren't trading. I took it off of him. I suspected he was using again."

"So why did you give it back?"

"Because I heard you. And there you were and I wasn't going to get into a fight with a drug addict who's beaten up his own mother in the past—"

He watched as her eyes flew wide. She'd been so sympathetic before, how had that shocked her?

"—he's unpredictable and often violent over his next fix. I wasn't going to risk it with you standing there." *Shit.* That sounded like he was blaming her and he wasn't. They'd learned to take responsibility for their own feelings and their problems when they'd all attended sessions with Mario's first stint in rehab. Well, Mario hadn't.

But Luke had. "It wasn't worth the fight. And he would get the drugs somewhere eventually. When I heard you, I just wanted him to leave."

He could only hope that would be enough accountability. She was angry, and rightly so.

"Why are you driving around town like that?"

He gave her what he could. "I'm looking for the arsonist."

There was a pause. He could see the gears turning in Ivy's head, and he could see the moment they clicked into place.

"You think you know who it is? Did you lie to me?"

"No." The word was soft, but at least he could say that with confidence. He'd been careful not to lie to her. Though he hadn't been sure why at the time. Now, he knew.

Despite the fact that she was following him, he trusted her. He wasn't sure he could trust her not to tell anyone. But he could trust her judgment.

"So you didn't do it? And you don't know who did?" He might trust her, but her tone made it clear she didn't trust him.

All he wanted was for her to believe in him. Hell, someone had to, right? "Not well enough to say anything."

"So you have a suspicion." Her accusation was soft and clear.

He only tipped his head. There was nothing he could say. No words that wouldn't be a lie. And somewhere along the way, he realized he couldn't lie to Ivy Dean.

"Then why did they burn down my house, Luke?"

CHAPTER THIRTEEN

L uke wasn't quite sure how to answer Ivy's question so he shifted gears and answered a different one. "Let's head back to my car. It's cold."

She rolled her eyes at him like a teenager. "I'm sorry. When I got dressed this morning, I didn't intend to be walking in the woods."

"Look, if you're going to tail someone, you need to be dressed for anything. And honestly, this—" he waved his hand up and down, indicating her khaki skirt and her shell pink sweater set, "—doesn't exactly keep you hidden in the woods. It's not quite camouflage."

He didn't comment on her absolutely inappropriate shoes as she led the way back through the woods. It seemed she'd followed him straight into the old meetup site and he felt like a fool. He'd had no clue she was behind him until he'd heard her gasp. Luke didn't ask himself how he'd instantly known the sound belonged to Ivy Dean, librarian extraordinaire and not-so-secret agent.

After he'd spotted Ivy behind him several times in the past few hours, he'd dismissed the idea that she was following him.

But when she made herself known as he'd confronted Mario, he'd had to admit she was more tenacious than he'd given her credit for.

"Why did they come after my house, Luke?" she pushed again.

"Let's get somewhere warm." The old hangout spot hadn't been very deep in the woods, just far enough in that a group of teenagers coming from different directions wouldn't necessarily be seen from the road. He'd wondered if the arsonist was one of his brothers, if he would come back here and … maybe stash evidence, maybe hang out? Luke really hadn't known what he'd expected to find, but what he had found didn't really surprise him.

He'd wondered now if catching Mario the way he had meant that Mario had bought the drugs just moments before he'd shown up. Why else would his brother have drugs on him that he hadn't already taken? So maybe now there were deals going down here. Hell, he thought there had probably always been deals going down back here. He'd simply been naive.

As they cleared the edge of the trees, Luke looked up and down the street, spotting Ivy's much nicer car stashed in another turnout a little further down the old road. Once again, she shivered and the thought of putting her in his old beater wasn't quite what he was going for.

He wasn't normally ashamed of the car. He simply spent his money on other things. Unlike Kalan, who drove a sleek sports car and flaunted it, Luke was a cosigner and often mortgage payer on his mother's small home right now. The shitty Chevy represented what was left over after sending Mario to rehab and making sure his mother had a roof and his own rent was paid. He wasn't quite ready to fold Ivy Dean into the passenger seat.

"Why don't we head back to my place? Or yours?"

Ivy shook her head. "Not to Jo's. She's home today sleeping."

She didn't comment that maybe Luke should be, too, since he worked the same job as her friend. But she stalked away, getting into her own car. It was clear as he turned the key and started the engine that she was going to make him go first. She was still tailing him; Ivy wasn't going to let him shake her off. When Ivy Dean wanted answers, she found them.

Maybe the car ride would be a good chance to put his thoughts together and be more organized before he opened his fat mouth. But he found himself pulling up her driveway as her garage door lifted, probably triggered from a remote in her car. He pulled into the open space in front of the house and followed her through the garage door into the kitchen.

He, too, shivered a little bit, not quite dressed for the cold snap that had decided to invade the town today. They'd had an ugly ice storm not that long ago. But the weather had kicked back and been relatively nice. That was about to be over.

Ivy walked through the kitchen, obviously wanting him to follow. They'd painted this space an inviting muted peach. The living room was a soft shade of sunshine. Ivy liked color—and that wasn't something he would have guessed from the outfits she wore to work.

As he stepped inside, the large empty space to his right let him know that she hadn't found a new refrigerator yet. The cabinet doors they had stained together were now hung. Ivy had been working even when he wasn't here. He got the impression that she merely slept at Jo's, then filled her hours at the library, earning her paycheck, and came back here and filled every spare minute with the task of putting her home back together.

He was in an apartment, so he didn't have that kind of investment, but he admired her for hers. As much as he'd been amazed by her mad carpentry skills that she'd never quite let on beyond that "barn raising" comment, he'd held his tongue. Now wasn't the time. She'd managed to hold onto her mad all the way from the edge of town.

She stalked into the middle of the living room, still an empty space that only made her anger bigger. There was no coffee table, no chairs, no TV, and he wondered if he could scrape together the cash to replace the model Jo had told him was lost in the fire. But Ivy wasn't thinking about furniture.

She turned, arms crossed in the middle of the sunny space, and stared him down, her own expression as cold as the wind that was kicking up outside as the sun fell. "Why did someone try to burn down my house, Luke? Because it belonged to your old friends?"

It hit him that he'd lied to her about that.

He told himself he wouldn't lie to her, but he'd been fudging the truth too much. It wasn't all for her own protection either, some of it was for his.

"But it wasn't your friend's house, was it?" she demanded, moving side to side until he finally looked right at her.

Shaking his head no, he watched as everything snapped together for her.

"This was *your* house."

Why did she have to be so damn smart? Even the chief hadn't caught on to it yet. Or if he had, he hadn't called Luke on it. So maybe it was that Ivy was smart and had an incredibly low tolerance for bullshit.

He nodded. "The arsonist is targeting places that I know."

"He's after you?" Ivy demanded answers where he didn't really have any. "He came after me because of you?"

"I don't think that's it."

"Which part? That he's after you or why he came after me?"

"None of it," Luke said. Seeing that she didn't believe him, he tried to explain. "I mean, the arsonist could be after me, as in, trying to kill me and make it look like an accident. Honestly, it could be that he's trying to frame me."

He watched as her eyes flew wide. She clearly hadn't considered that possibility. Even though she'd seemed to put

58

together that he was intricately connected to the series of fires around town.

"Were all the fires in your homes?"

He shook his head but said, "We moved a lot. So there are more houses to hit if they want to do that."

"That's what you're driving past when you loop the town." The way she said it told him this wasn't the first time she'd followed him around. *Shit.*

"They took out a place where I held a summer job. But Tiago worked there, too."

"Tiago?"

"My oldest brother. My brothers lived in the houses with me and so did my mom. For a while so did my dad. But he left so I don't think this is about him."

"You don't think the arsonist *is him* or you don't think they're *targeting* him?"

Luke threw his head back and his arms out to his side. This was frustrating as fuck. "That's the problem! I don't know. I don't know any of it. My brother, Tiago, is a fucking mess. He's been in and out of prison—"

"For arson?"

"No. And that's the problem. If it was for arson, I would have put the chief on him in a hot second. But my mother swears Tiago is cleaning up his act. She's sworn this before, but Tiago went right back to prison, because he hadn't cleaned up his act at all. But if he has this time, and I'm the one who sends him back …"

The words trailed off as he paced his irritation out. There was no explaining the cluster that was his family. Ivy nodded, somehow understanding the subtle and deep damage that brothers could do to each other.

"I don't know if one of my brothers is doing this. Or if somebody is targeting me, or one of my brothers, or if one of my brothers is targeting one of my other brothers just because he's mad." He sucked in a breath. "But you saw Mario. Mario has got problems. If he goes to prison, he's never going to get the treatment he needs!"

Ivy stared at him for a moment before Luke asked, "What?"

Her expression didn't change. "If Mario has drug problems, that's one thing. But if he's been setting fires, he goes to prison. Fuck his drug problems."

Not quite the expletive he'd been expecting.

She noticed. "I'm sorry. Did you think I don't know how to swear?"

He kinda had thought that.

"Somebody burned down my house Luke, or they tried to and they mostly accomplished it. And they tried to do it *with me inside.* So if this is your brother, I'm sending him to prison. If it's something else, but it's because of you, I need to know."

She did need to know. He just didn't have any answers for her.

Once again, Luke held his hands out to his side. The pressure in his head obscuring anything he could have said. But then Ivy looked at him again, and he knew she wasn't going to let it go.

CHAPTER FOURTEEN

"Can you help me? I don't want you following anyone or getting in any danger, but maybe you can look some things up."

"Oh my God." Ivy rolled her eyes at Luke. He didn't want her getting in the way was what he meant.

Luke had been explaining all the complicated possibilities that he had wondered about the arsonist. But to ask her that as though she should or could just tuck herself into her books and stay safe was ridiculous.

She knew that being a librarian was her job. But it was different when the fire was on her doorstep—it had been an inescapable ring around her home. Had the RFD not shown up when they did, she wouldn't have survived. That was a sobering thought. But she was already up to her neck in it.

She was getting ready to tell him in no uncertain terms that he couldn't just set her aside on her own case when her phone had buzzed. Pulling it out of her pocket, she huffed out a breath. "You have got to be shitting me."

She was swearing too much these days. Life number two was bleeding into life number three.

Luke backpedaled. "I just can't have you telling people what I just told you. Fine, if it's Mario, you're right, he should go to prison." He barely took a breath. "I mean, I guess you can tell whoever you want, but if you do, it will destroy my family, which is why I haven't said anything before. My mother spent too many years working too many jobs for me to destroy it all now."

Ivy was barely even listening. She looked up at him and sighed. "It's not you. It's the siding guys."

"Oh." She watched as all of the tension left his body and turned to irritation on her behalf. "What about them?"

She held up her phone as though he could read the tiny email message on the screen. "They've postponed me … *again!*"

She watched as his frown disappeared, and he turned and looked out the front window. She'd had the large window re-installed at a very hefty price. While the insurance had covered most of it, everything it covered was incomplete. So another chunk had come out of her savings. That meant no fridge yet and no TV.

Now, Luke looked across the street, a frown pulling at his brows as though he were watching a dust storm rolling in, or tornado touching down on the neighbor's house. "They can't postpone."

"Oh, they can. They just did." Her irritation bled through her tone. Sometimes, the old ingrained ways of always being nice and polite tried to force their way through. And sometimes, like it always had, her own more forceful personality showed. Now, she was at full scale irritation. This was too much and if she didn't get mad she'd crack and lose it.

"No, Ivy, they have to show up and do it. The weather's about to change. They have maybe two more days, and it has to be finished."

She didn't understand. The siding company seemed to not

care. There wasn't one in Redemption, and they kept saying they couldn't come all the way out for the day without having other jobs finished first.

But Luke was still talking. "We're due for our first big snow."

Ivy looked at him oddly. He'd said it as though looking at the sky gave him enough information to predict the rest of the week. But she tapped on her phone, checking the weather app she had.

She seemed to be the only person in town who didn't feel the snow in their bones or smell it coming on the wind. She figured, around here, most people had lived and died by the storms. If they didn't, their crops did. So it was genetically ingrained in the families to know when bad weather would come their way.

She simply didn't have the touch but, *shit,* he was right. A big ice storm had come through a short while ago, but a warm snap had bounced back. Now, winter was bearing down on Redemption, Nebraska. Hard.

"Is it bad to have my house without siding?"

He shook his head in a short tight way that said, not only was it bad, it was *very bad.* "I mean, you're wrapped, but the siding provides protection against water. It makes the water roll away from your home …"

His tone let her know that if the water came right now, she'd be in worse shape than she already was. "And snow?"

"More than a foot and they probably won't come do the work. The job is pretty seasonal."

"Well, they aren't coming! What do I do?" Her ribs felt like they were shrinking. Her jaw clenched involuntarily, the way it sometimes did if she suddenly had too much sugar. Her sinuses felt like there was powder in them and she fought hard not to cry. "How do I even file a claim for that?"

If the siding didn't get put up in time and the house got more damage … Scrambling her way through all the options, she tried to think everything through. If she sustained damage from a storm, it would mean a second claim, a second deductible, and more to fix. She couldn't handle any more. It would be even longer before she could move back into her own home.

Ivy didn't even realize she was shaking until Luke pulled the phone from her hand and looked for a moment for a place to set it down. But the room was empty. Her bookshelf and all her prized personal library had burned. The pictures of Ivy and Jo when they'd gone hiking last month had been burned to a crisp. So had the one she'd had taken the first day when she'd put the key in the lock and opened the Redemption Public Library for the first time in a year.

She'd inserted her key and watched as one patron strode up to her and asked if she was opening the library. The picture had been taken at an upward angle, because her first patron had been a kid with his mother in tow. She'd asked him his name and if he wanted to take her picture.

She could reprint those. But right now, it was all gone. There were no bookshelves. No TV, no coffee table, not even a chair.

She was shaking harder by the time Luke gave up and slipped her phone into his own back pocket. Reaching out, he enveloped her hands in his. His hands were large and warm, wrapping around hers. She wasn't sure if he was trying to comfort her, or if he was merely trying to hold her still.

He reached up and wiped her cheek, the wetness smearing a tear that she hadn't even realized had fallen.

When she was a kid, these big bad things didn't faze her, because she believed in her family. Though bad things happened, her family always stayed together. Only she'd realized together wasn't always the answer.

So now she was alone.

But that was wrong, Ivy told herself. She had Jo. She wouldn't be out on the street. She had friends. She could couch surf for a while if she had to, until she got a new apartment. She could afford an apartment even if all of her savings was gone.

As Ivy walked herself through a worst-case scenario, Luke wiped her face one more time. Rough fingers brushing against her cheek as he whispered, "Don't worry. I'll take care of this."

Her shoulders hunched up under her ears involuntarily, the tears kept coming. And she could only ask, "How?"

CHAPTER FIFTEEN

"Yes!" Ronan Kelly yelled as a cheer went up around Ivy's house.

Ivy stood in her front yard, her jacket wrapped tightly around her, her fingers icy.

Luke had been right: The weather had turned already. Though the snow hadn't arrived, it was a good fifteen degrees colder today.

The cheer wrapped around her house and filled her own chest as they all stood and watched Ronan tap the last corner piece into place. The siding was cheap vinyl, a snap together kind, but it was what she could afford. And Luke was right. It did look good.

It looked good right now because it was new, but it would weather and age quickly, not the kind that was built to last. Her house was now covered in a pale gray wood-grain look. Not the bright white, higher end kind the company was supposed to put on. But her house wouldn't suffer the damage and the guys had saved her a ton of money.

She felt Luke's arm wrap around her shoulder and pull her close. "We did it. You're safe from the storm now."

The smile on his face was full of genuine pride and Ivy didn't quite know how to respond. She leaned into him and whispered a soft, "Thank you."

This was one of the things she'd loved growing up: communities taking care of each other. It was one of the reasons she'd chosen Redemption. When she'd settled down here, she'd known that a library that had been closed for almost a year was not her cup of tea, but a small town that needed a library that she could reopen had been. She'd dusted all the books. She'd loved the place. She'd hired several part time employees and opened up a volunteer program from the high school. She'd gathered money for prizes for the local kids, and she'd helped find a few missing persons along the way.

She'd made the effort to familiarize herself with the town and the people in it, and the records of their past relatively early on. Now, the town had come back to help her.

Luke had called the company that was supposed to do the work. And, brooking no argument, he'd canceled her order for a full refund. He'd picked her up at seven that morning and taken her into Lincoln to pick out siding. It had all been so stressful that she had startled when he asked her what color she preferred. In her old world, no one asked if you needed help, they just showed up and did it. And you got the help the men dictated you needed.

Her father had been the one the locals looked to and making her own decisions had been foreign to her then. When she was stressed, it came back to her to take what was handed and say thank you. So Luke pressing her for a choice had felt a little odd, but she'd pulled herself together and chosen.

By noon, everyone had shown up. Ronan had volunteered the Kelly family work truck. The Kellys—as she'd learned from Luke—often did their own construction work. Ivy had even heard rumors that Patrick and the boys had built the house that Patrick and Mrs. Kelly now lived in.

From the way things had gone today, she could believe it. A-shift was off, and they were all at her house for at least part of the time. Some of B-shift had shown up, too. Leslie and Ann were both here, and Jo had been waiting on the front step when Ivy and Luke returned with the truck bed full of pieces.

Ivy dove in and put pieces into place. Her new work gloves were getting broken in and the feeling of satisfaction replaced the panic of the day before.

When several of the guys said things like, "Hey! You know how to use a nail gun." It was Luke who laughed and repeated, "Apparently, Ivy here can raise a barn."

She'd simultaneously stiffened and tried to laugh it off. That was not the information she'd wanted to spread in Redemption. She shouldn't have told him.

But the guys had laughed, and it passed without becoming a nose-first dive into her past. During the day, others had come and gone as they were able. Now, as the sun was starting to set, the team put the last piece into place.

She even had new gutters and drains. They'd insisted on replacing some of the eaves, too. Ivy had to fight the urge to just cry with relief for most of the day. She kept her feelings at bay by telling very heart-felt thank yous and making sure her hands were never idle.

Now, her home was safe, even if the snow came tonight. Even if it came as cold, wet sleet, her house would be protected and she'd been saved from further damage and more hassles and money.

She still had her bedroom, aired out, sheets washed, and put back in place. Her entire closet still had to be washed, but she had a place to sleep and she'd already turned the heat back on.

Jo stepped up next to her and nudged Ivy in the side with her elbow. "The way you're looking at this place, I can see you're thinking about staying here tonight."

Ivy laughed. "I was."

"But you don't have a fridge," Jo told her, still looking at the house.

"I know. And I think it's going to be a bit before I can save enough to order one." It didn't matter. Her home was livable again. Not great, not what it had been, but livable.

"Ah, that would suck—living here without a fridge. So I guess you're lucky, that that's not going to be the case." Jo grinned oddly as she turned and looked down the street.

Ivy frowned as Jo spotted something and then jumped up and down and waved her hands to get the truck's attention. Jo was even newer to town than Ivy and she hadn't quite yet learned that everyone knew where everything was and where everyone lived. She didn't need to wave down whoever was coming.

Patrick Kelly pulled up in the same truck they'd used that morning. Only, this time, a huge hunk of silver was strapped into the bed. Clearly a refrigerator, it stood upright like a monolith, old orange tie downs anchored it in every direction, to keep it from tipping.

Jo frowned as Patrick rolled down the window to talk to her. "Seems like you could have laid it down and made it travel better."

But Patrick laughed and it was Ivy who explained, "You don't want to lay a fridge down, not for any amount of time. It might not work when you put it back upright."

Jo turned and looked at her, wiggling her fingers as if to mock her knowledge. "It's a good thing both of you know that!"

Luke, on her other side, turned and looked a little surprised. Ivy shrugged at both of them. She had raised a lot of barns, she'd helped build more than one home, and she knew a thing or two about appliances. She'd been raised to repair instead of replace. As Leo Evans was fond of trying to get them all into more sustainable living, she'd always been happy to be able to say that she wasn't throwing things in the landfill.

She now walked the few feet to where Patrick was hopping out. "What is this, Jo? Patrick?"

The older firefighter, occasional Captain, and clear leader, turned and looked at her and said, "This here is what's known as a refrigerator, young lady."

Jo snickered and Ivy rolled her eyes. "Did you buy me a fridge, Jo?"

"I did!"

"Jo, I can't take a gift like—"

"Shut up, Ivy."

Everyone around her laughed as Jo turned around and made a snapping, shut-up motion with her fingers. "It's a gift and you will take it. It's not brand new, it's used, so you can get off your little high horse about the money."

Patrick turned to Ivy and bowed. "We sold it to Jo on the cheap. It's been in our garage since Ronan and ... since Ronan remodeled his place."

Ivy understood, this was a family piece. It had belonged to Ronan and Soirse—the name Patrick hadn't been able to say. She'd heard that Ronan gutted the house in the year after Siorse and his son Paddy had died. The family must have felt unable to dispose of it, but felt she was a good home for it.

Tears pressed at the back of her eyes. God, she'd moved to Redemption, sight unseen, knowing no one. She'd stayed in a shitty little apartment outside of town for a while, making sure she wanted to stay and keep the job. Then she'd found the little house. Establishing herself with a loan and making her downpayment on her own.

But now she had friends bringing her fridges. The combination of the fire stealing everything, and the town people coming together to give as much back to her as possible, was more than her emotions could take. She was swinging wildly.

It didn't help that the whole time she'd had to keep her

mouth shut. She was still undecided about what she would do with the painful knowledge about Luke's brothers and the fires.

"I'm going to stay with you tonight," Jo announced.

Ivy almost asked if Leo would mind, but she knew that if Jo had offered to stay, she'd already told her new boyfriend. And neither of them was one to get in the way or override the other's decisions. Ivy admired that. She didn't intend to marry, but she might one day want a partnership like Jo had.

Leo loved Jo just the way she was. Jo, of course, was tall, athletic, and beautiful, and managed to move to town and snag one of the hottest guys around within just a month. Ivy, on the other hand, had had no such luck. Not that she'd wanted it.

Beside her, Jo was grinning. "We're going to order a pizza. And we're going to run to the store for some ice cream. And we're going to put it in that nice new fridge."

"It won't get cold that fast," Ivy told her.

"Oh no," Aiden said, "it's probably still cold. Dad used it as the garage fridge. Don't worry, he needed to move it because he got a big freezer. It's barely been unplugged for an hour. It should be chugging right along in time for y'all to have your ice cream tonight."

He'd smiled at the two women, and slowly the firefighters and the locals who'd come to help out their neighbor stepped up and wished her good luck. They gathered up their supplies as the night began to settle in around them. The days were short, but Luke was right and he'd managed to get it done for her.

She watched as he joined the small crew doing the heavy lifting on the fridge.

Did she now owe him her silence? Was he trying to buy it?

He couldn't understand that she'd been silent for far, far too long before and she would never do it again. If he was trying to manipulate her, he would have a shock in store. She hated thinking that way of the man who'd been nothing but kind to her. Of the man she was starting to feel she was truly seeing for the first time. But she wasn't able to shake the old fears.

The fridge was slid into place, the guys handling it carefully, and not scratching the new gray tiles she and Luke had laid last week. When it was in place and chugging softly, they all told her congratulations, and that they loved the work she'd done. Then they'd gathered in the front yard in the dark to say their goodbyes. The Kellys took their empty truck and backed down the driveway. Even Luke left.

Jo grabbed her hand, tugging her to the front door. But, as Ivy followed along, her cold fingers twined in her best friend's, she turned and looked down the dark street, an uneasy feeling nagging at her.

CHAPTER SIXTEEN

L uke didn't make the conscious decision to turn the wheel, he just found himself headed toward her house.

He hadn't seen Ivy in two days. He'd worked a full shift. Helped put out a car fire, checked the wiring in an attic because it "smelled funny" and saved a full-blown house fire from happening, and he'd helped pull a puppy out of the river. That had been a rousing shift. That there'd been no sign of the arsonist helped.

The night they'd celebrated getting her siding up, he'd left Ivy with Jo. The next morning, both he and Jo had showed up early for A-shift. Jo had been brighter and cheerier than he'd expected, given the slumber party and ice cream from the night before. It made him feel better, that Ivy had done okay her first night back in her own home.

But he hadn't asked his fellow firefighter about the woman he was thinking of far too much. That morning, he'd gone home and slept off as much of the long shift as he could. When he'd finally woken up, the daylight was fading, but he'd still driven around town, checking out his own past here in Redemption to see if he could find something.

Maybe he could catch a spark before it became a flame. And if he was very lucky, maybe see who started it and stop the whole process before it got too ugly.

But he'd had no luck. His mother hadn't even been home. By the time he'd knocked on her door it was fully dark. Though he wondered where she might be at this hour, it wasn't his place to ask.

He drove a little more of his regular route, thinking it was time to mix it up, or people would get suspicious of him. With the snow beginning to fall, just as predicted, he wasn't able to see anything.

Would their arsonist slack off with the winter coming on?

Some did. He both hoped this one did and that he didn't—that he would mess up soon and they would all sleep easier once it was over.

Only Luke had a sinking feeling that he wouldn't sleep easier even after the guy was caught.

The chief had speculated about who it might be. He and Sebastian Kane had even reached out for a profile, but so far no one had had any answers. So here he was, far too late at night, turning up on Ivy Dean's doorstep unannounced.

Even as he told himself it was inappropriate to be there, he climbed the front steps and knocked and waited. As he looked down and tried to see if any of the black char remained ground into the cement or if she'd managed to clean it all off, he heard the shuffling sounds on the other side of the door. Looking up, he saw the shadow behind the peephole and thought maybe it wasn't wise of her to be a target. Someone standing on the porch could see she was home, even if she decided not to answer the door.

Had the arsonist actually tried to kill her? And if so, would he be mad that he'd failed?

But when the door opened those thoughts fled. Ivy didn't

even say hello, she just stared at him through bloodshot and puffy eyes.

"What happened?"

She shook her head, not able to answer him in words as she inhaled sharply through her nose, as though she were holding it all behind the pressed line of her lips.

"Ivy, you can tell me." His heart felt the push and pain of seeing her like this and he didn't know what to do besides offer help. But what help did she need?

She shook her head again, her lips pressed tight and, for a moment, he thought maybe she couldn't speak. But he tried one more thing. "I told you about my brothers. You can tell me anything."

He hadn't even realized that Ivy had stepped back, leading him into the open space of the living room and closing the door behind him. As he heard the lock slide home, her shaky voice told him, "My brother died."

Luke tried not to look shocked. Clearly, Ivy was upset, but he hadn't even known she had a brother. Come to think of it, she'd never mentioned siblings or even a mother or a father. So he simply turned to face her, standing awkwardly in the empty space and trying to look like he fit. "Tell me."

"He was an asshole."

Once again, she'd shocked him.

"His wife is probably sad that he's gone, but she shouldn't be. He treated her like crap and left her with four little kids. Two of them I didn't even know about."

Holy crap. No wonder she was crying. He was stunned by the news himself and found himself asking, "When did he die?"

"Nine months ago."

And she hadn't known?

This time, her hands lifted, waving as haphazardly as her words. Her shoulders rolled with a deep breath and an exhale that said maybe she would finally let it all out.

Looking around, Luke motioned for her to sit. The kitchen had been so burned out, it had allowed for a little bit of redesign. They'd added a small bar to the existing counter and he saw that she'd gotten stools for it. Even if she didn't yet have chairs or a TV or a table, there was a place to sit without pulling her into her office or her bedroom.

It pushed at him again, that he wanted to get those things for her, to fill in the house and replace the things that he still felt partly guilty for her losing. But this was the only option, so he pulled out one of her own barstools and motioned her toward it.

Then he went to the new silver fridge and found two bottles of hard lemonade. *Alcohol.* He hadn't expected that either. He opened one very empty drawer to find three knives, a cutting board, and the bottle opener he needed.

He wondered if he knew Ivy dean at all. But now wasn't the time to question that. She was leaning forward with her face in her hands, and he could still see that the tears were coming fresh again.

He wanted to ask how her brother had died and she'd not known for nine whole months. But clearly, that wasn't the issue. He tried something gentler. "Was he your only brother?"

Had she said? He didn't remember.

Ivy shook her head. "I have thirteen brothers and sisters."

He shouldn't have been taking a drink right then. He almost leaned over the sink so he didn't spit it onto her floor, but managed to get it swallowed. Maybe he shouldn't drink while Ivy Dean revealed her secrets.

Luke couldn't think of anything to say to that. And it didn't matter because she quickly filled in, "Well, I guess I only have twelve now."

Fourteen children. He thought it was harsh being one of four. He'd envied the families that had just one or two kids because they seemed to have more time and more money to go around.

Though he wouldn't trade his brothers for anything, his parents had definitely overshot with how many kids they could support.

His mother had always complained about feeding four boys and here Ivy was one of fourteen. He softly pushed the bottle toward her, the black label again reminding him that there were things he didn't know about her.

Luke watched as one slim hand came out and wrapped around the bottle. She lifted it and took the longest swig imaginable, draining half of it in one gulp. When she swallowed, she thumped the bottle down on the table and turned to stare at him. The red in her eyes only made her seem more determined.

She asked him, "Do you really want to know? Because it's not pretty."

CHAPTER SEVENTEEN

Luke didn't know what he had gotten himself into, but he nodded that he wanted to. He hadn't done it just to comfort her. It was the truth.

If there was more to Ivy Dean than met the eye—and it was clear that was the case—then he did want to know.

"I grew up in the middle of nowhere, Iowa." She took a breath. And another sip as though that in and of itself, might be enough. It was the only non-shocking thing she'd said so far.

He almost prompted, "with thirteen brothers and sisters," but she continued.

"It was a very religious community on the outskirts of a very small town. At the time, I just thought we were godlier than everyone else."

Oh, shit, he thought.

She turned ever so slightly, her eyes completing the arc to catch him and maybe to assess his expression. Was she deciding whether to tell him what came next? Luke kept his expression neutral and friendly, hoping she felt she could trust him.

"Looking back, I'd have to call it a cult. The women were only allowed to wear pastel colors. We made our own clothing and the men's. We baked our own bread. We buttoned ourselves up to our neck and wore skirts down to our ankles."

"Are you Amish? Or Mennonite?"

He shouldn't have asked. She shook her head.

"No. That's actually far too …" she searched for the right word. "*Christian* for what we were."

"You weren't Christian?" He shouldn't have said that either.

"We called ourselves Christians, but I don't think there was actually anything from Jesus in it. I sure can't see it now that I've been allowed to read things for myself."

Oh, fuck. One of those. He decided to dip his toe in. It might explain a lot if he was right. "Powerful church leaders, subservient women?"

"Got it in one." Ivy smiled and tipped her drink at him as though he'd won a party game rather than a glimpse into her shitty childhood. "Girls didn't get educated past the fourth grade. The boys did. Some of them were even allowed to go away to college. But the women were just there to serve …" She waved her hand as if to indicate everything. "We were supposed to be modest so that the men didn't want us. And when the men did want us, we were supposed to take care of it. We existed only to cook and clean. I was raised to be somebody else's servant and not my own person."

So many things snapped into place for Luke in that moment: The cute khaki skirts that hit just below the knee and on wild and crazy days, just above. The sweater sets. Even the library made more sense. A woman like Ivy, denied knowledge, would certainly become ravenous. "Is there more?"

The laugh that bubbled out of her started cute and sweet. But it quickly turned sour, then bitter and harsh. "Alder, my oldest brother, the one who passed away this year—"

Luke nodded again. It seemed that was all he could do.

"—He was a real asshole. As the oldest male, he was the heir apparent to my father. My father was a church elder, thus very well respected in the community, so he wielded a lot of power with his opinion."

"One of the leaders up there with the minister?"

This time it was Ivy who nodded, though she couldn't make eye contact with him. "The one others tried to be like. The one that the other men listened to and the woman obeyed. As the oldest son, Alder could do no wrong. His wife, Julie—I don't know—I think maybe she was just the meekest, most agreeable woman they could find. She was just 'good' and 'pretty.'"

Luke watched as Ivy's eyes darted to the side and tears formed. Was there something about Julie in particular that made her sad? Or was it just that these were the woman's most important attributes?

"They had had two kids ..." She paused, sucked in a breath, and tried again. When that didn't work and the words still didn't come, Ivy shot down half of what remained of the hard cider.

Luke was beginning to get worried. Did she have any food in her system? Hell, did she even have any food in the house? He didn't want to stand up and leave her even to walk a few feet and look in the fridge. So he softly mimicked her motion, taking a much smaller drink of his own—in case he needed to drive later—and sitting next to her.

"I left. Obviously," she told him, sitting so still that he wouldn't believe she was talking if he didn't hear her. "And every year on the anniversary, I look them up. Try to figure out what's new. They're hard to find. Nobody has social media profiles. They don't make the news very often. Unless," she gulped, "they die and get an obituary. But once a year, I stay up all night, searching everything I can."

Luke put it together before she said it.

"That's why I wasn't in my bed on the night of the fire."

That was the anniversary. That was why she'd fallen asleep in the small back room with her computer.

"So I got interrupted this year. I had to put the house back together." She waved her hand around again, only this time she almost hit him. She was definitely getting drunk. "It's not the anniversary anymore, but I hadn't finished so I tried again, and this time I went through by each name, not just the family. I found Alder's obituary. I knew from a previous search a couple years ago that he had two kids, but they've had two more sons."

Luke wanted to ask how her brother had died, but he didn't dare. Ivy went in an entirely different direction, and he let her. Clearly, most of it was too painful.

"We got a new Assistant Minister when I was about twelve." She took another deep breath and Luke hated the pain that flashed in her eyes. "He sexually abused my little sisters, Peony, Violet, and Rose. Lily and I were older. And by sheer luck of the draw—" her voice cracked, "—he wasn't interested in us."

Luke's chest felt like it was caving in. Ivy had carried all of this for so long. As far as he knew, she hadn't even told Jo. "You found out?"

She nodded slowly and carefully. "We all did. Honestly, a few of us had our suspicions about the little girls, but it was Peony who told us one night. She was a few years older than the others, but he'd gotten her too. She said she didn't think it was right that they weren't married."

Ivy's voice pitched up suddenly, "I don't know how she figured out that that was the kind of thing that married people should do! Because my parents sure as hell didn't educate us on any of that."

Small swears now. He imagined the family getting excommunicated for pulling their daughters out of the church or the minister getting driven out of the community. "What happened?"

He heard and felt her massive intake of air.

"Nothing … *nothing* happened. My father and Alder told Peony that it didn't matter. They told the girls to stay quiet and told Peony to forgive him. They said that the minister had made a *mistake*."

If she had turned around and hit him with a flat palm right to his sternum, hitting at just the right moment to stop the electrical impulse that made his heartbeat, Luke wouldn't have been more stunned.

The women in Ivy's community or church or cult weren't just subservient, they weren't *anything*.

The anger boiled up in him as he thought of anyone treating a child that way. And then he thought of anyone treating Ivy that way—bright, beautiful, driven, and so intelligent Ivy. She had been stuffed in a tiny box, and told she wasn't worth anything other than serving a man. His rage flared hot and bright. But there was no one to hit. Ivy had saved herself and she didn't need him.

He hadn't heard of Ivy dating at all since she arrived in Redemption. She'd run the library and befriended all the town's citizens and especially the children. She'd flat out taught some of them to read, he knew. She ran the library as a beacon of hope for them all. And he'd seen the way the kids were with her. He'd figured she'd made them all love books, and they all loved the librarian. And if they struggled, she helped them.

He knew now, if they had a secret, she would defend them. They loved her not because of her sunshine, but because she understood their darkness.

"I tried to protect Peony. Tried to keep her away, so she wouldn't have to be alone with him. When I told my mother that he was trying to do it again, my mother said he wouldn't do that. But Peony said he did!"

Her voice cracked again. Luke's heart cracked right along with it.

"I told my mother! And she told me that Peony would just have to forgive him. Then they separated us, so I couldn't protect my sister!"

The pain and the tears tore at her. She was crying full out and there was nothing he could do to make any of it better. Luke couldn't fathom any pain of that level in his heart. He couldn't imagine a mother trading her own daughter this way.

But as a firefighter, he'd been inside so many of the homes in town and so many were unexpected. Some were full of secrets and wonderful surprises—bright colors, toys strewn about, and happy children. But some homes had held dark things he hadn't been able to shake.

When Ivy turned and opened her mouth to tell him more, Luke knew it was only going to get worse and he wasn't going to be able to bear it.

CHAPTER EIGHTEEN

"I would never have left Peony." The words came out on a broken cry that she couldn't hold back. Despite all the pain, Ivy knew Luke understood.

Yet, obviously, she had left her sister.

This was the part she never told anyone. In fact, she hadn't ever told anyone about her family. When she'd left them all behind, she'd decided that they were part of a past she didn't want to be connected to anymore. Her family was *life number one*, and she'd immediately entered *life number two*.

She could tell Luke wasn't blaming her, but he also didn't understand.

"When I was sixteen ..." God, she needed more alcohol. She lifted the bottle and drained the last of it, wishing it weren't empty. But since Luke didn't hop up and grab her another, she figured it probably wasn't the wisest move. She was just going to have to suck it up and deal with the hurt. "Several of us snuck out. We drove into town, changed clothes, got fake IDs and went to a club. Looking back, it felt so wild and crazy."

But she knew now that it wasn't even as much as the average teenager did. It was just shocking in her crowd. "I didn't do anything but wear a short skirt and a T shirt. I wasn't dressed down half as much as most of the women there. I ordered one mixed drink—in fact, I didn't even drink more than a sip."

"That was it?" This time he seemed shocked by how tame she was.

"That was the extent of my rebellion."

"But it wasn't just you …"

Ivy shook her head. Lily had been there and so had Rowan, along with several other kids from their church. "I didn't finish that drink. I went back for a coke and I had the nerve to kiss a boy in the back hallway. It was my very first kiss, and it was interrupted by Lily running in and telling me that our dad had showed up at the club."

She felt it all again, the sudden fear, the ice in her veins, the knowing that she would be in harsh trouble. She'd thought she was so brave and bold and—aside from the one sip—she hadn't even been drinking.

No matter that she'd liked kissing him, the terror of what her father would do changed everything. "I pushed him away and I froze. I should have run. I should have gone out the back door, and never let them know for sure that I had been there."

She took a deep breath.

"Lily grabbed me by the hand and I told her to hide, but she just looked at me and said *we can't*. I didn't want to face dad, but she and Rowan grabbed me and tugged me along. We all three went boldly out the front of the club, past the bouncer. Right past Dad and Alder, too. Dad was yelling at us. Everybody in the club was looking, and I remember being so embarrassed. I remember thinking, in that moment, that that was the worst thing that could ever possibly happen to me."

She turned to look at Luke and saw that he understood.

She'd been so, so wrong in thinking that, and it wasn't long before she figured that out. "They followed us out of the club, put us in the car and drove us home. I was even embarrassed to be climbing into this big old powder blue Cadillac. At the time, I thought we were Godly and saving money by driving this old car. And now, looking back, it was just this posturing my dad did. See how he was better than you that he didn't have to buy new cars? Everything was about being better than someone else."

She sighed. She couldn't do this. She should stop. Luke had already figured out that she'd left her family so far behind that she didn't even know her brother had died nine months ago. But she couldn't let him think she had done this herself.

"We got home, and my dad lined the three of us up in front of the other kids. With everyone watching, he said all kinds of horrible things. He encouraged the others to say it, too. But Rowan was told he'd misbehaved. At the time, I didn't even catch it. But now, looking back, Dad told Rowan he had *done* something bad. Rowan would have to pray and repent. But what he told Lily and me was that we *were* something bad. Mother said we'd ruined our futures and no one would want us."

She picked at the label on the bottle so she wouldn't have to look at Luke. But the story had started and it was going to continue, even though she didn't want it to. "I remember being relieved that no one would want me. The worst thing I could imagine would be getting married and handed off to some guy that—if I was lucky—I would like him. Most likely, I wouldn't. And it wouldn't matter."

Her unsteady fingers wrapped around the bottle, lifting it for another drink before remembering it was already empty. When she set it back down, it thunked harder than she expected, letting her know she was more upset that she was willing to admit.

Even now, all these years later, just thinking about it was like getting a knife and digging it deep in her own skin. "Dad asked whose idea it was, and I still think Lily just panicked. It had been her idea. I had totally gone along with it. I will fully admit that. I thought it was a fantastic idea, but I was not the one who originally suggested that we head out and catch the bus and buy clothes and hit a club.

"At first we were all silent, but Dad pulled his hand back." She saw Luke flinch now the way she had fought so hard not to that night. "Lily said it was me."

Luke's eyes flew wide and his whole body jerked. "Did your brother stand up for you. Did he not know it wasn't your idea?"

Ivy tipped her head as if to mock him. "Don't you remember? He was already excused from this shit show. He just had to do a little prayer and repent for his bad behavior. He was not part of turning the women against each other."

"Shit." It was the softest of whispers. He probably hadn't meant for her to hear it. But she did, and she agreed.

"I'll be honest, I wasn't the perfect kid. I back talked, and I wasn't good at being meek. Neither was Lily, but she hid it better than I did. For whatever reason, that night was the final straw." Ivy paused as something she'd read clicked in her brain.

"Do you know the hypnotist's dilemma?"

Luke hadn't quite followed her sudden subject change. But she tried to explain.

"They invite everybody up on stage and ask them to do a simple task—like make a fist. Then the hypnotist comes along and pushes on each fist, and one by one, he sends people off the stage, telling them they don't qualify. He chooses people randomly. The idea being that even the person you thought was going to make the cut, didn't make it. And if you want to stay, you have to fall in line."

She took a breath. "Looking back, I wonder if maybe my father wasn't employing the same strategy. Kick out one of the kids and show the others that no one is safe. Obedience is necessary. I'll bet it was very effective at keeping them in line after I was gone."

Luke blinked and said the words that were in her head. "But you don't know because you weren't there."

She nodded. "I was fully kicked out of the house and the family by midnight. I wasn't allowed to say goodbye to my brothers and sisters. No one was allowed to contact me. He told them while I was gathering my things that they were to think of me as dead, for surely the good Ivy that should have resided inside me had died or I wouldn't have behaved this way."

Another sigh. Another wish for something that would ease the pain. Ivy could have used a hit of something good to take the sting out of this story.

"My mother cried. She refused to hug me ... even when my father wasn't watching. She didn't say anything to me, just turned her back."

"Holy shit." This time, Luke didn't even try to hide it.

At the time, Ivy had told herself she was strong. Lord knew, in her family, they'd all taken enough knocks that they were tough. But looking back, no sixteen-year-old should ever have had to deal with that.

Luke's voice was soft. "It makes more sense now the way you reacted to what I told you about my brothers. But I need you to understand that, as bad of things as my family has done, we would never do that to each other. And that's why I can't tell the chief about my suspicions, not until I know more."

Ivy nodded. But her nod was one of agreement. Her agreement meant that she understood that Luke felt he couldn't turn suspicion on his brother. Ivy wasn't sure she felt the same way.

CHAPTER NINETEEN

I vy woke the next morning, somehow both refreshed and utterly drained.

She had been up way too late, but that didn't matter. She had a job to do and she wanted to be good at it. So she was here and she would give her best, even if that wasn't as good as her best on other days.

As she unlocked the doors to the library and opened the space, she was thinking of the job. Sometimes it was the job she loved and looked forward to, but right now it was the way she earned money. Ivy was thinking of money to replenish her savings, money to buy another coffee table, replace her big fluffy armchairs, and get a TV. Though she'd managed a new dinner table she still needed chairs for it, and ... And. And. And.

Even so, the library was still a bastion of hope for others if not for her. Within a few minutes, she had several patrons inside. "Good morning, Mr. Gentson!"

He'd requested the newest from Stephen King and before he asked, she pulled it out from behind the desk where she'd held it on reserve. His smile helped wake her up. One of the local moms came in with her two young children in tow. For the first time, Ivy noticed that the woman was pregnant again.

Every time she thought she'd shaken the past off, something grabbed at her. That many children in that short of a time period? It gave Ivy the shudders, but she hid it. Smiling at the woman, she told herself that she didn't know that Layla's situation was the same as her family's and that she couldn't undo what was already done.

That was a lesson she'd learned a long time ago. So she pointed them to the children's section, saying hello to the two little ones as they passed by. They offered cute gap-toothed smiles, and she felt her heart melt. She was where she belonged.

After she'd told Luke as much as she could last night, he'd put his arm around her for just a moment, she'd sunk into him, feeling that at last she had a rock she could lean on.

But he wasn't her rock. He might not even be a rock at all. He was possibly harboring the arsonist who'd tried to kill her. And he'd never quite answered the question of whether whoever it was—brother or not—might come back and try to kill her again.

She'd been tense for weeks, wondering if she might be in danger. And she hated how the fire had taken everything from her. Ivy had to remind herself it hadn't gotten everything, and the arsonist hadn't gotten *her*.

She'd vowed the night she left home that she was the sole owner of everything she had—her belongings, her reputation, her feelings. Leaning on Luke felt both wonderful and unsteady, as though she were handing over some of her precious control. She knew it was okay to do it, she knew that what she felt was an overreaction from her past ... but that didn't make doing it *feel* okay.

A little tired, and more than a good bit overwhelmed, Ivy went through the usual motions of her job. She wasn't up for designing extra reading contests or finding new ways to reach into the community today. She could run this library with her eyes closed, and at eleven, when her part timer came in, Ivy turned over the front desk. Some of the volunteers just shelved books, but everyone who was paid knew how to do every job. When Ivy had had to miss shifts from the fire, it had paid off. There was a certain pride in being indispensable, but there was more pride in knowing that she'd set the library up to run without her.

"Thanks Shannon, I'm going to be in the back. I'm heading into the record room to do some reorganizing." She didn't like to lie, so she would do some organizing while she was there. But most of what she did was dig through some old files and city records.

Half an hour later, she had the names and birthdates of Luke Hernandez and his brothers. Santiago, was the oldest, Luke second, then Mario, then Carlos. There had been a fifth boy born to Mrs. Hernandez—a small, premature baby that had been named Jose—who, according to the records Ivy found just a little while later, had been stillborn.

Luke hadn't mentioned a fifth Hernandez son. Had he not known about his little brother? Or was it one of those things the family just didn't talk about? This was that odd kind of knowledge that she couldn't unknow. She'd found it through researching him and so she couldn't quite ask him about it either, not without admitting that she'd been digging into his family's past.

Tiago had a string of arrest records, mostly petty things. He'd shoplifted, gotten into bar fights, and he'd once stolen a car. At one point, one of the townspeople had pressed charges for him breaking in and stealing about ten thousand dollars from the man's home. Tiago had served some time for that one but had been released for good behavior—it seemed he was always getting released for good behavior—a few years ago.

Ivy sat back, her pencil clattering to the note paper. She

hadn't wanted to take notes on her phone. It was linked to the internet. And she knew from her own searches on her family, that so many things that people thought were private could be uploaded from any connected device.

For example, the minister who'd assaulted her little sisters was eventually jailed. One of the other families in the church had decided that their daughters weren't, in fact, worthless and had pressed charges. The minister had been convicted mostly based on the testimony of the children and text messages he'd sent someone about what he was doing.

For Ivy, reading everything about the story of the other family had been both cathartic and deeply painful. She'd found more than one newspaper article where they'd spoken up about how their group—they'd named no names—had kicked them out for turning on the beloved minister. At least he was gone, and hopefully her own sisters were now safe.

Ivy also had to remind herself that children grew. And her younger sister was older than she remembered. Older than she'd been herself when that minister had come to town.

Ivy also had two younger siblings that she'd never met. It turned out her mother had been pregnant the night her father had kicked her out. Had her mother felt trapped and unable to protect Ivy because she'd had another baby on the way? Or had she simply believed as her husband did?

Ivy had long ago come to terms with the fact that she would probably never know the answers. She didn't crave them anymore, but it sure would have been nice to get them someday.

And it would be nice to know more about Luke's brothers. In fact, she *needed* to know.

Tiago didn't strike her as an arsonist. Despite the chain of arrests, none of them were for fire. None were for things like animal torture or assaults or the other things that arsonists and serial killers tended to start with.

Her fire had clearly been premeditated, not reactionary or spur of the moment in any way.

In each case, there was accelerant at the scene. In the three she could find out about the accelerant was different. One had been gasoline. Another had been oil from the garage of the shop that had burned and a third had been kerosene. In all cases, the place had been ringed with accelerant and set ablaze.

Did Mario Hernandez have the wherewithal to do this? He'd been ready to fight Luke for street drugs the other day. Ivy would imagine a drug addict would make mistakes and not be able to elude the investigators for long. The fourth brother, the baby, Carlos, wasn't even in town. He lived in between Lincoln and Omaha and was climbing his way up some ladder at a car dealership.

Had Kane and Taggart not found this information? They were the arson investigators. Should she take it to them? Tell them about the Hernandez boys?

If someone died and she hadn't done everything she could, would she be able to live with herself? But what did she even tell them? That Luke had a suspicion … one that she thought didn't hold much water on deeper inspection.

Honestly, his family was a mess. But his didn't hold a candle to hers, so who was she to turn them in when even Luke didn't have a strong suspicion?

She pushed away the old birth and death records and pulled up articles. Maybe she could learn something by looking up accelerants or arson. While it was fascinating, it didn't do much for her suspicions or Luke's. Not until the third article sparked another thought in her mind. The problem with arsonists, was they knew how to set fires and not get caught.

Her heart caught as she thought of Luke.

As the writer pointed out: who knew how to set fires better than a fireman?

CHAPTER TWENTY

L uke let his spoon drop, splatting into his bowl of cereal and sending milk everywhere.

He used to have a schedule. He used to have a life that he thought fairly well of. But now, everything was up in the air.

It was growing dark, but he'd just woken up. He was eating cereal at the end of the day. Though he was hungry, he'd only stared at it and let it go soggy.

He was due at the station at eight am the following morning. The way the chief liked to run things, was that everyone was, at worst, on time. Luke was usually early.

Would he be able to get back to sleep? He didn't know.

B-shift would have gotten off this morning. They might be out at Snafu drinking this evening. Maybe he could join them, just for social contact.

He got dressed, figuring he could weave his way to the bar by way of his usual circuit around town. He still wanted to check all his old haunts and hope that his timing was simply miraculous and that he caught a spark before it became a problem.

His stomach was growling because he hadn't even finished his stupid cereal, but he climbed the front steps and knocked on the door of the tiny house. His mother was in tonight, and he stayed for a few minutes, unable to watch the ash from her cigarette grow to an enormous length. He couldn't avoid thinking about the damage she was doing to her lungs. But it couldn't be any worse than the damage from the cheap wine that she drank constantly, or the cheap food that she put into her body.

He told her he loved her, hugged her, and headed out the door. He should have gone straight to the bar. But once again his steering wheel seemed to have a mind of its own. And he found himself on Ivy Dean's street again.

He'd decided the night before that he was going to get her a TV. It seemed the least he could do for leading an arsonist to her door ... even if he wasn't really admitting that yet. He'd hit up the local store and ordered one to be delivered as soon as it came in.

With a smile on his face, even though it would be several days before she got her present, he pulled into her driveway and knocked on her door. She was still in her work clothes—soft, slim, pale green pants and a matching silk shell. The neck on it was high, the button in the back a little pearl. The short sleeves fluttered around her arms.

For a moment he didn't know what to say. He should have been better prepared for this. But she motioned him inside and it was as natural as anything to follow her.

"You keep showing up on my doorstep, Luke Hernandez."

He liked the way she said his name, the way it rolled off her tongue with just a hint of the appropriate accent. He imagined her calling him *Luciano* and it made him smile again. He found a few words and hoped they worked "I thought maybe after the night you had last night, you'd want to come out. Maybe go to Snafu, grab a beer?"

The last part came out as a question and he was relieved when she smiled at him.

"I could but I haven't eaten anything yet. I should do that before I drink anything."

At that moment, his own stomach decided to growl loudly. At least Ivy had the grace to laugh at him. He probably turned five shades of red as he remembered the stupid soggy cereal that he put down the drain.

"We can get food there," he offered immediately, trying to cover the embarrassment with words. He jumped in again, "I'm buying."

But she shook her head, waving her hand toward the kitchen. "I already have something in the oven."

Well, shit. He'd just ruined his whole plotline for the night, hadn't he? But Ivy always seemed to know how to make things right. "Why don't you stay? Have dinner with me. I owe you after the way you watched me cry last night."

She didn't owe him anything, but he didn't quite know how to say that either. It seemed they were owing each other a lot these days. And no matter how he counted it, the debt was always heavy against him.

He agreed and found out that he'd arrived at a quite opportune time. Within a few moments, she was pulling a small roast chicken from the oven. The glass baking dish was filled with tiny carrots, potatoes, mushrooms and onions, all scattered around the chicken and smelling heavenly. By the size of it, she'd probably planned to eat it for the next three or four meals. He would scarf down that much in one sitting.

Luke almost refused, but Ivy didn't give him the chance. She was pulling plastic plates out of the newly refurbished cabinets and dishing out the hot food. She put two thirds of it onto one plate for him. He'd thought he'd come over to ask her out and even offered to buy, but in the end she was feeding him and the debt weighed against him again.

They ate, not speaking of any of the hard topics of the past several weeks. She didn't mention her past or her family and he didn't mention his own brothers or his concerns. He didn't tell her that, as the weeks passed, he grew more and more tense that it was time for the arsonist to strike again. Or that the light dusting of snow that seemed to be covering the streets these days wasn't going to be enough to keep a firebug at bay.

When asked something that made the conversation hit a snag, Ivy would just shift the topic asking something different. It should have been awkward, but she made it less so.

In the end, they both finished their food at about the same time. So he stood to help her clean up. It was the least he could do. Wasn't he always doing the least with her?

When the dishes were in the dishwasher, not full enough to run, she closed it and turned to him. "Shall we go?"

"Do you want to change? It's Snafu. You could loosen up a little bit."

He hadn't meant it in a bad way. Just that she was clearly in her work clothes. But the expression on her face told him he'd stepped in it.

"Really? You do understand this is *loosened up* where I come from."

"I didn't mean—"

She sighed at him then her lips pressed flat with anger. "I know you didn't mean it that way, but you don't know anything about it."

Didn't he? She'd told him last night. "I just meant you always look so proper." He had held back the word *prim* and gave himself a pat on the back for it. "When you were wearing Jo's clothes. It just ..." he searched for the proper term. "It suited you."

He couldn't go wrong with that, could he? But he must have.

She turned around and stared at him. "What would you have me do?"

Shit.

He tried. He really did. "You never wear jeans."

He liked her in jeans! If he was going to step in it, he might as well jump in the puddle with both feet and make a splash. He didn't want to say, *You don't wear anything sexy.* But her expression hardened and she stared at him.

"Really, you think I should loosen up?"

There was nothing he could say. He'd come over unannounced, eaten the food she prepared for herself. And now he'd managed to completely insult her.

She was not going to go out with him now and let him buy her a beer.

But even as he was thinking his way through all of that, she said, "Have you ever done coke off a hooker's ass, Luke? Because I have!"

He knew there was no way to hide his expression. Just in case the things she'd said before weren't shocking enough, she'd tossed another grenade at him and he wasn't catching it well. She'd *What?*

"When I left my family and went out on my own, I got a job waiting tables. And I was good at it. So I moved to fancier and fancier restaurants, where I began partying afterwards with the patrons. I've done all kinds of drugs, Luke."

He blinked at her.

She had had the grace to say, "No. I'm not an addict. Unlike your brother, I just don't have—" she raised her fingers for air quotes "—an addictive personality."

When he didn't speak, she went on, lobbing her stories at him like lit sticks of TNT. "And thank God, because I tried *everything.*" She sucked in a deep breath as she mistook his concern for disapproval, her lips flattening again. "How exactly should I loosen up? Should I fuck my way around town? Should I get some tattoos, Luke? Well, you're too late for either of those!"

One hand reached up to the back of her neck, and then quickly her arms crossed, grabbing at the hem of the pretty silk shell she wore. She twisted her back to him as she stripped it, revealing a twine of inked Ivy and Lilies that snaked across one shoulder and down her side. Black ink scrolled through it as did tiny words he couldn't make out.

But she was reaching to the front of the silk pants and unbuttoning them, pulling one side down, revealing more ink: crossed swords on a tantalizing hip bone. And as she boldly faced him—the shell discarded on the kitchen counter behind her—in only a white lace bra, he saw another tattoo on her breast. This one snuck down under the edge of her bra.

It hadn't been disapproval that she'd seen and now he couldn't even form words to tell her she'd been wrong. He had no way to fight her anger and tell her she didn't need it.

He didn't have any issues with any of it.

It was bold and sexy and unexpected. And his whole body clenched at the idea that Ivy Dean was hiding this from everyone ... except him.

What he did next would change everything.

CHAPTER TWENTY-ONE

I n a moment of pure fantasy, Luke leaned in.

Ivy was mad at him. She might be standing there in her bra, demanding that he see her tattoos and understand that she wasn't the prim, buttoned-up librarian she might appear. She demanded that he see her as she was ... and he was noticing.

He hadn't flirted with her. He didn't sweet talk her. He didn't brush her lips lightly with his and try to coax her into a kiss or something more. He simply lost his damned mind and sank right into it. Into her.

The kiss was fierce and demanding from the first touch.

She didn't quite trust him, he knew. He'd almost gotten her killed.

He didn't quite trust her either. She had the tools to destroy his family with a few well placed rumors.

But he wanted her. His hips ground into hers, finding the rolling sensation of her moving against him as a reward. Her fingers were wound tightly into his hair, holding his head so she could ravage his mouth. Luke was more than willing to be her victim.

His hands gripped the new tile countertops, his mind

flipping through scenes of him finding her expertly using the tile saw, laying each piece and then grouting the whole thing with a pastry bag. The woman knew what she was doing and his fingers clenched against her handiwork before reaching to her hip and clutching her hard enough to leave marks.

Luke couldn't regret it. His mouth sought hers, his tongue battled for dominance, and he loved every second. When he stopped to draw a breath, she expertly maneuvered him, swapping their places and pressing him backward against the counter.

Her mouth traced his jawline as his head tipped back in ecstasy. If anyone had told him he'd be getting ravaged by Ivy Dean he would have … well, he would have had fantasies that didn't even begin to rival reality.

No longer holding her in place, Luke's hands slid up from her hips. He didn't have to hold onto her, Ivy wanted to be here … or at least she needed to be. His fingers traced the top edge of her bra, her breasts silk to the touch as her sudden intake of breath heaved her chest up for a moment.

That one gentle, reverent touch hadn't been enough. He reached around and ripped at the clasp, having no idea if he had suavely removed it or torn the thing by brute force, but he didn't pay attention as it hit the floor. His hand reached into her hair, holding her head back as his mouth traced her neck, her collarbone, and finally tasted the pink tip of her breast.

He wasn't normally such a beast. But Ivy was giving as good as she got. He was going to have fingernail marks down his back tomorrow and he not only didn't care, he loved it.

The sweet suction of his mouth on her was thwarted by his shirt getting tugged up and over his head. Ivy wasn't playing nice. As one hand tossed the shirt away the other reached for the snap on his jeans and it occurred to him for the first time that they weren't playing at all. Neither of them was going to come to their senses and call this off.

Her fingers slid along the skin of his hips, pushing everything downward. His muscles had been on fire with need, but he entered flashover, everything igniting at once. Any thoughts were incinerated. He was operating on pure need as he reached for her pants. Finding them still unbuttoned, he growled with need as he saw the crossed swords on her hip and leaned down to nip at them.

His feet were caught and he kicked at his shoes and clothing, suddenly naked in Ivy's kitchen. But her hips were wiggling as she let the silky pants slide down long bare legs, panties going with them. He could smell her. He couldn't think. He wanted her. He needed her. He couldn't resist.

Pushing her to walk a few steps backward, he had her against the edge of the new dining room table. A sturdy, butcher block piece, it held her easily as he lifted her to the edge and then pushed her backward until she was draped, naked, open, and inviting across the top.

Her hair splayed out around her like she was a mermaid. Her body with all its visible tattoos and hidden scars was his, if only for a moment or two.

He must have looked at her too long, because her ankles hooked behind his knees, pulling him closer. He didn't need to be pulled, he wasn't going anywhere.

She spoke his name, a sound somewhere between begging and demand. If he'd ever had the ability to resist her, it was gone now. With his own hand, he positioned himself at her entrance, pausing for a split second to savor the moment. Ivy's legs open, her body laid out like a feast on the table, her eyes glazed and hot with need. For him.

He pushed into her. Hot and wet, the sensation wiped every shred of self knowledge from him. There was only now. Only her. Only this.

Her hips moved, taking him deeper and forcing him to comply. Her legs wrapped around him, holding him inside as her hips rotated, pushing and pulling against him until they were moving in a rhythm neither of them had complete control of. His tension built, and he tried to savor the sweet feeling of being inside her. She felt like heat and danger and home all at the same time. But nothing about this was letting him stop and linger.

Ivy arched her back, changing his angle and making his eyes roll. Luke fought to keep moving against her, to give as good as he got. When he managed to open his eyes again, she was propped up on her elbows, bare breasts heaving with her gasping breaths, eyes demanding.

She reached up, lacing her fingers into his hair and controlling his head until their lips were locked. He was pressed, full body, against her, inside her, over her … and yet she'd still invaded him.

They moved as though they were made for this. Each fighting for dominance and each conceding that they'd never quite achieve it. Their groans and cries probably reached the neighbors', but Luke didn't care. He couldn't hold back as the blackness crept in around the corners of his vision and he both felt and heard her cry out her release. The feel of her around him changed and he couldn't hold out anymore as his own body convulsed with what had to be the most sweeping orgasm of his life.

Collapsing forward onto his elbows, he tried not to crush her as his lungs fought for air and he gasped repeatedly as he fought to both return to reality and to never come back.

Slowly, he felt her melting away underneath him, her own senses likely returning as her head rolled to the side almost as if she could fall asleep right here in his arms, still laid out on her own dining room table.

But as his head slowly lifted and he looked her in the eyes, Luke knew there was nothing he could say. He had to get out of here.

CHAPTER TWENTY-TWO

Ivy woke up in her bed and immediately her hands went to her head. She was wearing her pajamas, sleeping alone in her home, and her alarm was going off. She could try to believe that this was any normal morning. But it wasn't.

Reaching out, she slapped at the alarm clock as memories of the night before flooded back in. When was the last time she'd even had sex?

She tried to remember. It had been in life number two. Life Number Two had been tight jeans, low cut tight tops, friends who actually turned tricks for a living. They'd been high end call girls and Ivy had enjoyed the occasional limo with a Hollywood star funding everything. She'd been to after-parties galore and partaken of plenty of hedonistic pleasures.

But one night at the restaurant, she'd waited on a group of librarians coming from a conference. They'd been ecstatic about their trip and happy to see each other again and told her all about it. When she'd asked about their jobs, they had encouraged her. Like magicians, they pulled out their phones, referencing everything, giving her tips for things she hadn't considered. They told her what degrees to get, what the best schools were, and linked her to loan sources that would help fund someone like her through the high cost.

Ivy had spent six more months after that waiting tables. No more hookers and blow for Ivy Dean. Every penny went into savings. That fall, she entered New York University's Library Sciences Program. Life Number Three had begun.

And she hadn't slept with anyone. Not since the night she'd waited on those librarians. Until now.

Rolling over in bed, she knew she could burn the time until her snooze went off. Ivy tried not to think about Luke. About the sizzling heat of his touch and her complete inability to control herself when he kissed her. They'd gone from zero to sixty thousand degrees in a moment.

Forcing her thoughts back to the librarians, she wondered if she should reach out again. She had stayed in touch with two of them, letting them know when she graduated NYU and when she'd gotten her master's. She'd told them of the job in Redemption. They'd been cheerleaders all the way as she'd once again cut herself off from most everything and walked away from Life number two. This time it had been of her own free choice.

But last night, she'd whipped out her tattoos in a fit of anger. Feeling the fire as Luke had touched her, and doing ... *Oh my god, what had she done?*

Life number two was bleeding into life number three. As much as she was attracted to him—clearly too much—she still wasn't completely convinced that he wasn't the arsonist. She didn't believe he was, but her feelings had led her horrifically astray before and she couldn't trust them.

The alarm began screaming at her and once again her hand flailed out to hit it. This time she forced herself out of bed and climbed into the shower, her body deliciously sore in previously unused places. She wasn't even sure if Luke had fled her home, or if she kicked him out. It seemed to be a mutual thing.

But he was gone now, and she could at least pretend that last night hadn't happened, even if she couldn't shake the memories that rushed back at her.

She got dressed, ate breakfast and drove to work. Ivy tried to turn her brain off as she checked into the library. This was not her usual MO. But she made it through the day as normally as possible, then picked up fast food on the way home. That wasn't normal for third-life-Ivy-Dean either, but what was she going to do? The leftovers that she was intending to eat tonight hadn't existed after she'd fed them to Luke.

She brought her bag of cheap food home and sat at her bar … she couldn't sit at the table. Between it having no chairs yet and being covered in sweaty steamy sexy memories, it wasn't as though she could just unwrap her burger there and ignore the things she was trying hard to ignore.

So she sat on a barstool, played on her tablet, and tried to keep her brain from straying to the man she'd been magnetically attracted to for quite some time now.

In life number two, Ivy had known how to fuck someone and walk away. Was that what she was going to do here? Could she even do that?

It seemed that there would be no way that she could simply not see Luke Hernandez again. Even if she shifted her way out of his circle, they would surely run into each other. Maybe that would be okay. She could be polite. He could be polite.

But what if she uncovered that it *was* one of his brothers starting these fires? Or even his father? What would she do then?

Her phone pinged and she saw the message from Jo. The shift must have hit a down patch.

—Holy shit, what did you do to Luke last night?

She froze. Had he gone into work and told everyone? That didn't seem like Luke, but fucking a man she didn't quite trust on her kitchen table didn't seem like her either. Quickly, she tapped back a non-commital message.

—Why? What did he say?

Only as she hit send did she realize that she'd basically admitted everything. *Fuck me.*

No, honey. Luke already did that, she reminded herself.

—Oh, he's just off his game big time. Alternately smiling at himself and then frowning at nothing. I figured it had to be about you.

Jo chased that message with a string of emojis that mocked her. But Ivy put her head in her hands and didn't respond. Last time she'd incriminated herself.

She sighed and tried to think of other ways to catch or clear Luke's brothers. Ivy wouldn't admit to herself that solving that mystery would make room for her and Luke to be together. They *weren't* together. But she worked on it anyway.

Tracking down Santiago Hernandez Senior had been difficult at best. The only thing she'd found so far was that the bastard had left his children when Carlos was barely out of diapers. Probably around the time the fifth son had been stillborn. Was there a connection? Did it matter?

There was no evidence she could find of any child support or even any contact after the day he left. She finished her burger with no more pings from Jo. Her thoughts scrambled as she celebrated having won yet another round of her matching game.

As the screen played an ad she wasn't interested in watching, Ivy looked out the window. While she'd been eating, the day had gone from dark to pitch black. She'd left her new curtains wide open. They were cheap poly fabric, but the cranberry color had contrasted nicely with the pale, creamy sunshine of the walls. She loved the way the color popped and told herself that when she got chairs, she would get pillows that matched.

But as she looked out the large front window, her thoughts

were not on matching pillows, but on the way her blood suddenly cooled as she scanned her own front yard and looked at the street. There was nothing she could put her finger on. Nothing she'd seen. But she couldn't shake the sudden sensation that she was being watched.

CHAPTER TWENTY-THREE

I vy turned the key to the empty building. She liked being the only one here. Wednesdays meant they opened at noon and stayed open until nine at night. It was yet another change Ivy had brought to the tiny library.

The beauty of opening a library relatively from scratch was that she got to implement her own ideas. She wasn't changing set schedules that the townspeople already knew. She'd seen this at other libraries and loved the idea of late night book borrowing. So she tried it. The other good thing was that she didn't have to work the late shift herself. Usually Shannon did. And Wednesday mornings were her chance to take care of things without anyone else around.

But today, as it had been since the fire, the library wasn't getting quite her full attention. She'd exhausted all the knowledge at her fingertips. But she was now one of the magicians she'd aspired to be and when she ran out of material, she turned to people.

For a moment, her heart clenched as she'd immediately thought about picking up the phone and calling Marina Balero. The detective had been a friend—helpful, smart, kind, and caring. Exactly the kind of officer you wanted in a small town. *And she was gone.* Murdered while solving a case, Marina had given her life to keep people safe.

Though Ivy knew many of the other officers, she wasn't sure who she could trust to give her the kind of information that she needed without turning it back around to the Hernandez family or maybe even Chief Taggart.

Was she making a mistake? Though she told herself she hadn't decided *not* to tell the chief, she also hadn't told him and that was a decision, too. It had been several weeks since her own fire and she could tell Luke was getting antsy about the arsonist striking again. That in turn, made her antsy about it.

She'd almost died. And she was concerned the next person wouldn't be so lucky. Still she hadn't quite brought herself to hand over all of her information to Sebastian Kane and Chief Taggert to fully run the investigation.

So she pulled out her phone and called an older number.

"Ivy!" the voice answered, clearly glad to be hearing from her.

She should have called for a better reason, she thought. But she hadn't, and she needed him now. "I hope I haven't caught you at a bad time."

Former detective Orlando Tavares was now on the road with his fiance, Chloe Goodman. They worked together as part of the privately funded missing persons investigation unit. Nebraska's own Reiner Institute funded them and touted their incredible success rate. "Don't worry about it."

Ivy noticed that he didn't say *it's not a bad time.* Then again, they hunted missing children, so maybe there was never a good time. She didn't know how they dealt with what they saw, but somehow they did.

Ivy had helped them with cases on several occasions. When they had missing kids local to the area, she pulled records and fed them information and answered questions the best she could. She liked the work and felt that she was doing her part to reunite children with their families. Though she hadn't thought of it as building up points, it was definitely time to cash in her chips. "I need some help with some background information and I've exhausted all my resources."

She could hear in the background as Chloe's voice asked, "Is that Ivy Dean?" He must have nodded or motioned *yes* because Ivy immediately heard, "Hi, Ivy!" from the background and she told him to tell Chloe that she said hi, too.

"We have an arsonist in town." There wasn't time to beat around the bush.

"We heard. How can we help?"

She explained about the particular places the arsonist was hitting and her theories about the Hernandez family and about Luke's own suspicions. "Can you pull records without alerting anyone?"

"You haven't turned this over to Taggart?" he asked.

This was the shitty part, where she couldn't even point her moral compass in one direction or another. "One of Luke's brothers is in need of rehab again. Another, if accused, could easily be found guilty whether he is or not … with his record, he'll just go down for it. Then, if we put him away and we're wrong, the arsonist is free to strike again … In fact, Luke is very concerned that his brother isn't the right guy. Honestly, I think he's concerned the brother is into something illegal, but if it's not the arson, Luke doesn't want to touch it and he doesn't want to be the trigger for it. He's really concerned about what happens if we get it wrong."

"Okay, gotcha," Tavares readily agreed, making Ivy feel that maybe her own reasoning wasn't quite so crazy.

She fed him everything she had to get them started and then set him and Chloe loose to dig up police and federal records.

Only a few moments after hanging up with Orlando and Chloe, her phone rang.

"Hello, Miss Dean. I'm here at the front door."

"I'll be right there, Mr. Gentson." She made her way quickly around the counter, weaving her way through the short hallways, not wanting to leave the older man standing and waiting too long. She unbolted the door and glanced around quickly. The library faced the main street and several cars passed by, meaning at least a few people in Redemption now knew that Mr. Gentson was here.

She had told the elderly man that she wanted to interview him for an oral town history. Which was actually a plan that Ivy had, so it was a fudge, not a lie. As a child, she had been taught that lies were bad, then it was demonstrated lies that suited her parents or the elders were fine. It had taken her a while to develop her own code. As an adult, she'd found many good reasons not to tell the truth. Some to save her own skin but many out of kindness to others.

In this case, it was to protect Luke's family.

She knew the older man had so much useful information about the town, and she would use this interview in that process. So she now had no issues telling him he was here as part of her project and no trouble saying that to anyone who might have seen him come in during closed hours.

Motioning him to sit down in one of the big comfy chairs at the center study table, she told him, "You're my first interview for this project! And I'm honestly not sure which way the project is going to go. I do know I want it to do a few things. I want to really capture the memories of those who grew up here over the decades and I want it to include things that we can't find in the books and records."

He was nodding along, seeming pleased to be part of the work. She hoped he never found out that she was also milking him for information. But if his stories helped her locate the arsonist, he might like getting that credit. The man appreciated being appreciated.

It took them a good hour to get through the basics of when he was born and who was in town then. She took copious notes and asked clarifying questions. Then she asked about prominent families in town. She started with the Balero family, then the Millers, thinking maybe she could throw the Hernandezes into the mix and he wouldn't notice.

"Okay." She smiled, hoping he couldn't read her ulterior motives. "You've told me about the prominent families. What about the notorious ones?"

Sure enough, two families later, he said, "The Hernandez boys."

Though there were several families named Hernandez, Mr. Gentson was talking about Luke's family. But she was confused by the names. "There's no Diego in the family."

"Oh, the Santiago Hernandez I'm talking about is the father of the last batch. His brother was Diego, and his other brothers were Carlos and Pedro." No wonder she'd been confused, several of the names had been recycled in the current generation. But she didn't even have to probe, he volunteered what she needed and Ivy gave a silent cheer.

"That next round of Hernandezes was just as bad. I always wondered what kind of trouble they would cause when they grew up. And here we are."

Ivy felt her suspicions start to gel.

CHAPTER TWENTY-FOUR

"Thank you, Mr. Gentson. You've been a huge help."

Ivy led him out the front door, though the library had opened while they talked and she'd moved them into the back room. She'd even cut him off partway through the interview when people started needing books checked out.

She'd not "finished" per se, and he would have to come back, but he'd told her all sorts of things about all kinds of "bad seeds" all over town. Watching as the old man made his way to his car, she noticed he was leaning more heavily on his cane than he had on the way in. The interview, as tame as it had been, had worn him out.

Ivy worried about him in more ways than one. He had been instrumental in finding some lost children just a short while ago. He was kind, friendly, and always willing to be helpful. On the other hand, the information he had just given her about the history of the town spoke to a deep bias against Latino people.

That hurt her soul in addition to simply being ridiculous. The Hispanic population in Nebraska was so high that having a bias against them would mean being at odds with a very large portion of the locals.

Nebraska, as late as the 1990s, actively recruited southern border immigrants, inviting them to not stop in the southern states, but come all the way north and settle on the open plains and corn fields. It worked, and Ivy now saw the results of that in the faces around her—even in Luke's.

She would have to take everything Mr. Gentson said with a grain of salt. However, even accounting for that there were disturbing things the man had said, it was clear that Tiago's troublemaking had begun when he was young. No one was watched the boys—they'd basically raised themselves which made her all the more impressed by Luke's success. Carlos, too. It seemed he had only managed to get himself straight by leaving town.

Ivy checked out a young woman's stack of thrillers even as her brain replayed some of the things Mr. Gentson had said. "It's no wonder Mario's got problems!" He'd smacked his hand onto the laminate surface of the table. "Tiago dealt drugs for a while, probably got his own little brother hooked."

Ivy hadn't written notes for that one, but mentally noted another thing to follow. She'd not found drug arrests in Tiago's history but there weren't necessarily public statements for every time he'd been picked up or questioned.

Mr. Gentson had also had a sour expression when he'd told her, "Mario and Carlos used to tease the neighborhood dogs. They were horrible little children. Evil if you ask me. There were rumors that somebody had found Mario having cut open a squirrel to see what was inside it. I don't think it died of natural causes." Ivy hadn't been able to hide the way her whole body had pulled back with the revulsion.

Mr. Gentson had nodded at her as if to say, *See, he was right. Those Hernandez boys were terrible.* "That Luke kid ran with a rough crowd, stolen cars, lots of *weed.*" He'd emphasized the last word and she wondered if he would call it the "devil's lettuce" or something more ridiculous. She wondered what he'd say if she told him about all the drugs she'd done. *Weed* had been the least of them.

"That Luke never got caught," Gentson had said and there was something in his tone that made Ivy wonder. But the older man followed it up with, "I never was quite sure if it was because he wasn't really doing any of it, maybe just hanging out with the wrong people. Or if he was so slick, that he always weaseled out of it and left his friends holding the bag for what he'd done." Ivy nodded along, knowing that people spoke more when you agreed with them.

Mr. Gentson at least had the decency to follow up with, "Luke, though, he's made something for himself. Went off to community college, came back and tried out for the firefighters." He said it as though it were a cheerleading squad and Ivy smiled as she tried to cover a laugh. "Surprises me, but seems he's been a good addition to the station. Taggart seems to like him. And I like Taggart."

And didn't that just say it all? Mr. Gentson decided who he trusted. And he trusted the people that those people trusted, whether or not it was the right thing to do.

Between helping the few patrons that wandered through the place on a Wednesday afternoon, she dashed back into her office and pulled her notebook out of her bag and jotted down everything she could remember about the Hernandez boys. When she finished, there wasn't much left to do, just help the steady trickle of patrons and stare at empty walls.

So she worked her way through the library, doing some of the things she normally did on Wednesday mornings, so that her workers didn't find things amiss. Though they were giving her a pretty clean pass these days, so she knew that anything that wasn't done would get written off. Still, it was time to get back to normal. Sitting around and waiting for the arsonist to strike again would only make her a crappy librarian … and who even knew how long that would last?

Turning her attention fully to the job, the singular focus that she'd lacked for several weeks felt good, even though she hit a long stretch with no one but herself in the building. The only sound that cut the silence was her phone ringing.

The name on the screen said Orlando Tavares, so she jerked the phone to her ear and greeted him quickly. "That was fast!"

"You did catch us at a good time. We're in between cases and it was easy enough for us to just sit down and pull the records for you. We'd just been finishing breakfast when you called." His voice sounded cheerful, and she was glad that he and Chloe were doing well with the work. "Anyway, it's all gathered up, but I didn't want to send it until I talked to you. Sounds like this info is a little hush hush?"

"That it is." She hadn't fooled him at all.

"So where do you want me to send it?"

She rattled off her personal email because everything that went through the library system could be checked by the city records. It was, after all, a public job. She thanked him and tried to turn her mind back to the work. When she heard the ping, she didn't dare open it on one of the library computers, she herself had made sure everything researched on library systems could be traced. She couldn't have any of her employees finding what she'd dug up or even learning that she was digging if they were the ones checking search histories.

So she was on her phone as she heard the chime over the front door, indicating that another patron had come in. Her eyes grew wide as she'd read through the sealed juvenile record. How had Orlando and Chloe gotten this?

Her heart was racing, but she closed everything out—just in case someone saw what was on her phone. The rest of the day went by in a blur. She traded out with Shannon later, not having gotten the break she was supposed to have taken before she opened. With her stomach grumbling, she drove through for fast food again and headed home.

At least she was finally able to sit down, open the email, and read through the reams of information that Orlando had sent. He had even included a couple of notes. "Chloe suggested I look up old burglaries. So I included these reports."

Chloe was known for her hunches. It was part of why she was so good at finding missing children. She and Orlando were the perfect pair—she was an ex FBI-agent, him an ex-detective who knew his way around the area and the people and the cultures here.

Chloe had once asked Ivy to help her look up her own ancestry, as she hadn't known much of it herself. It was Ivy who had traced her past to the Goodman family from regions in both Northern and Southern California. It was Ivy who told Chloe the interesting thing about the Goodmans was that they ran a witchcraft shop in Los Angeles. And for the first time, Chloe had wondered if her ancestry played a role in her special gifts.

So now, when Chloe suggested Orlando look into the burglaries, Orlando had listened to Chloe's hunches and Ivy took it all, even though she didn't quite see the pattern.

Yet.

Several hours later, with all of it churning through her head, she had hopped in her car and driven halfway across town. In a small set of quadruplex buildings, the pink stucco chipping and the numbers often hanging by a single nail, she found the door she was looking for and knocked.

A sleepy-eyed Luke Hernandez seemed as surprised to see her as she was to be here. He wore only sweatpants that he seemed to have hastily pulled on to answer the door. He blinked as though he wasn't quite awake and unknowingly reached up and scratched at his bare chest.

And, with that move, Ivy forgot what she had come for.

Her bag was slung over her shoulder, but she forgot about the contents as she stepped boldly past him. As she brushed against his skin, she felt the warmth from where she'd clearly roused him from a deep sleep.

He still hadn't said anything but was sloe-eyed as he pushed the door closed behind her and turned around. Forgetting everything she'd prepared to say, Ivy heard her bag fall to the floor with a *thud* as her arms wrapped around his neck and she kissed him with everything she had.

CHAPTER TWENTY-FIVE

Luke kissed her back. Had she already forgotten what he tasted like? Because she knew it was good, but she'd not remembered it was this good.

Her tongue swept into his mouth, searching for more, for whatever it was that only he seemed to have. Maybe she'd been lying to herself, telling her brain that it wasn't this good, that her body didn't flare with desire just from getting close enough to smell him.

She couldn't have let go of him if she'd tried. It didn't help that Luke's arms were around her, too. The bulk of her heavy coat had been necessary against the cold, but it was only in her way now. He was half naked and her clothing was far too much barrier for what her body craved.

He pulled at her coat and she heard it fall to the floor but didn't bother to look. Her hands were too busy roaming his skin, her mouth was too occupied with his. She pushed him up against his own door, intending to ravage him, but he gently moved her back.

Ivy froze.

Did he not want ...

But his eyes and his fingers went to the front of her white button-down shirt and he began popping each button one by one.

He wanted her. She could feel the flare in her own eyes, smell the need on him that equaled her own, and practically taste the need in the air. She wondered if he could see it on her. But he wasn't even looking; his eyes were following the path of open shirt and exposed skin that he created.

When he hit the bottom of the row, she was struggling to pop the buttons at the wrists of the shirt that she'd carefully lined up and fitted into place one-handed this morning. He was right, she was the very definition of "buttoned up." Would it be so wrong to dress in a manner that Luke could more easily peel her clothing from her body?

Or would this be the last time? Were she and Luke just a passing phase until their need was sated?

She dropped the shirt to the floor and dove for him. Their mouths met again, and this time her bra was the only thing stopping full skin contact. Her hands skimmed up his chest and she pressed herself against him, wanting to devour him. Wanting him inside her and making her scream.

But as she took a breath, she realized that Luke wasn't ravaging her.

His hands skimmed along her arms, the lightest of touches leaving tingles and goosebumps in their wake. Though he was pushed against the door, he took her hands in his, holding them overhead as he leaned into her and his mouth made a leisurely trek, tasting every corner and testing every inch.

He was supposed to be her conquest, and instead he was leaned against the door, no longer caged, but leading an expedition. Her heart thumped in odd time and fear traced her veins along with the fire she couldn't ignore. She overcame it by tugging her hands free and pushing into him again.

Their mouths dueled, and she was more content with this

speed. His hands cupped her jaw, holding her in place as he— finally—rolled his hips against hers and let her know how much he wanted her.

But again, he pulled back and pushed her away.

"Luke?"

Had she misjudged?

"Shhhhh." He whispered the soft sound and kissed her again, this time a simple, sweet lingering of lips that again had fear curling fingers around her heart. "Slow down."

Her breath skipped. She wanted to say *no*. She didn't know how to slow down. Life number one had been devoid of anything to do with sex or lovemaking. She hadn't even seen it on TV, and aside from her first kiss in that club—which she now realized wasn't even worth a spark—she'd had no experience. Life number two had been about exploring everything denied to her. But there had been nothing slow or sweet or hotly seductive about it.

Her eyes opened and found his. He was asking her to trust him.

Half of her knew she couldn't.

She couldn't trust anyone.

The other half of her begged for it. "I don't know."

The words weren't even loud enough for her to hear, but Luke didn't seem fazed by it at all. "You can. Come on."

He reached downward and before she knew what was happening, he'd scooped her behind her legs, lifting her from the floor and carrying her—romance movie style—through the small space.

She laughed at the absurdity of it then froze. She'd broken the mood. She'd ruined—

But Luke was laughing at her, too, and none of the heat had left his eyes. Expertly maneuvering her through the doorway and into the dark back room, he set her softly and gently on the bed.

He'd figured it out. He'd figured *her* out. She'd screwed and fucked and sated her needs, but she'd never done this.

"I've got you." His whispered words flowed like rivers over her exposed skin. His fingers touched her knee and slid up her leg.

She moved by feel, the apartment still mostly dark, and the room nearing pitch black. She pushed her fingers into the waistband of his pants and began to push downward, but his hand clenched her wrist and stopped her. "Slow."

Sucking in a breath, she placed her hands on his hips and wondered if she was gripping him tightly enough for him to feel her tension. She had to be. He was reading her like a book.

His mouth traced her lips. Then, as she moved to kiss him back, he skipped away, tracing her jaw up to her ear as his fingers worked magic on her skirt. She felt the soft touch as he dropped it to the floor, sliding his silver touch along her arches as her shoes fell away. She was only in her underwear, not an unfamiliar state, but still feeling so exposed to him despite the darkness.

But then, as he kissed her and seemed to know exactly how to pull her under, she closed her eyes and felt his touch. He skimmed her legs reverently, teasing her and making her gasp. She grabbed for him. Though now, instead of controlling the course of their lovemaking, she was reaching to hold on as her world rocked.

Luke was steady as he removed the last of her clothing and his, as his fingers found her hot and wet and ready for him, but he still didn't enter her. He didn't even come close. He touched her, tasted her, drove her to the brink and made her cry out. Ivy could feel the hard length of him against her leg, it was the only thing that kept her from doubting that he was just playing with her, trying to take control and prove he could drive her to need him.

But he could.

She did.

He hooked a hand behind her knee and pulled her leg up over his hip, though she pressed against him, begging him with her motions, he didn't give in. She wasn't driving this and she was lost—lost in the sensations he pulled from her and lost in her need for him.

She didn't need anyone and it was petrifying to let him be in charge. But the way he touched her made it worth giving up her control.

He slowly entered her, holding her hip to keep her from bucking against him and taking him all in one motion. His other hand played with her hair, and he kissed her as though they were sitting on the couch and watching tv. Soft, casual kisses that belied the storm he was brewing under her skin.

"Luke!"

"Shhhhhh." He moved further inside, causing her back to arch even though it didn't change what she felt. He pulled out before filling her completely and she thought she might cry. If he stopped now, she'd be left devastated. And she'd put herself into this position.

What if he ...

But he moved again, filling her and stealing her breath with a sensation bigger and bolder than any she'd known. His breath sighed heavily into her ear, reassuring her than this was just as wild for him as it was for her. She wasn't the only one.

"Ivy."

He drove home, plucking her like a too-tight piano string. She cried out as the sensation flooded her system. But she didn't come.

He moved again. Whispered her name again. Drove home again.

And again, and again, until they were together one writhing ball of need and desire and flame. When at last he pushed her over the edge, she screamed his name and no amount of shushing her could have prevented it. She didn't have the wherewithal to doubt him at that point, but she felt his own release through hers, heard his cries, felt the undulation of his whole body.

She breathed him in, still wrapped, warm and sweaty and sated, around him, until she began to come to her senses.

What the hell had she just done?

CHAPTER TWENTY-SIX

Luke stared at the ceiling. He was sure as hell awake now.

It had taken quite some time to be sure he wasn't dreaming. He'd been dead asleep between shifts, not sure he'd heard the knocking on his door at first. He'd stumbled his way out, almost falling and cracking his head on his coffee table as he'd hopped into his sweat pants.

Firefighters knew how to sleep, and they knew how to wake up. And they also knew how to do a good handful of things without actually waking up. His first thought was this was someone selling donuts, to raise money for their scouts. A pizza delivery to the wrong place. Maybe the mail carrier with a package he couldn't leave in the box at the front of the unit.

It could have been any of them. Luke had no idea what time it was. But to open the door and find Ivy standing there had been beyond unexpected. It convinced him that he was dreaming after the shit he'd pulled the other night—just leaving in the middle of the night. Add in that they hadn't spoken to each other since and he was still trying to figure out how to apologize, to ask if she'd kicked him out, or figure out if he'd been the asshole.

Then, she didn't say anything, had just fused her mouth to his and pressed herself against him. Her hands roaming along his bare skin had been even more convincing that it was just a dream. So he'd kissed her back.

He wasn't quite sure when he realized that it wasn't a dream, Ivy was actually there. But by then it was far too late to stop and ask questions.

Now it became clear, as their breathing leveled out and she squirmed beside him, that she was about to get up and walk away. She was tucked in the crook of his arm, her head against his shoulder, and he tightened her against him, this time doing what he should have last time. "Stay."

Her fingers clenched against his side, but at least she stopped acting as if she was about to roll over and say something about a good time but she couldn't ... "Luke. I know you won't believe me, but I didn't come over here for this."

He chuckled, unable to fight the rumble that started low in his chest. She could have fooled him.

"I had things to tell you but—"

"You saw me and you couldn't resist me?" he teased, rolling his head toward her and watching as she rolled away, unwilling to look him in the eyes. His stomach growled and he felt more than heard her slight laughter.

"Food," he declared, adding, "and unlike you, I don't just happen to have a roast chicken with all the trimmings about ready to come out of the oven."

She shook her head against him, her hand coming up and splaying flat across his chest and making him forget what he was hungry for. "That was pure coincidence."

She shifted slightly as she spoke so he turned onto his side, keeping his one arm behind her. He moved the other to drape it across her hip. This time, he was going to make sure that no one fled.

"I'm sorry I left the way I did last time." His voice was low and full of gravel. Apologies didn't come easy, but he also knew if he didn't say it, it would hang forever between them. And he liked this—the nakedness of it, the lack of space between them.

She still didn't look at him. Again, she shook her head as if to shake it off. "That wasn't just you. I freaked out. I practically pushed you out the door. I mean, I don't need my neighbors seeing you leaving in the morning."

This time he laughed out loud. "So it was better for them to see me leaving in the middle of the night with hair that clearly said what we'd been up to?"

That at least made her eyes snap up to his. "Really?"

"Yes, but it was dark." He shrugged it off now, though he had initially intended to make her understand that the neighbors probably had figured it out. Now, he didn't want her to think that because it obviously worried her. For a woman who spouted the things she had, throwing her past at him as though it would hurt, she sure was concerned about what her neighbors might think. Leaning forward, he kissed her again, in the soft, casual way that he hoped conveyed he wanted something more than just this late night need. He wanted to be more than just an itch that Ivy Dean scratched.

She kissed him back and leaned in, her simple touch making him want her again. He felt the change when she pulled back. "There are things that I have to tell you."

He nodded, understanding she meant the things that were in the bag that she brought with her. Important information. "I have things I need to tell you, too."

She nodded softly as though waiting for him to tell her.

"I want more than this sneaking around. I want more than getting kicked out at two a.m. with my T shirt on inside out."

"It wasn't two a.m.," she protested.

"You know what I mean. I was hoping you would go out on an actual date with me." His heart pounded. How long had it been since he'd done anything other than hook up? How long had it been since he'd been with the same person more than once?

He laid there naked in bed, still smelling the scent of sex between them and the silence stretched out as he waited for Ivy to answer.

CHAPTER TWENTY-SEVEN

"I feel like I'm being watched."

Luke tried not to let the shock show at her words. Ivy sat at his old cheap table in an old cheap chair that looked like it had been stolen from his mother's first home. Ivy's place—even burned out—had been in better shape than this.

They sat in front of bowls of cereal. She'd not really turned him down, but she'd not agreed to a date either, saying only, "I don't know. With everything going on between us, I'm not sure it's the right thing to do."

Now he was hung up on that idea. Though he was listening to her, at the same time, he was trying to figure out how to get her to say yes. But this? It grabbed all of his attention. "What do you mean?"

She pushed the small, half-eaten bowl of cereal away. He kept this place warm and right now, he was enjoying the benefits of that as she sat there in only her underwear and one of his t shirts. She was wearing his clothes, eating his cereal, in his shitty apartment in the middle of the night.

They should be dating. But again her words pulled him back to the present with fear.

"I haven't seen anything I can put my finger on. It's just a feeling I've been having. And I don't know if it's some stupid paranoia, because my house burned down or if I'm actually sensing something and I just can't articulate it." She was looking down at the table top, as though ashamed of her own concerns.

Reaching over, he put his finger under her chin, a simple gesture that he hadn't done for simple reasons in a long time. He flirted when he could. He took it further when the offer was on the table, his moves always calculated to make sure that the person he was with wanted to be with him. And if she did, Luke went all in. Then he walked away when it was over.

But nothing here was calculated. He simply reached out and touched her. He'd wanted to see her eyes. Being with Ivy was like nothing he'd experienced. If he'd been choosing who to sleep with, it never would have been the town librarian. Never a woman he'd respected the way he did her. Not someone he admired for the way she had managed to come into a town and find a place at the heart of it. She hadn't grown up here, but she'd managed to put her finger on the pulse of what made his hometown his home.

She'd even helped solve cases, and he believed she could solve this one, too. Still, beyond all that, he simply wanted to be with her.

Though as she looked at him, he broke eye contact and rolled his eyes, looking up at the ceiling. "Damn it, Ivy."

He looked back at her in time to see her eyebrows rise, wondering why he was cursing her. "I want you to go out with me because you *want* to go out with me."

Ivy just shrugged and opened her mouth. But Luke waved his hand as if to cut her off, telling her to shut up. "If someone is watching you, you need to have someone with you. You need to have someone who's constantly stopping by. So that whoever is trying to get to you sees that you're not alone, that they could be dropped in on at any moment. Ideally, it's someone who stays overnight and someone with some power, like an FBI agent or a police officer."

He hated saying that part, but Ivy caught on and grinned at him. "Or a firefighter?"

Half of his mouth pulled up in a smile. "It wouldn't hurt. And I sure as hell don't want you shacking up with someone else."

"So, we *what?*" she asked. "We go out, get seen together publicly? We become boyfriend and girlfriend?"

"That's the idea." He said. But it wasn't all of it. "I don't want you with me just as a cover but also I don't want you unsafe. And I don't want you with anyone else."

There. He'd said all the words out loud. Let her untangle them. His frustration was that they were all true. Any of them happening would preclude some of the others.

He was looking at the tabletop, studying the grain that had been painted on when her fingers fisted into the front of his t shirt, pulling him upward. He barely managed to look up in time to catch that Ivy was coming toward him.

Her kiss was fierce and strong. He was grateful his cheap table was tiny and she'd easily been able to close the gap. Her lips tasted of sugar from the cereal and her mouth tasted of a heaven he hadn't quite known existed.

"All right," she said, releasing his shirt. "Let's do this."

But he was protesting again. He needed Ivy to want *him,* not just safety.

She tipped her head at him as though to chastise him. "Let's be honest, it's the perfect excuse to do what I want to do anyway."

His heart soared. After all, the woman wore twinsets and hid those sexy tattoos from the world, she made choices based on appearance. But if she wanted to be seen with him, he could live with that.

He slid heavily back down into the seat with a thunk, the jolt almost sloshing the milk out of her cereal bowl.

Then she frowned at him. "I take that back. I don't know if you're going to want to be seen publicly with me after I tell you what I learned."

CHAPTER TWENTY-EIGHT

"Carlos and I were both at my mother's that night." Luke pointed to one of the papers that was spread out on his table before him.

Some were prints that Ivy had made of police reports and charges and court documents that Orlando Tavares had sent her, others were handwritten notes. The yellow pages held crisp blue pen in neat cursive strokes that spoke of her homeschooled background.

Ivy pulled the page over closer to her and made a mark in the upper corner. She'd made little notes on each, T, M, and C, for each of his brothers. She crossed C off of the report for the fire that had started the night Luke remembered.

He had to wonder if she might have had an L up there, too—if she might have needed to rule him out. Or at some point along the way had she actually done it? It seemed odd to be sleeping with her, to be asking her out, and to not be entirely confident that she knew he wasn't their arsonist.

"Am I off your list?"

"You are now," she told him with a cute smirk, and he didn't ask when "now" had occurred. "Orlando said that Chloe told him to pull burglaries and it took me a while to figure out how it helped, but, look …"

Ivy pushed one of the reports toward him. Quickly scanning it, Luke read about another arrest for yet another petty theft.

"Jesus, Tiago," Luke said it out loud, even though he hadn't meant to. All his misery at his oldest brother's inability to get his life together or even just stop committing crimes seeped into the two words.

He hadn't even known about this most recent arrest—hopefully there weren't more. He wondered if his mother did but forced his attention back to the table and the way he and Ivy were trying to rule out suspects. "What does this have to do with the arson?"

"Because it puts your brother in a holding cell for twenty-four hours around the time of this fire being set." Ivy pointed to the report for the fire at one of the abandoned houses.

They sorted through the other documents and quickly crossed all three Hernandez brothers off of their list of suspects.

Luke felt his heart settle inside his chest. "Thank you."

"For what? This is my fire too, now. I mean, I'm happy to help but, please understand that this—" She waved her hand at the table and all the notes that surely represented hours of her own precious time. "—It wasn't entirely for you."

He was looking down. Though he'd known that, it was still hard to meet her eyes. He shook his head as though shaking her off. "It doesn't matter why you did it. I've been afraid it was one of my brothers all this time. And I'll sleep so much easier now."

Finally seeming to understand, she slid her fingers over his and held on. It was Luke who turned his palm upright and laced his fingers through hers. He looked at the two hands together—his large and rough, hers slim-fingered, dainty with neat nails. A hand that spoke of a life of refinement, a life she built for herself from absolutely nothing.

Even Luke had always known that, if he lost everything, he

could crash with one of his brothers. He could go back to his mother and beg a room. It would suck, but a roof would exist over his head and food would be on the table, even if he had nothing. So how had Ivy clawed her way up from being tossed onto the streets at sixteen with no life skills? She'd been so naive that the world should have simply swallowed her whole, yet she was the one with delicate, unmarred hands. His looked like he'd been scrambling for purchase his whole life.

Though their hands looked so different, he wanted to believe they belonged together. He wasn't sure when he'd gone from wanting to live a simple life, where he worked, paid his bills, and occasionally got laid, to wanting to be with Ivy. And he had no idea when that had transformed into *needing* to be with her.

He only knew that it had happened.

"Thank you." He had to say it again.

Her smile was soft and sympathetic. This time, when he looked her in the eyes, he expected a smile. But Ivy was on to the next task, and he'd better keep up.

Her expression fell. "The problem now is that we don't have a suspect at all."

He looked at her, still worried about these supposed-to-be-sealed juvenile records. "I don't know how Orlando got his hands on those."

Ivy didn't either.

"I remember Carlos and Mario getting picked up by the police as kids, but my mom handled it. She pretty much kept me and Tiago away from it. If I remember correctly, the lawyer got it pled down or something."

Ivy wasn't working from memory. Easily putting her finger on the document she wanted, she plucked it from the pile and read it. "It looks like he got it down to a misdemeanor."

Then her eyebrows rose. "This was originally a class D felony, Luke." She was pointing to a spot on the page.

But Luke didn't look. That sounded bad. "I remember Mario confessed and went to therapy for it."

For all that he was pleased that his brothers weren't arsonists, the search had brought out new information about their pasts that bothered him. Mario had killed an animal as a kid. Those horrifying acts indicated bigger problems. Tiago had been arrested recently, something Luke hadn't known about.

He would have to ask his mother. Was she keeping up with her children? Or had she simply decided they were all adults, and could make their own shitty decisions?

He didn't have answers. When the silence settled in, he noticed that Ivy's own expression had fallen, too. "I don't know what to do about that." She shrugged. "But what do we do about not having a suspect? If it's not one of your brothers, then who is it? The fires are too close to your family history to be a coincidence."

He didn't know. He'd been thinking about this for several months, and he had a few names to toss out. Like with his brothers, calling these guys under investigation would mean upending their lives. It would possibly end an uneasy truce between his past and his present.

Maybe he should have moved out of Redemption like Carlos had. He was understanding his little brother better now. Their mother had hated it that Carlos left town, even though he was barely over an hour away, but Luke was thinking that maybe the youngest was the smartest. He'd always been a little too clever.

Except, if Luke had left, he wouldn't have met Ivy.

She asked him her next question, clearly not having the same existential crisis that he was. "So the question is, who else followed that same path? Is it an old friend? Is it someone after one of your brothers?"

She waited a moment, while he debated who to throw under the suspicion bus first. But then she said, "I feel like we should have some ideas to take to Taggart. Because it's definitely time to take this to him and Kane and let the arson investigators know what we suspect and what we found."

What she found.

She was a damned genius.

Luke nodded. The heaviness that had lifted from his heart was replaced with a new one. He knew he had passed the background check when he had been hired to work at the Redemption Fire Department. Getting notice that he'd been hired meant that his own juvenile record hadn't held him back. That had been a weight off of his shoulders. It should have stayed sealed forever.

But somehow, Ivy had put her finger on the right button and cracked the seals on those. When they took this to Taggart, Taggart would know more about him. What if it changed what his chief thought about him? Would he lose his job?

Even the way that Ivy looked at him couldn't change the fear that settled as a cold hard fist in his chest.

CHAPTER TWENTY-NINE

"Everything is good?" Ivy checked one last time with Shannon, but her assistant only nodded at her and made a motion for Ivy to get away.

She was headed home from work early. She and Luke had set up a meeting with Chief Taggart. Ever the librarian, she had tried and tried again to organize all their reports and her notes into a trail that made sense. She'd been at it until two in the morning when Luke had finally put his own hands over hers and stopped her frantic organization.

"Taggart will change it all. Just take it to him in a big pile. It will be okay."

He'd almost laughed at her, but she'd still been concerned.

Maybe he was okay with this, but she'd read all the reports. There was damning information in there about Luke. A good number of reports of him getting rounded up with his friends. He'd been questioned about stolen cars, drugs, even home burglaries. But nothing had ever stuck.

He'd seemed smart enough to clean up his act by the time he turned eighteen. Neither she nor Orlando had found any records on him after that birthday. She'd asked him, "Why do your records end six months before your eighteenth birthday? Did you just know you couldn't afford a record as an adult?"

She wondered if he would answer. It was such a personal question ... and the only reason she didn't have a record was because she hadn't been caught. No one arrested the Hollywood stars nor the half-dressed women tagging along and fucking them.

"Carlos and I were in a car accident."

She felt her eyebrows rise. His expression said the memory was not a good one. But when he kept talking she didn't stop him. Her own curiosity outweighed the need to comfort him.

"Carlos was driving—underage, mind you—and he ran us right into this telephone pole. At the time, it seemed like he did it on purpose."

"*What?*"

"No," Luke was shaking his head. "You know how memories get messed up with accidents. But he nailed it, square on. Wrapped the car around the pole, us both in the front seat."

He took a deep breath and continued. "It was an old car, there was no airbag, and he was slumped over the steering wheel. I thought he was dead." Luke didn't look at her. He didn't look at anything, just stared into the middle distance. "I tried to wake him. I now know not to move an injured person, but I shook him. He didn't move. Nothing. But a police officer came by."

This time, when he took a breath, he lifted his eyes to hers. "That officer had hauled us in so many times that I don't remember. We were horrible to him, awful. Cussing him out, Carlos liked to insult the man's wife."

Oh, shit. Ivy consoled herself that she knew the end of the story already and that Carlos was still alive.

"He took one look at us, and even though the engine was smoking and the whole car was about to blow up, he told me we were going to be okay. Then he carefully talked me through everything, managed to get my door open as he called in the accident. He put me on the grass and climbed in the passenger seat and saved Carlos himself. When they put my brother in the ambulance and we still didn't know if he would make it, Officer Beasley put me in the front seat of his patrol car—I'd never been in the front before—" He laughed a small self-deprecating sound, "and drove me to the hospital. Then he waited with me on those stupid orange plastic chairs that are so fucking uncomfortable. Even when my mother showed up, Officer Beasley stuck around. He bought us snacks and he waited until we knew Carlos would make it. And he never once said a damn thing about what little shits we were to him."

Ivy breathed out her own relief. "That's a good story."

"I went into the station the next week. I waited an hour for him to be free and I apologized to him for everything. Then I asked him how to become a cop."

He sat me down and said, "I saw how you looked at the jaws of life when they pulled your brother out. And I saw your awe when the car burst into flames and the firefighters put it out. I'll help you become a police officer if you want, but I think you should be a firefighter ... And here I am."

Luke shrugged, but Ivy fought to keep her jaw from falling open. "Can I include that in the town history?"

That was a shitty thing to say. "I'm sorry! I'm not trying to make it about me or minimize what you went through, but it's just such a wonderful story!"

She was almost crying. What he'd been through and what an amazing person he was to recognize the moment that had been handed to him. At seventeen, he'd apologized for the way he'd treated someone else and started to turn himself around. She knew the path to becoming a firefighter wasn't an easy one. Regardless of the way Mr. Gentson had tossed it around, Luke had spent years getting educated to the point where he could even apply for the job.

Luke laughed and looked at her like she was nuts. "Beasley was there when I showed up for my first day and said now I was his colleague. Then he apologized to me, for all the times they'd pulled us over simply because of who we were."

"Jesus." That was history, she could feel it in her heart.

"I guess you can tell the story in the town history. Once Taggert knows, I'll either keep my job or not."

She shook her head at him. Taggart loved his men. He didn't hire and keep anyone that he didn't want on the team. Jo had been new just a few months ago, but her presence had illustrated some unsavory facts about another firefighter. The chief had removed him, not Jo.

Ivy had high hopes that—despite Luke's concerns about revealing his own ugly past—the chief would understand the man he had become, and not the kid that he was.

Hell, if she was judged by life number two, things would be very different for her today. Lord knew she hadn't put all of her drug use and crazy partying on her NYU application. Just the GED that she had gotten and the work that she'd done. Luke would be the same.

They'd gone to bed and she'd fallen asleep in Luke's arms for the first time—even if it was just for four hours by that point. So now, she was running on fumes, but she still had things to do.

She pulled up in front of her house to see a large package on her doorstep. Was it wrong to be so suspicious? She'd received deliveries for a while as she ordered replacement items, but she wasn't expecting anything today.

She'd carefully parsed out every penny and ordered what she absolutely needed until she ran out of what she felt free to spend. So finding the box with large letters on the sides and the clear logo of a TV company made her wonder.

A printed note was taped to the front of it. Reaching out, she gingerly plucked it from the tape.

Deliver to: Ivy Dean.

That was followed by her address and information about the tv that was in fact in the box. It was large but not huge, more money had gone into quality than width. Beneath all that was an additional sentence that it was paid for by Luke Hernandez.

She rolled her eyes at no one and, still standing on her front porch, grabbed her phone and called him.

"Hey," he answered with a smile she could hear. "You about ready to head over?"

She didn't even address his question. "Luke. Why are you buying me a very expensive TV?"

Then the thought occurred to her, "Is it because we're sleeping together?"

"Noooooo!" The word was drawn out, multisyllabic, and he sounded truly offended by her suggestion. While it made her feel better that that hadn't been his reasoning, she felt worse now. She needed to apologize. But honestly, she'd known too many women who weren't officially sex workers … They'd simply worked out arrangements. Though they had no single man who could be referred to as a sugar daddy. Their rent was paid one month by one man. Loaded credit cards appeared in their hands. Lavish gifts were bestowed.

For all that she had done, Ivy had never quite been willing to exchange sex for favors or money. "Luke, I don't need you to—"

"Obviously, you don't." He interrupted, his tone abrupt and maybe a little angry. "I want to say it was just a gift, but …" His voice lowered. "Honestly, I feel guilty that you lost everything. So just let me get you the fucking TV."

She would have fought him on it, if not for the tone of defeat in his voice, if not for the anger that came through that she knew wasn't really directed at her.

"I'm sorry," she said, though whether she was sorry for her improper conclusions or for the fact that she would never have taken the TV until he browbeat her into it, she didn't know. Maybe it was all of the above.

She held out what little olive branch she could. "Why don't you come back with me after our meeting? Help me set it up?"

There was a long pause that worried her, but then he said, "I'd like that."

It wouldn't hurt her to have anyone watching see him arrive on her doorstep and stay for a while. "Okay, I've got to hang up and get this behemoth inside."

"Are you heading over here soon?"

"Yeah, I just came home to change." They said goodbyes and she decided to change out of her heels before she brought the tv in.

She thought about how she wouldn't have changed clothes after work had this happened last week. She was happy in her twin sets and her skirts. But Luke had gotten her to thinking: She wasn't so much happy with the clothing itself as she was with the way it made people perceive her. And maybe she didn't need to be perceived as utterly proper and untouchable.

So she put on the pair of jeans that Jo had gifted her, leaving the twin set sweaters in place. It was cold and she wasn't quite ready for a full makeover. She'd done two of those already in her life. But maybe she could just add new pieces without worrying about the town of Redemption knowing that she was trustworthy, that she wasn't making poor choices, that they could ask her their questions and put their secrets in her hands.

She zipped the jeans and added a cute pair of boots, then declared herself done. But as she headed back out to the porch to bring the TV inside, the hair on her neck rose. For a moment she struggled with the box, holding the door open with her foot, trying to lift the awkward weight and ultimately just sliding it over the threshold.

When she got the TV inside, her nerves didn't settle. Ivy realized she wasn't simply concerned about her new belonging getting stolen. The sensation of being watched was still there, even though she'd stepped in and locked the door behind her.

Scanning the street and her yard, she checked for unusual cars or movements coming from the stand of trees between two of the houses. She was just two houses down from a little strip of woods that led into the greenway that connected the town.

Despite her checks, she didn't see anyone. Even her neighbors weren't out. And she was left with the eerie feeling that the birds being silent meant something.

But was she simply paranoid or was there really something out there?

CHAPTER THIRTY

"I called Shannon." Jo told Ivy with a smirk on her face as she stood on the front porch where she'd knocked just as Ivy was getting ready to leave for work. "There's nothing you can do about it."

That was the problem with small towns. Everyone knew everyone else.

Ivy had told Jo about her schedule, about how much she liked her assistant Shannon Deleon. Jo also knew exactly who that was and how to get in contact with her and when to knock on the door to catch Ivy before she left.

"What exactly are we doing?" Ivy asked.

"You and I are going to the new spa that opened up. We are having hot rock treatments, facials, and massages. We are supporting the local business." She added the last one with a self-satisfied grin. Jo knew Ivy believed in supporting the locals. And the spa had opened up recently, trying to bring in business from Redemption and the surrounding areas.

Ivy had to admit that it sounded wonderful, but she didn't have the funds for something like that. Or she did, but they were already earmarked as savings for replacing her big fluffy armchairs. Jo seemed to understand that the two of them—especially right now—were playing the roles of rich man, poor man.

"I've got it covered." Jo just reached out and grabbed her hand for a moment. "It's my treat to you. You've seemed tense these last few weeks."

She wasn't wrong. Though the town had moved on from her housefire, she hadn't. She had her siding up and she was fine in the snows now, but she wasn't sleeping well. She and Luke were both following along, dating, kissing, spending the night ... and waiting for the arsonist to strike again. She hadn't been able to let her guard down.

Jo on the other hand ... Ivy smiled. "You seem good. Leo looks good on you."

"Maybe." Jo looked mellow but she was smiling a bright genuine smile. She'd been uptight and standoffish when she'd moved to town. But Jo was Jo, always moving forward, always fighting. Though she hadn't lost any of that, she'd certainly been able to step into her work and into the town and begin to trust them.

Ivy liked to think that she was part of the cause. She didn't think Jo had ever quite had a friend the way the two of them were becoming. She knew she hadn't. She also knew it was time that she told Jo about her past. Luke knew about her, and just the fact that she'd told it to someone was enough to know that, at some point, it would get out. She didn't want Jo to find out from someone else.

"Let me change," Ivy told her, then she looked her friend over. Jo had just gotten off shift, but she was in her big camel coat, her jeans and cute boots showing from beneath the hem. "You're not too tired? You're sure you want to go now?"

"It was an easy shift. I slept a full night. Besides, you're right, I've mellowed. Leo has been good for me."

Ivy couldn't agree more.

"You've been more tense." Ivy felt her shoulders fall, Jo wasn't going to let it go.

"Let me change," she said, and it probably didn't go unnoticed that she'd changed the subject again.

In her own room, she stepped out of her work clothes and into her jeans and a sweater. Jo would definitely recognize the jeans, but Ivy had never been above hand me downs.

"Oh," Jo declared when Ivy walked out. "I love those. They look better on you than they ever did on me."

Never mind that Jo was noticeably taller, and that Ivy had cuffed the jeans when Jo had lent them to her originally. But once Jo had sworn they were hers, she had hemmed them.

Jo noticed. "Did you get them hemmed?"

"No, ma'am. I hemmed them myself."

"That looks professional."

Ivy laughed again. Jo was more than capable but, having grown up the way she had, she'd not been taught ordinary household or repair skills. Ivy, on the other hand, had been taught every plausible household and repair skill. Jo could hold a hammer because she'd been actively trained to do it as a firefighter. Ivy could because she'd been practically raised with one in her hand.

She could bake bread from scratch and easily hem jeans in a professional manner. One of the first things she'd bought after she'd left home was a sewing machine. Though she wasn't a big fan of sewing, she'd known it was too valuable of a skill to lose. Many of her Hollywood friends had no idea that she'd sewn the majority of her own clothes. Hemming the jeans was nothing.

Jo motioned Ivy out the door and into her little Mercedes. They headed to the spa, a short drive. Ivy had considered telling Jo about her history, but the drive wasn't long enough to unload the shitshow that was her past.

They were parking before she knew it, and within moments they were inside, Jo's credit card handed over. They had robes on and were waiting to get their toenails done—something she'd not expected from Jo.

Though Ivy was delighted, she almost complained. "Jo, I'm not going to make it back in time to open the library."

"Of course, you're not," Jo scoffed at her. "You can go when you're finished. Shannon knows the deal and she said you're fine to stay as long as you want."

Shannon wasn't her boss, it was certainly the other way around. But Ivy figured Shannon was enjoying being in charge for a while. She'd certainly handled the place with grace and zero notice when Ivy's house had burned. So Ivy put her faith in her assistant and turned her attention to watching as her feet were wrapped in hot towels and her toenails painted.

Jo had raised her eyebrow and nodded at the bright teal Ivy had chosen. Leo might have mellowed Jo, but Luke was opening Ivy up.

She shrugged at her friend, Jo had already seen the tattoos.

Later, they'd been put into a single room with two tables. Jo had booked them into a couples massage, laughing that it was what was available. "Apparently, Wednesday morning is when you go to the spa in Redemption."

Ivy hadn't cared. "At least the business is doing well and will hopefully stick around." So far she was enjoying having a spa nearby.

In a short while, they were both on the tables, face down, half covered with sheets, and getting hot rocks placed on their backs.

"I've never had this before," she told Jo.

"It's super weird, but I love it." But when the masseuse left them alone, Jo spoke up. "I just noticed the tattoo on your back is ivy and lilies."

It was too good of an opening, Ivy thought. So she dropped a bit of a bomb. "I have thirteen brothers and sisters." Well, shit.

"Actually, only twelve now. I found out last month that my oldest brother died a while ago."

"One of those deeply Christian fundamentalist families?" Jo didn't gasp at the number of brothers and sisters, or the fact that Ivy's brother had passed and she hadn't been notified. She shouldn't have been shocked that her best friend had figured her out. Over the years, no one else had. Maybe she'd been too wild or too closed off, but it felt good to be understood.

Ivy nodded. "They kicked me out when I was sixteen and I haven't had contact with anyone since. Lily was …"

She couldn't quite bring herself to say it. But Jo nodded, one hand coming out, and Ivy accepted it for a quick grasp of understanding.

Lily had been everything. Lily had been the one who understood her like no one else ever had, or ever would. Lily had been the one that Ivy would have bet everything on being here with her now. So her betrayal had cut the deepest.

"You don't have to tell me." Jo comforted her, seeming to recognize the scuffling in the hall meant that someone was coming back to them and that Ivy wouldn't necessarily want to share her story with everyone.

"I will. You should know," Ivy said. "We should plan a slumber party. You bring the ice cream and I'll tell you the whole sordid story."

Jo nodded. "I'd like to hear it."

Ivy knew it wasn't that she wanted the gossip. Jo wanted to know more of her friend. But as she looked over, she saw her friend had slowly turned her head and was looking at the door.

Too many people were walking down the hall, making noise, and making Jo frown. "Why haven't they come back for these rocks?"

Ivy had to admit that hers weren't that hot anymore.

Jo sat up abruptly, the rocks falling to the bed and a few clattering to the floor as she did it. Ivy turned her head, but even with the noise her friend had just made, still no one came to their door.

Jo exhaled oddly as Ivy slowly turned, looking the other way. Unlike her friend, she wasn't simply willing to sit up and toss the rocks away. She had no idea if they were expensive and she cared.

"Ivy! Get up!" Jo snapped at her.

Ivy did as she was told. The odd sensations nagging at her suddenly becoming clear as she did.

She saw and smelled it. Even as Jo said the words, dread curled low in her stomach.

"There's smoke coming in under the door."

CHAPTER THIRTY-ONE

"At least this is good," Ivy said as, together, she and Jo headed for the bathroom that was attached to their massage room.

Jo was already inside, making short use of the supplies.

There was a shower in here in case anyone wanted to wash off the oils. *Perfect.* Ivy followed suit, grabbing one of the big fluffy bathrobes and climbing into it. It wasn't just covering her nakedness, it would protect her from the fire that was clearly beyond their door. The only question was: how far beyond?

Jo turned on the water and shoved Ivy in first, ever the firefighter.

"Sweet Jesus!" Ivy yelled. It was freezing.

But Jo was quick to point out that she'd be thankful for the cold in just a few minutes. Grabbing another large bath towel, Jo shoved it over Ivy's head and let the water soak it, too.

"You'll breathe through that one," Jo told her as they switched places, Ivy now dripping onto the floor.

As she glanced out into the main room, she saw the smoke still curling in from the hallway. With another towel in hand, she stole a little of the water from Jo before heading out and stuffing it under the door.

There were no windows back here. *Of course not.* You wouldn't want anyone peeking in on your massage, but now the only way out was through the fire.

Jo stepped out, now just as cold and soaked as Ivy. Then she immediately ducked back in and Ivy heard the shower turn on again. Jo emerged a moment later with a stack of wet towels.

Ivy pointed into the corner. "Shoes."

There wasn't enough time to get fully dressed, but they shoved their feet into what they'd been wearing on the way over. Ivy was suddenly grateful for sneakers with thick soles. There wasn't time for socks.

Jo grabbed her and hauled the two of them to one side of the door. Reaching out, she pulled the knob and opened the door. Smoke thick and oily whooshed into the space, and Jo tugged them both down to the floor while she waited a beat to let the room adjust to the intrusion.

Ivy understood. One of the nights that she and Luke had been curled up on the couch watching TV, she'd asked him all kinds of questions about firefighting. Just out of curiosity, or maybe because an arsonist had torched her home.

He'd told her, "Anytime you open an airspace, you invite the fire."

Jo was staying out of the way now.

Ivy felt her friend's hand wrap around her wrist through the wet squish of the thick robe. When she felt the squeeze, she understood the signal and began moving even before Jo tugged her along.

They crawled down the hallway. There should be an emergency exit to her right. The smoke was thick and they moved slowly on hands and knees, the heavy robes not making it any easier. Jo had been right: The ice cold of the water was quickly replaced with heat.

She couldn't see through the thick smoke and she struggled to pull breath through the heavy towel. It was tempting to pull it off and gulp, but she knew this beat the alternative.

They felt their way along, Ivy seeing only thick oily smoke through rapidly blinking and watering eyes. When the floor got too hot, Jo handed her extra towels to cover her hands as they crawled.

They ran into another woman who wasn't covered. She was dressed in pink scrubs, indicating she was an employee. Coughing as though a lung was coming up, she motioned them to turn around. "Go back!"

Jo made a motion back to Ivy, the heavy hand on her shoulder telling her to stop. Ivy couldn't see much of anything anymore. She'd pulled the towel up over her eyes and was working mostly by feel and a few wet-eyed peeks.

She heard Jo explaining to the woman, "There's an emergency exit ahead."

"Yes. It's blocked!" The woman argued back with another epic cough.

"I'm going to go check it out. I'm a firefighter." Jo said it with such conviction that Ivy almost laughed at the big fluffy wet beast that was her dearest friend. But there wasn't enough air to laugh.

Jo pushed the remainder of the still wet towels she was carrying at Ivy. "Wrap her up. Stay here." And with that, Ivy was alone with the new woman.

Ivy motioned with one of the towels, putting it up over the woman's face and wrapping it around her neck like a scarf. She held up another towel, the last one, and hollered above the sound of roaring static. "For your hands!"

She watched as the woman went at the towel with gusto. Pulling the first towel down to get one tooth firmly into the fabric, she ripped it clean down the middle, making two smaller towels that she then wrapped around each hand. Ivy wished she had that kind of strength.

By the time she got the woman situated, wrapped up as best she could, Jo was back. Crawling in on her hands and knees, she motioned them to get moving the way they'd come. "It's blocked. The door itself has already caught."

For the first time, as the three of them turned and headed toward the front door, Ivy felt an ice cold fear snake around her heart. No one had said it, but it was clear to her this fire had been deliberately set.

It had been set and she had been *inside.*

Was it a coincidence?

She didn't have time to consider that. Her first—in fact, her *only*—job right now was to save herself and the others who were in here with her.

Jo banged on closed doors as she went but only one of them opened. She moved them all out of the doorway, waiting for the smoke to equilibrate into the empty space. Luckily, it was another massage room. Also luckily, the woman who had been in there had the same thought they did. She'd covered herself in wet towels.

She hollered out, "Damn, I hoped you were the fire department."

The smoke hadn't gotten to her lungs yet, Ivy noted.

Jo hollered and coughed back, "I am the fire department!"

Then she gave instructions to join their little group of survivors. At least, that's what Ivy had decided they would be. She'd just gotten her damned house refurnished and she wasn't going to die like this now.

The four of them began their way toward the front of the building, all of them shuffling along on their hands and knees. Ivy was holding onto the tail of Jo's robe, another hand clutched to hers. She could only believe the other women in the chain were hanging on tightly behind them.

They made painstaking progress. There was a roaring static

that assaulted her ears. She couldn't tell whether it was the fire crackling and consuming everything around them or if it was just the churning of her own noisy thoughts. Ivy wanted to believe she heard sirens, but she didn't think she would be able to even if they were right outside the building.

As they got toward the front, she saw splashes of orange and yellow light as she finally caught sight of the fire. It roared beyond the windows. And Jo yelled out, "Lobby!" as though that was enough.

Ivy looked up again, blinking away the smoke and ash that tried to invade her eyes. Was the fire even inside the building? Or had the arsonist just ringed the place? Had the flames already made it through the walls? She didn't know.

They moved further into the space, and she felt Jo come to a halt in front of her. Behind her the other woman bumped into her. One by one they came to a stop.

Lowering her towel, Ivy opened her eyes fully into the smoke and the heat. She felt the heat searing them but could see that they were trapped.

Jo had turned to the employee asking if there was another door. The woman shouted back, it was difficult to be heard through the thick towels and the crackle of flames.

Ivy heard, "Yes."

But even as she said it, a dark figure emerged from the other hallway. Low and crawling and coughing its way along, it was clearly not the firefighter Ivy wished to see.

She couldn't see anyway, and she lifted the towel back into place over her head. Her hands were probably blistered. She'd been so excited to protect her feet with sneakers and she'd spent the whole time crawling on her knees.

Her lungs were seared now too, even though she'd not breathed the air except through her wet towel. But she could hear as the other employee shouted.

"That way's blocked, too!"

CHAPTER THIRTY-TWO

The click and static of the scanner on the seat beside him made Luke's heart race.

He didn't recognize the address, and he wasn't on shift. But his fears about the arsonist targeting him or one of his brothers had more than offset the relief of figuring out the criminal wasn't a family member. He'd been listening in to dispatch whenever he was alone. Even Ivy didn't know he was doing it.

For the first time, he'd caught a full-blaze fire.

He'd been on his way to get his oil changed, but he pulled a quick U-turn and headed toward the other side of town.

The trucks were already there when he pulled up in front of the small spa. Luke watched as Ann stepped down from the driver's seat of the first rig and the small red pickup that was the Chief's pulled up nose to nose with the truck.

Ignoring the trucks for a moment, he found his view blocked by the Chief's truck, so he stepped out of the car, but stayed back. Taggert saw him but hardly paid notice. Luke and Ivy had handed over everything they had to the local arson team. The Chief could hardly be surprised to see him here.

Moving across the front lawn, he thought he saw flames on

all sides of the building. Flames burned differently depending on what they encountered inside the house, whether the air was on, and what kind of ventilation it had, so he couldn't say it was arson just from the glance. But he was thinking that it was.

The mulch beds burned hot and a line of fire tracked along the driveway, right next to the house. It licked at the brand new siding, making his stomach churn with the reminders of Ivy's house going up much the same way.

This fire already had so many odd substances, all burning wildly, that his heart clenched as he could no longer deny what was happening: the building was ringed in accelerant. His only consolation was that this time the chief knew all about his brothers, knew that they'd been cleared, and had been investigating anyone associated with the Hernandez family who might have been following their path.

Still, Luke was afraid something about him might have put a target on this house. But he didn't recognize the location even now that he was here.

He was about to volunteer as a medic if anyone came out. He could do that without being in his turnout gear. But even as he thought of it, two ambulances cut down the street, sirens wailing for the other cars to get out of the way.

It looked like whoever had called it in had given clear information.

He watched as the team began their search, checking out the building and trying to find places to vent or see if it was safe to enter and search.

From across the lawn, he saw a woman frantically waving her hands over her head. "I think they were open today! I think there are people inside!"

Craning his head, Luke saw what the firefighters would have already spotted: cars parked in the lot behind the building. He nodded to the woman, then headed quickly over to talk to her. He could do this, even if he wasn't on shift.

"I'm a firefighter, ma'am. Off duty right now, but I can relay any information the team needs." She was nodding gratefully at him as he said, "I assure you, they are checking for people inside right now, and their next move will likely be to go in. See where they are dousing the front? That's where they'll go in."

She sighed with relief and was clutching his arm to thank him, when he saw the small silver Mercedes parked in the back. He only knew one car like that in town. It was possible it wasn't her, but ...

Luke barely motioned to the woman before he bolted across the lawn. This time he cut through the firefighters' workspace between the truck and the house and he didn't care.

Taggert was frowning as he got there.

"I think Jo's inside!" Even as he said the words, he hated that he was grateful that Ivy would be at the library by now.

Taggert's eyes snapped to his and Luke added, "I saw her car in the back."

"Good." The Chief's bold declaration stopped him cold.

Why was this good?

The man must have heard his thoughts.

"Jo will get them out."

Luke sighed. Taggert was right. Jo wasn't going to die in a fire, she'd be too mad to die. And she sure as hell wouldn't die in a fire at a damned spa. What was she even doing here, unless she, too, had seen it and run inside to help?

He watched as the firefighters took too long to inspect the place. When it was him, he always felt as though he were working as fast as humanly possible, from this perspective B-shift almost looked like they were dicking around.

But he knew it was always better to go in safe than to go in fast and make things worse. The team did their job and quickly decided that the front lobby was the way to go. He heard them shouting to each other that all the other exits were blocked and this was the biggest section of openings—doors and windows—on the building.

The Chief sent him to question everybody standing around watching, but in a few moments he'd ascertained that so far no one had seen anyone come out.

The spa was in a little house that had been converted for the business. The area had once been a row of small starter homes and had recently been gentrified to businesses. The lawyer next door and his assistant were out on their lawn watching the blaze, as were the employees and patrons of the medical supply shop next door.

As they watched, the hose line advanced forward, and Luke itched to get his hands on and help douse the fire. But he wasn't dressed for it and he'd only be in the way.

As soon as the fire was out by the door, he watched as the guys got the "key" in hand—a large battering ram that opened any door. They hollered to anyone inside to stay back. With three swift hits, the door flew open and the firefighters immediately fell back.

No flames reached out for them.

But even from where he stood, Luke could hear the shouts of the excited people inside. His heart had been beating double time, and now it slowed a little bit. They were alive.

There was a breath of waiting time, then the firefighters rushed in. One by one they brought out the people. Some had white towels wrapped around their hands, all had them over their faces. The last two were in white fluffy robes, clearly doused. Smart, Luke thought. Jo's handiwork likely.

He looked around for her as the people who'd been inside were hauled over to where the medics waited. As he watched, one of the women in the white robes peeled the towel from her face. Luke felt his jaw drop open as he ran forward.

"Jo!" he yelled.

"I'm good. I'm good," she told him, her words swallowed by a paroxysm of coughs. That didn't surprise him, but she looked okay at first glance. Ash and debris covered her bare legs, and she likely had some burns.

Even as he looked, the woman next to her—much in the same condition—peeled her own towel from her head.

Luke spotted the blond hair and he simply *knew*. His heart felt the squeeze as the towel came off and he saw Ivy's sweet face. Only there was terror in her expression, as she called out in a gravelly voice. "I can't see!"

CHAPTER THIRTY-THREE

"This isn't uncommon in fires," Luke heard the doctor say in a clipped tone. The man was standing over Ivy as she sat on the hospital bed, and Luke didn't doubt that she knew it. The physician continued in his overly aloof tone. "And we're concerned that there may have been something in the accelerant that caused this."

Luke pushed his way into the room. Ivy heard his footsteps or sensed him—a thought that would have made him smile had her own expression not been so wobbly.

The doctor continued to drone on about the damage Ivy's eyes had taken, seeming to not even notice that another person had entered the room. Luke recognized the doctor and he wasn't a fan. "Miss Dean, you'll need to leave the bandages on for a while."

Ivy's fingers laced together on her lap, as she quietly fidgeted her way through her anxiety. The doctor didn't notice, but Luke did.

"Ivy, this happens a lot with smoke exposure. I've had it, too. I was in bandages for a day." Okay, his hadn't been as bad as hers was. He'd simply been in a situation where he'd run out of air and had to remove his face shield. And he'd worked hard not to open his eyes. "It clears up on its own. It has every time I've seen it."

As he watched, she relaxed, the blue and green pattern on the gown showing the lines of her shoulders and making it clear just how tense she had been. She sat in a pile of white sheets with starched pillows behind her. As she nodded at him, Luke turned to the doctor.

"She's been sitting there trying to figure out how to do her job if she's permanently blind. You need to tell her she's going to be okay!"

"Well, I can't promise anything," the doctor replied, a small frown on his face.

"But you can tell her the statistics. When's the last time you saw someone who had their eyes damaged by smoke who didn't regain at least most of their vision relatively quickly?" Luke was angry now. How long had she been sitting here thinking that she might be permanently blind?

They hadn't let him in until just then, and even then, they hadn't really 'let' him in. He'd simply overheard the doctor from the hallway and had enough.

The doctors had likely been giving her this "we can't tell you anything" line since she'd arrived a few hours ago. Without her eyes or her phone or precious library, she wouldn't have been able to find the information for herself. Because Lord knows if she had any tools she would have found everything she needed in a heartbeat.

"Thank you, Luke." She turned to face him despite the bandages over her eyes. "I'll be okay."

"Yes, you will," he replied, coming and sitting on the edge of the bed with her so she could feel him close. The doctor frowned at him again, but Luke frowned back harder. This time he asked. "When do you expect to take the bandages off to check her eyesight?"

"At least tomorrow. It's evening now. So probably tomorrow morning."

That was at least a good time estimate and, from the way Ivy's body released just a little more tension, he knew it was information she'd wanted, too.

Ivy nodded in response to the doctor's words and when the doctor left, she reached out seeming to know where his hand was. Luke placed his fingers through hers, watching as once again her shoulders softened. The stress had to have been horrible.

For a moment, he was glad that he hadn't known she was in the fire until they'd brought her out. He was also glad that she couldn't see his own shoulders and the tension that he carried there now. His wasn't relieved by the fact that her bandages would come off tomorrow—he'd already known that.

His concern now was that Ivy had been targeted again. If the arsonist had come after Ivy, then it wasn't about his family, it was about *him*.

Now that she seemed to be calmer, Ivy launched into a discussion. "Why the spa? I mean they were lucky Joe was there!"

Luke grinned at her even though she couldn't see it. "Honestly, they were lucky they had you, too. You always know what you're doing and you're competent in an emergency."

Her smile pulled at one side of her mouth, but he had to say it, even though he didn't think it would make her smile. "I think they might have gone after the spa because you were in it."

Those harsh words stilled the soft fidgeting of her fingers, and he hated that he had done it to her.

"The location doesn't mean anything to you?" she asked softly, already sensing that he didn't understand why that address had been targeted.

"No, I don't remember anything from there."

"It's only been a spa for a little while," she prompted. "In fact, the whole area has only been rezoned for businesses within the last ten years."

He marveled at the fact that she knew that, given that she had not lived in town before the small area had gentrified and transformed, and that she'd had no reason to know about the history of this particular street until she'd been caught in a fire there this morning.

"I don't have anything," he admitted, and he hated that that was all he had to contribute. "The only thing I can think of is that you were inside."

He didn't think the place meant anything to his brothers or even his mother. They sat quietly, a moment of careful thought on Ivy's part and worry on Luke's that he'd spoken too hastily. His fear knocked on the door and he wondered what would they do if Ivy didn't get her sight back? But as he was reminding himself that he didn't know anyone who hadn't recovered, he managed to keep his mouth shut.

But Ivy was still on their last topic. "What about your mother?"

"I don't think she was frequenting that spa ... or that she's ever been there." Luke almost laughed at the idea. His mother didn't have the kind of disposable income for spa days, and if she did, she would have spent it on cigarettes or whiskey. In fact, if she had forty dollars, she'd buy four bottles of ten-dollar vodka rather than one good bottle of forty-dollar whiskey. If her nails were painted, she'd done it herself. And he didn't think she'd ever gotten a massage in her life.

But even without being able to see him, Ivy was grabbing his attention again. "No. That's not what I meant. Ask her if she knows the area. She's lived here her whole life, right?"

Luke was catching on. He'd been a bit slow on the uptake on that one. "Yes, she has."

He stayed with Ivy for a while longer, but it seemed both of them were anxious to know what his mother had to say.

By the time they'd gotten Ivy and Jo out of the fire and treated, it was late enough in the evening that Luke was relatively sure his mother would be home from her shift. It was Ivy who encouraged him to go and, twenty minutes later, he was standing on his mother's doorstep.

He was so wound up, that he was almost incapable of offering a decent greeting before asking a question. She stood on the threshold, cigarette poised near her lips, once again the ash burning long. "Oh, yeah. I know that place. I heard about that fire."

He wasn't surprised. Word traveled fast. At the factory where she worked, his mother stood on a line she was getting too old to stand on and gossiped with the locals on either side of her ... all day.

"What do you mean your girlfriend was in it? I didn't know you have a girlfriend."

Luke was surprised. She knew everything else, it seemed. He figured the whole town would be abuzz with their relationship —he and Ivy were not low-profile citizens. He'd thought he *needed* the town to be abuzz.

He'd believed the knowledge that Ivy was seeing a firefighter would keep her safe. That clearly hadn't worked. And he wondered now if he might have made the biggest mistake of all: he might have put a target on her.

And even as that idea clicked into place—yet another horrifying realization today—his mother said, "Yes, I know that place. That's where your father's girlfriend lived. Right before Jose was born."

"Jose?" he asked, more surprised that his mother had mentioned the name for the first time than that there had been a fifth Hernandez boy. Luke only knew about the baby because Ivy had told him. He didn't even remember his mother being pregnant when he was young. But then again, when had she been home?

But she ignored the question and continued to talk about the location. "I went over there and dragged his ass home more times than I can count. Hugely pregnant, too. The whole town probably saw."

She waved the cigarette for emphasis and flicked the ash to the side, not seeming to care that it landed on her own porch.

Luke nodded. But if the whole town knew that didn't help narrow their suspect pool at all. "I don't remember any of that."

"Why would you? You were at home, and I just showed up with your daddy. I think Tiago is the only one who even caught on."

With that proclamation, Luke felt his heart clench.

"I tried to keep it from you, boys, all of it. You know, I'd do anything for you."

Her words struck a chord deep inside him.

He'd not considered her a good mother, though he knew she'd done her very best. But the idea that she would do anything for them made sense. She had worked her own fingers to the bone supporting them. She'd hauled their father home when he strayed. And when that had been too much, she'd likely kicked the man out.

But the idea that she would *still* do anything for her sons reached deep into Luke and twisted inside his chest. He needed to search his memories.

They'd missed something.

CHAPTER THIRTY-FOUR

The first thing Luke saw when his eyes finally came open was park ranger Leo Evans. Not the most romantic awakening, Luke thought.

Leo spotted him and didn't even say anything. He just sucked in a deep breath and cracked his neck from one side to the other. Not surprising given the hospital chairs they'd slept in.

Jo was in the bed next to Ivy, laying face down. The robes they'd used from the spa had not covered the back of her legs, and she had suffered severe blisters. Ivy—being shorter—had remained more covered and didn't have anywhere near as many leg burns.

The two friends had wanted to share a room and that meant the two men were now facing each other after spending the night in very uncomfortable chairs on either side of their beds.

Jo shifted and Ivy's voice piped up with a command. "Don't roll over!"

Once again, Luke caught Leo's eye. Both of them were trying to laugh as silently as possible. Jo had not taken kindly to being told what position to sleep in to let her legs heal best. They'd all been on her case to stay face down and keep the wounds upright. It had taken all three of them to make her stay put.

Luke hadn't even realized Ivy was awake. The bandages still hadn't come off of her eyes and she hadn't moved much. Maybe she'd been letting him sleep.

Even as he wondered about it, another doctor walked in. He was grateful. He knew this doctor, too, and she was kinder and gentler than the other.

As they unwound the gauze from her eyes, Ivy chided her friend. "If the first thing I see is you sitting in the wrong position, Miss Joely Huston, I'm going to be very angry."

"I just moved my head!" Jo called back angrily, the two of them using the kind of tone only best friends could.

In a moment, Luke had forgotten about Jo as Ivy was blinking, her blue eyes squinting as she adjusted to the first light she'd seen in close to twenty-four hours. But the fact that she was squinting meant she was seeing light.

As Luke smiled at the revelation, Ivy turned her head to him. It was plausible that she'd heard him shuffling around. It was also plausible that she'd heard him laughing at her first directive to Jo. But he was medic trained, and he knew the signs. His grin only widened as he saw her eyes focus on him.

"It's a little blurry," she told the doctor and Luke knew she was likely calculating what strength of lenses she would need.

But this doctor was better than that. "It'll be that way for a little while. Maybe an hour, maybe a few, but I suspect it will return to normal quickly."

She ran a few more checks, shining the light into Ivy's eyes, double checking her reaction times. Then she smiled and declared, "I think you'll be good as new. I'll come back in a few hours. We'll check again, and I hope to be signing you out."

She next headed over to Jo, who grumbled before she was even asked anything. "I don't need pain medication."

To which the doctor replied. "How about we just give you

some anyway? In a lot of cases, people are grumpy because they're in pain even if they don't realize it."

Across the two beds, Luke watched as Leo's mouth dropped open. Jo was still facing Ivy, so—over her back—Leo looked up at the doctor and nodded and gave a thumbs up.

Luke fought to keep a straight face since he was in Jo's line of sight. But it was Ivy who looked her friend in the face, now able to focus on her and said, "Take the damn medicine, Jo."

"Fine, fine." Jo grumbled as she rolled over. "I'm going to miss my shift."

"Jesus, Jo," Leo sighed. "You're going to miss several, and it's going to be just fine. Seriously, you're missing shifts because you worked a live fire without gear. You get a pass, baby."

This time, no longer in her line of sight, Luke did laugh.

He felt better as Ivy turned and smiled at him. It was difficult to hold back what he'd learned at his mother's, but he'd managed it all night, mostly because Ivy was asleep. Now the nurse came in, and the two women placed orders for hospital food breakfast. Leo headed out, claiming he needed to brush his teeth and change his clothes.

Ivy leaned forward and whispered, "I'm okay if Jo knows."

Luke nodded and moved his chair to the space between the two beds, watching as Jo shuffled to be part of the conversation.

Jo might have been born a pampered rich princess, but he got the feeling that, even in the cradle, all her family's efforts simply hadn't stuck. She looked him in the eyes now and said, "So tell me about this arsonist and tell me why you know things the rest of us don't."

He and Ivy explained what they'd found out. And, while he wished Jo had some sudden lightning strike of an insight, she hadn't.

By early afternoon the two women had been released. Still, the process had taken well over an hour from start to finish before everyone who needed to had signed off and Jo and Ivy were finally headed to the cars. They were wheeled out by staff members as Luke and Leo both pulled under the awning to drive them each home.

As they were finally released onto their own two feet, Jo in loose sweat pants that allowed for the bandages on her legs and Ivy walking of her own accord now able to see clearly, Jo looked to Leo. "We're following them. They've got things we need to see."

Luke simply nodded. It wouldn't hurt to have more eyes on it.

The hospital wasn't in Redemption, and it took them a while to get home. Again, Luke watched as Ivy breathed a sigh of relief when she saw her house stood intact on her street. And again when she opened the garage door and walked into the kitchen and everything smelled fresh and not charred.

She hung her keys and her purse on a hook that she had placed by the door and ushered everyone in. It took her only a few moments to head into the back office, into the two rooms where Luke had offered to take down the cheap dividing wall and make it into one room again. She told him she was putting that *on the list*. But she had other things to do that were more pressing.

She'd quickly brought out a file and laid out the paperwork on the butcher block kitchen table that now had four chairs around it. Luke tried hard not to think about the things they'd done on that table. And Ivy's no-nonsense approach to the problem in front of them at least helped most of the time.

She pointed to each piece, looking at Luke for permission, before opening the sealed juvenile records, his own and his brothers'. But he didn't hesitate to share the information now. Ivy had been attacked twice. There was nothing in his history he wouldn't give up to make that stop.

Laying everything out on the table, Ivy and Luke watched as Jo and Leo looked at it for the first time. They took a few moments, picking up sheets and reading, checking over Ivy's notes and then looking at something else before Leo put his finger on one of the open juvenile cases.

"This," he said, "I think this is more damning than you're giving it credit for."

CHAPTER THIRTY-FIVE

"What do you mean?" Ivy glanced across the table at Leo, glad that she could finally see clearly.

She'd been worried for a while, at least until Luke had come in, that she might not see again. Luke had been right, she'd been replanning her whole life around possibly being blind.

Now Leo's finger rested on the document detailing how Mario and Carlos had been arrested over the squirrel as kids. "This torturing animals is introductory sociopathic behavior. Maybe psychopathic, depending on how you define it."

Though Jo and Luke shook their heads not understanding, Ivy nodded. "There are no strict distinctions between the definitions of the two words. Lots of therapists use them interchangeably and lots of people say they are different, but no one agrees on exactly how. So when you say psychopath—" she looked at Leo, "—do you mean actual violent behavior?"

"I don't know about violence, but definitely deviant. We deal with wildfires out in the parks all the time." This time Leo turned to Jo and Luke. "And people start them for all kinds of reasons. Many are accidental. Many are stupid—so stupid, that calling them accidental is far too kind. And some are deliberate.

It's the deliberate ones that are what I think of when I say psychopath, I mean *intending to cause harm*. Whether or not that's actual pain to another creature? I don't know."

Ivy nodded, she wasn't really asking. "You think this arsonist falls into that category. But we've crossed off Carlos and Mario here. Targeting me makes it look like it was either Luke or one of his brothers."

Luke held up his hands as if to say *hey now!* and Ivy reached out and playfully swatted at his shoulder. "You were on shift too many times. You've alibied out."

She was glad she could now feel comfortable in that assessment.

"I always thought Tiago looked the best for it," Luke volunteered, and Ivy could hear the tinge of regret in his voice at having put his own brother under the gun, even if it was only around her dining room table. "He's got the biggest string of arrests."

"But that's exactly what makes me think it's not him." Leo argued many of the same points that Ivy had before. "None of his crimes matched the kind of thing that we would likely see in the history of someone inflicting pain on others. And Tiago keeps getting arrested."

Ivy caught on then, and watched as Luke did, too. "If Tiago was our arsonist, the chances that he would have made it this long without making some kind of mistake is low."

"Exactly," Leo filled in.

"So who's left?" Jo asked, sitting in her chair, though both Ivy and Leo were standing. Ivy thought Jo's legs were giving her more trouble than she was admitting to but she didn't call her friend on it. It wouldn't be appreciated and probably Jo was doing the best she could.

"Mario's got a drug problem," Luke said. It wasn't news to anybody. Mario had a record and they could see where he'd gone into rehab twice.

"Is he using again?" Jo asked bluntly and Luke nodded. "How confident are you of that?"

"Well, I came up on him right after he'd purchased." Luke ground the words between his teeth. "I took his drugs from him and watched him get ready to dig through the forest floor to get them back. So yeah, really confident."

But it didn't make Mario their arsonist.

Together, the four of them started from scratch, retracing where Luke and Ivy had alibied out each of the brothers.

"You and Carlos were with your mother when the fire at the old convenience store was set?" Jo pointed to one document.

Luke double checked the date and nodded. When they finished, they agreed, as Luke and Ivy had the first time that each of the brothers wasn't available to set all of the fires.

"But look here: Tiago, Mario, and Carlos … all three of them are only alibied out for one fire each." Leo pointed out. "How good are you at determining the origins?"

Both Jo and Luke jumped into the answer on that. "Pretty good, we think." "You're talking about Kane and Taggart. Kane is relatively new as an arson investigator, but Taggart goes way back. He trained at Quantico."

"So they would have found timing devices, anything like that?" Leo asked.

Ivy was impressed at his fire knowledge. Though, as he pointed out, they dealt with them a lot in the park system. She jumped in. "These fires are classified by ringing the building in an accelerant and burning from the outside in. In several cases, we found a single burnt matchstick, not even a match book that would give us a location where the arsonist might frequent!"

Lord knew, she'd seen that often enough on TV shows and movies. But they weren't so lucky.

"No fingerprints on it?"

It was Luke who shook his head. "Ivy and I gave this information to Taggart and Kane a little while ago. They went back and searched the sites again and they actually found another matchstick. They've since tested all of them. No fingerprints or any DNA."

Crap. That should have been a good lead. A fingerprint would have solved everything. So of course they didn't have it.

They all stared at the paperwork in front of them for a while longer, each occasionally reaching out, picking up one of the documents, reading it thoroughly and, to Ivy's disappointment, setting it back down without having made some grand deduction. She really believed that having her friends here would help—more brains, more eyes, all of that.

She was about to get up and ask if anyone needed a drink or a shot of whiskey when Luke, looking dejected, said, "I think we need to expand the search."

"I agree," Jo offered, her expression grim. "But maybe not that far."

All eyes turned to her as Jo looked to Luke and said, "You said your mother told you that there was nothing she wouldn't do for her boys."

CHAPTER THIRTY-SIX

"Holy shit, Luke!" Ivy threw her hands in the air and almost pissed her pants ... her nice new pants for work. Luke had a gun aimed right at her head.

By the time she'd said it, the barrel was aimed down at the floor. "I'm so sorry!"

"You gave me a key ..." she reminded him, but she had come in while he was showering. She'd thought she'd sneak in and surprise him, and well, she guessed she had.

Her heart was still racing, her breath whooshing out of her as he clicked the release and popped the magazine out of the gun, quickly rendering it useless. But ...

"One in the chamber?" she asked with a raised eyebrow.

"Didn't get that far. I was just going for the threat."

"Well, you're very threatening in your happy polar bear towel." It must have been something he'd picked up at a camp or as a prize for something. She turned her head sideways trying to read whatever event the towel said it was from.

He looked down as if even he didn't know what he'd slapped around his waist when he'd heard her enter. With the gun and the clip still in one hand, both of them relaxing a bit, he said, "I didn't expect you."

She tipped her head side to side. "That got me revved up."

She'd been on her way to work and she'd simply stopped by. She hadn't slept well without him there and she didn't want to tell him that. Ivy had known he'd just gotten off shift and it was Wednesday, so she'd made the turn and hoped to find him still awake.

As she'd put the key in the lock, she'd experienced a moment of utter fear—that she would open the door and find him with someone else. Instead, her fear had been correct, just dramatically misplaced.

"I should have told you I had the gun," he said, but Ivy was already crossing the floor.

She'd been hoping to hit him up before he fell asleep, and now with her heart doing double time still and her body on high alert, it felt like maybe coming apart in his arms was the only thing that would calm her down. Her fingers snaked into his hair and she pulled him down for a searing kiss.

Luke's arm came around her, starting to pull her up tight against him until she realized he was still wet from the shower. "Whoa …"

She whispered it as she bit and tugged at his lower lip and backed away. "Follow me."

Her sweater was easily peeled and she dropped it on the floor. Reaching for the button on the front of her pants, she kicked off her heels and stepped out of them, Luke still behind her.

"Is this what you showed up for?"

"Is that a problem?" She looked back over her shoulder at him, the coy expression having the effect that she hoped it would.

"It is absolutely not. I'll just make sure to ask if it's a robbery or a booty call next time." He was grinning and she could see the front of the towel move as she turned to face him and dropped her bra.

It was heady, the power of making him react. It had always been heady making a man want her, but with Luke it was tenfold. She understood now why her family had always thought it was a sin that women could have that kind of power. Hooking her thumbs into her underwear, she tugged off the last of her clothing and stood naked in front of him.

What her upbring had missed was that Luke had the same effect on her.

She reached out, tugged at the towel and used it to dry him off. His eyes fell closed as his head tipped back and he stood statue-still under her touch. But touching him turned her on just as much as it did him.

He must have heard the towel hit the floor, because his eyes snapped open and his gaze focused on her mouth. She was biting at her own lower lip now, not even realizing it was a reaction to being naked and so turned on around him.

Luke started to walk forward, moving her back to the bed, but Ivy took control and tugged him with her, turning at the last moment and pushing him backward. She wasn't sure which one of them growled with the motion or why it tugged at her heart so hard.

His hands reached up to touch her breasts and her head fell back. In a moment she was on the bed, straddling him, moving her hips in a way that made both of them moan. Her hands rested on his chest, both supporting herself and holding him down.

When his hips bucked up under hers, she fought the urge to climb right onto him. Leaning over, she closed her lips over one nipple then traced a path up to his jaw. She found the lobe of his ear and bit down softly until he returned the favor on her nipple.

Her fingers curled into his shoulders as she found his mouth and kissed him hard.

When he tried to roll them over and take the top spot, Ivy refused. One shake of her head and he stopped, leaned back, and let her run the show.

She ignored the understanding she saw in his eyes, hating it. But she needed this, needed to bend him and make him come on her schedule. Rubbing herself against him again, she pushed up, lifted her head until her back arched and she hit the sweet spot. She was so close to coming. Given his heavy breaths and occasional groans, he was, too.

Ivy lifted herself on pure muscle, letting his erection lift itself. God, he was so hard, he wanted her so much. She didn't let herself think how much she wanted him, or how much she was beginning to *need* him. No, if she was being honest, she'd passed need some time ago, but she only had the bandwidth to ride him like a bronco right now.

She moved her hips slowly, too slowly, until she found the tip of him. Changing her angle, she sank slowly onto him. The buzz in her nerves and muscles growing louder with each inch she pressed.

When Luke bucked his hips again, she matched the movement, pulling away and not letting him slide any deeper. She was so wet that all she'd have to do was stay still and he could have fully seated himself. Instead, she leaned forward again, her hair swinging down until it brushed his chest.

He groaned and opened his eyes. She was caught in his gaze. There was nowhere to go, nothing she could hide from him. Luke saw everything and the fear of what he would know was a petrifying aphrodisiac.

She pushed downward, seating him fully inside her in one rushed stroke, as though she could distract him with sex. His eyes dilated, his breath rushed out as though he'd gotten the wind knocked out of him, and his hips bucked upward. This time she let him push, feeling the thick slide of him inside her.

It was supposed to distract him, break the connection of him seeing her soul. It only deepened.

Luke didn't move, content to sit with her sheathed around him, maybe forcing her to take the reins. Ivy lifted her hips, the burn in her thighs as welcome as the sweet sting in her blood.

She rode him slowly for a few minutes, moving up and down, arching her back and rolling her hips to claim the best angle. Still Luke watched her face, made it impossible to break eye contact as her senses heightened and tightened.

When she was wound to the point of bursting, her body stole control from her and she picked up her pace, riding her own need as sure as she was riding his body. Luke's hands grabbed her hips, fingers tightening until she would have bruises that would tell anyone who saw exactly what she'd been doing. He let her set the pace, but his grip held her close, grinding them together as the focus in her eyes began to fade and she looked beyond his precious face and into something that wasn't visible at the surface.

"Ivy!"

She screamed loud enough to rouse his neighbors. Then she did it again. Her back arched, her head fell back, and her body bucked with the release of her orgasm. When her consciousness returned, she could still feel her body clenching rhythmically around him. Her fingers gripped his thighs, her back like a bow, her chest heaving ... the movement of her breathing pressed her against him in a way that shot more small spikes of pleasure through her even as she came down from the high of being with him.

Slowly, her breathing normalized. Slowly, she returned to her body and heard him gathering his breath, too. She leaned onto his chest, and then over him. Tipping her head to keep her hair out of the way, she dipped in and kissed him.

The kiss was reassuring rather than seductive. It was deep and fulfilling, not needy and taking. She squeezed her eyes as reality and all the intrusive thoughts returned.

Luke's arms came up around her and, with a little pressure, pulled her down against him. His embrace was warm and comforting. His words were not. "Ivy, what was that?"

She shook her head. She didn't want to tell him.

CHAPTER THIRTY-SEVEN

"I have to get to work." Ivy rolled over, grateful that it was Wednesday morning, and that no one would notice if she wasn't there exactly on time. Because, on Wednesdays, there was no *exactly on time*.

Luke grinned up from bed, one arm tucked behind his head. "That was it? You just came over, used me, and now you're leaving?"

He thought he was being funny, she knew. But, as he said it, she realized that was almost exactly what he'd done the first night they were together. Ivy couldn't take offense at it, though.

He stayed there, reclined on the bed as she climbed into her clothing. More of her original things had been ruined in the fire than she'd thought. It had required paperwork with the insurance company to get them to pay out more, but she wasn't the only one to realize further damage after the fact, and she'd fought to get the payout. That's what insurance was for. She told herself it was about the money and ignored the fact that her house had been deliberately set on fire.

Some of her clothing, particularly the dryclean only pieces had not ever been able to be cleared of the smoke smell. She'd waited on the check, then replaced the old long skirts and loose style pants with work pants in more comfortable stretch fabric. She added skirts that didn't swing wide and hit below the knee.

But even as she was sorting through the nice new clothing that she'd thrown onto his old, worn carpet, Luke was sitting up in bed, not quite lazing back, a not-quite-grin on his face.

"Ivy." Something about the tone stopped her halfway into getting her legs into her pants. She looked at him and tried to ignore the tug of his expression, the seriousness of it.

She pulled them up, buttoning the front and zipping them.

"Ivy." He said it again. "You're so tense."

"Of course, I am!" she snapped. Then she closed her eyes and took a deep breath. It wasn't his fault, though he seemed to think it was. But he was a victim here as much as she was. She was just getting herself together to apologize when his words stunned her.

"I think we should maybe stop seeing each other for a while."

"What?" She didn't even have a bra on and she whirled around as quickly as humanly possible to face him, her incredulity clear on her face. "I thought you were my *protection!* But you're just dumping me?"

She heard the words coming out of her mouth, the sarcasm, the disdain dripping. But she couldn't stop it.

"Obviously it didn't work," he said.

But he'd said it wasn't about that. He'd said that he *wanted* to see her. In fact, he'd told her he didn't want to just be her protection, he wanted to be more. *And now ...?*

"And if whoever's targeting me thinks I've broken up with you ..." She let it trail off. But she waited and he didn't reply, he just looked away.

"What?" she asked, maybe just to fill the space. "So I can just sit at my house in the evenings alone? That sounds super safe."

But she didn't want him if he didn't want to be there. She

would sit at her house alone. Whoever was watching her be damned. She knew how to use a gun, too.

"I don't know what to tell you." He was standing up now, absolutely unconcerned with his own nudity.

"Is that what you *want?*" she asked. Was he simply trying to break up with her and the arsonist had become a convenient excuse?

Her heart clenched and ice froze in little tendrils through her blood. Luke being Luke, somehow seemed to see it. He walked forward, placing his hands on either side of her face and pulled her in for a kiss that said it was absolutely not what he wanted.

She breathed a little easier then. But she was still confused. "I don't think us being separated is going to change anything. It just makes us both alone."

"Okay." He said it as though he was conceding to something. But then he added, "Good. I want to be with you, but I need you safe. I just don't know what the best way to do that is."

He stepped back, reached into a dresser drawer, and magically pulled out a pair of pants that was either exactly the pair he wanted, or else he simply didn't care what he pulled out. He stepped into them.

The apartment unit stayed warm the way he liked it, despite the cold weather outside. The snow was coming down again. Ivy looked out the window, wishing she could see who was trailing them, targeting them. Because it wasn't just Luke's past they were burning now, it was his present.

There were so many unknowns.

The thought of stepping away from Luke was too much. They still hadn't figured out how the arsonist had managed to ring the spa with accelerant in broad daylight. Even as Jo and Ivy had knocked on all the doors they passed, the manager had taken the whole other side. But she wasn't a firefighter. She hadn't gotten down low quick enough. She'd inhaled too much smoke and gotten too many burns. She'd be in the hospital for a while.

Ivy and Luke were hoping that Kane and Taggart would get to her for an interview soon. But if they already had, Ivy didn't know about it yet.

Whether the arsonist was one of Luke's brothers, or even his mother—as Leo had suggested—didn't change the damage they'd done.

Ivy felt like they'd come a long way, but still didn't know anything. Luke didn't believe it was his mother, if only for the sheer reason that she simply didn't have the spare time or the wherewithal.

Though Leo had pointed out, "She's a smoker. That makes it easy enough to start fires." Luke had shaken his head at the time and reminded them, "But none of the fires were started with cigarettes."

They'd all agreed it was valid. But something had nagged at Ivy and, despite having an alibi for one of the fires each, the Hernandez brothers remained at the top of her list.

In fact, they were all leaning toward Tiago or Mario right now.

She'd spent the last week trying not to bring it up, to let Sebastian Kane and Chief Taggart do their job. She tried to have faith that they would figure it out. The problem was she had to have faith that they would figure it out *before* the next fire was set or the next person died.

The longer it took, the harder it was to keep that faith. The more she worried that the arsonist would strike again. That she —or worse, Luke—wouldn't survive the next time.

Jo had been injured. Ivy had been in the hospital, unable to see, for twenty-four hours. And the woman who ran the spa still hadn't gotten out. There was too much on her mind and, she knew, written on her face. Somehow, Luke read all of it.

"Ivy."

He stepped close now as she tugged her sweater on. She would have stepped into her shoes and turned to leave, but he pulled her into his arms and held her close.

"You can't control it."

She almost snapped back that she knew that. But he was right. She was trying to control everything the best she could. In life number one, everything had been about control and modesty. She was to be seen but not heard, and not even seen if she didn't have to be. She existed only to serve others. All control had belonged to someone else.

In life number two, the pendulum had swung wide the other way. There was no control and no modesty. She'd embraced hedonism and everything pleasurable, denying herself nothing, making no plans. She'd deigned to follow a schedule only to the bare necessity of maintaining a job, so that she could support whatever pleasure she could find on her off hours.

In life number three, the pendulum swung back. She still believed in pleasure, this time in moderation. But she'd gone back to control—embracing it to its fullest, glad that this time she was the one who wielded it. She'd graduated magna cum lauda because she controlled everything. Her modesty, and her desire for others to think well of her was another issue under her own control.

She hadn't even realized that's what she was doing until she'd fallen into bed with Luke and he'd wrested it away from her.

"You can't control it, Ivy," he said again.

She fell into his arms, the tears coming, because she knew that whoever was coming after them wasn't finished.

Luke knew that. She'd told him everything … almost everything.

What she hadn't told him was that someone was still watching her.

CHAPTER THIRTY-EIGHT

"You're home!" Luke stood up from the table as Ivy came in through the garage. "I hope I didn't startle you."

"No," she laughed at him, glad she could now find humor in the morning's events.

"Is it okay if I stay? I've been here about an hour."

"I saw your car in the driveway." She told him and Luke hoped that meant yes, it was okay to stay.

He hoped everyone who looked saw the car and knew he was here. So far, Ivy had only been targeted when she was away from him. If he could, he would stick to her side like glue.

But as he watched her pace the small house, checking everything, he saw her movements odd, a little off. Something was bugging her, something he didn't yet know about.

"I see you found my work." She waved her hand at the table where she'd left the papers out. He wondered if their arsonist had broken in and maybe found that they had been studying up. He hated that he'd looked the place through and tried to figure out what would happen if it burned again, what would go up first, what stood a chance to survive.

But he didn't tell Ivy any of that.

He kissed her softly and slowly and told himself it wasn't a good time to strip her naked and bury both their worries for a while. He waited while she put her purse and keys on the hook, then he pulled her over to the table. "I think it has to be Mario."

She looked at him a little sideways. "What makes you say that?"

He lined the pages up, pointing out each of the cases.

"But how would Mario know about the spa?" she asked.

"He stayed close with our mom. He and Carlos didn't know our dad much. But I remember him constantly asking about him. I remember him being angry about it as a kid." He stopped and tried to sift through all the tangled memories that made up his childhood and pick out the right ones to stop the arsonist. He tried to leave the others behind—the ones that would incriminate his other brothers or himself.

"I don't think I saw it at the time, but he was an angry kid. He had our dad around just enough to get used to him, but not long enough to have any real memories of him. If I was a therapist, I'd say it's probably part of what fueled the drug problem." He sighed harshly. He couldn't remember being mad about his father leaving. "Maybe Tiago and I saw the man enough that we knew we were better off with him gone. But Mario and Carlos, they didn't."

He hadn't thought about it at the time. Even as an adult, Mario just always had problems. Luke had simply reacted to each thing as it came up and never looked deeper. "I always brushed him off. It might explain why some of the targets seem to be a little more specifically at me."

Ivy nodded, following along. "What about this fire?"

"That one I don't know about. Maybe he set it and my mom covered for him."

The way she nodded, slowly and unsurprised, told Luke that he was late to the party. Ivy had already figured these things out.

But he'd learned something else today. "Kane and Taggart got in to talk to the spa manager in the hospital today. She's finally off the pain meds where she can speak clearly."

Ivy sat down across from him, almost excited. "Did she have ideas about how he got the accelerant around the building?"

"She said an exterminator showed up that morning. She'd thought it was odd and she asked him about it, since he was totally out of season. He said the owner had hired the company and they were doing a new thing, putting down chemicals in the winter. So it had time to soak in and form a good seal around the base of the house before the bugs came out. Something about people waiting until it was too late, until after they had a problem."

He watched as Ivy's mouth dropped open. "That's brilliant. He openly came and sprayed stinky chemicals on the building and they just let him ... Wait, then she saw his face!"

But Luke shook his head. "He was wearing a covering over the lower portion of his face. The spa manager apparently didn't think anything of it, because he'd already done half of the house and it stank."

He watched as Ivy sighed heavily, lowering her face in her hands. He'd felt the same. Each break hadn't been one. They'd been closer, and all of it would help convict the guy when he was caught, but so far no one had caught him in the act or doing anything that would be enough evidence to bring him in.

The entire town was getting worried now. Luke heard the rumblings.

At first it had been old houses, abandoned places. Then empty buildings. Even Ivy's house wasn't everyone's house. It wasn't public. Anyone could look at it and think they were safe. But hitting the spa when it was full? Anyone could have been there ... and the town was getting mad.

Luke just didn't know if they suspected *him*.

He took a breath and turned his effort away from things he

couldn't change, to things he hoped he could. "Here's the thing, though, the description could be Mario. It's too short to be Tiago, so we can rule him out."

"Do you think Mario has been sober enough to pull this off? The exterminator cover requires some coordination."

Again, Luke shrugged. He wished he had more to go on, but all he could say was Mario had been very high functioning in the past. "This isn't his first rodeo. And honestly, the fires started months ago. So it's plausible he started off knowing exactly what he was doing. Then he might be taking the drugs to counteract his conscience."

"You think the fires spurred the drug use, not the other way around."

Luke raised his hands, feeling helpless the way he had for so long now. "I wish I knew. It's just a theory."

"Kane and Taggart are on top of it now? You told them it's Mario?"

Luke nodded. "It's a matter for the police now. But RPD is tailing him. They'll catch him." His heart was breaking and Ivy seemed to be able to tell.

"I'm so sorry that it turned out to be one of your brothers," she told him. They sat for a moment, staring at all the evidence. Then she asked, "Are you still making your rounds?"

Unable to really put a voice to it, he nodded again and she simply let it go. Standing up, she announced, "We should make dinner."

For a while, they cooked together, him turning chicken breasts in a pan while she made vegetables. It felt so fully domestic, and so comfortable, that he forgot about everything else. The home he'd grown up in as a child had not felt like this and he knew Ivy's home hadn't either. But here, together, they could build something better.

He thought of all the times he'd gone into Lincoln and flirted or drank his way into a one night stand. All the times he'd walked away from it the next morning. He thought of a few girlfriends he'd had where he tried to make something work but in the end it hadn't been worth it and he'd given up quickly.

But this—here now, with Ivy—it was everything. He couldn't quite put his finger on why it was right. Why this felt so different ... aside from the fact that this was Ivy and he knew they belonged together. She felt like home.

He had a fatalistic sense that he'd found it only to have it taken away.

CHAPTER THIRTY-NINE

"I didn't want to say this before," Shannon whispered as she slid in close to Ivy behind the desk.

The last of their patrons had left and Ivy suddenly found herself cornered. Her coworker seemed to have something conspiratorial up her sleeve. Ivy liked Shannon. The young woman was intelligent, fun, and sadly, would leave relatively soon. Shannon was amazing in part because she was on her way to getting her own library science degree, and hopefully running her own place. Unfortunately, Ivy didn't think Redemption could support two full time librarians and that meant she would lose her best assistant. So when Shannon had something to say, Ivy did her best to make time and listen.

"I hate to bring up bad things. But now that you're okay and everything has died down, I wanted to tell you. It's probably stupid and just someone who was wearing clothing that you would wear ... But when you were in the fire, last week, I thought I saw a ghost."

Ivy felt her eyebrows rise and her mouth quirk. Ghosts were not a thing. Then again, when she thought about it, that was what she'd been told by her family. She always tried to stop and reevaluate, question where her beliefs had come from. She would probably spend the rest of her life questioning her childhood. "What do you mean?"

"We all heard about the fire pretty quickly. I think we heard about it maybe before it was out and I knew you were at the spa that day." The young woman's voice faltered.

"Oh, Shannon." Ivy hadn't even thought of that. Jo had set the whole thing up with Shannon to be a surprise for Ivy. So as soon as Shannon had heard the spa was on fire, she hadn't even had to think about it. She'd *known* Ivy and Jo were there.

Ivy stepped in for a quick hug, Shannon's arms going tight around her. It had been a week that she'd been holding that in, and Ivy just stood there in the hug, the two women supporting each other for a moment.

This, she thought, this was what she'd moved here for. Friends she was allowed to commiserate with rather than just serve her time with. When she stepped back, Shannon tipped her head.

"I thought you had died. Then when I thought I saw you here, I believed it."

"What?" Ivy asked. Though initially, she'd been ready to console her friend the last part of the statement had turned her on a dime.

"You were walking in and out of the stacks like you were looking for a book. When I called out to you, you kind of disappeared. Then I saw you leaving out the front door a moment later." Shannon was waving her hand, motioning exactly where ghost Ivy had gone.

"You were probably really upset," Ivy told her.

"I know. And then it seemed kind of weirder, since you didn't die. Oh my god!" Shannon's hands flew to her mouth. "Please don't take that the wrong way. I'm so glad you didn't!"

Ivy was laughing as she grabbed Shannon's hands to pull them from her face. "It's fine. I totally understand. I'm impressed you were upset enough by word of my demise to imagine you saw my ghost!"

"That's probably it," Shannon said. "And I'm going to miss you so much next fall! Anyway, it was a weird day all around and we were so glad to hear later that everybody made it."

"You and me both," Ivy said.

With no patrons in the library, the two of them headed over to the stacks. "Do you want to look up ghost sightings?" Ivy teased.

Shannon gave her a dirty look tinged with humor, but thirty minutes later she was checking out a stack of books on the subject.

Ivy tried not to laugh at her.

"Take care of yourself, Ivy," Shannon said, as she backed out the front door, books in hand, leaving her boss to finish out the evening and lock up.

Another patron or two wandered in, but sometimes she was left alone in the building and the silence. For the first time, she understood that the entire town knew what she was going through. They probably all knew the Hernandez boys were at the heart of it—at least as targets, if not as perpetrators.

She'd thought for a while that the whole thing was her problem. But that was the thing with a small town like Redemption: Everyone knew everyone else's business.

She had come in with an understanding of small town life that wasn't an idealized or romanticized version. Not everyone was good, quirky wasn't always great. In fact, she'd known that few people would actually be her best friends and that she would get to know people well enough to know she didn't like them. But she'd liked the idea that people knew what was happening. And she'd been there and helped others through their crises. But somehow, when her own crisis had hit, she'd simply forgotten that she was already a part of the community, and they would rally around her too.

Ivy stayed until the library closed at seven. With Luke at work, she was on her own overnight, and knew it meant she wouldn't sleep well. After doing her final check, she locked up behind herself and headed out to her car ... the lone vehicle in a parking lot lit only by a few old yellow sulfur lights.

Was she being watched again?

She truly felt as if she was. But she was also becoming convinced she was simply paranoid. She'd never caught a glimpse of anyone out of the corner of her eye. Not found footprints around her home. And she'd received no cryptic notes or even gotten hangup phone calls.

Still, she locked the doors in her car as soon as she was in and tried to breathe easier as she drove through for a burger, a habit that was becoming far too regular. A habit that she had told herself she would quit when the crisis was over. But she was now coming to understand that it might never be over.

The fires might simply fade away in frequency. Or, she thought as she watched the sky gathering snow it softly dropped, their firebug might simply be put on hold for the colder months. She could be tense all winter waiting for him to strike again when he wouldn't.

Tonight, she made Luke's rounds, seeing nothing. She'd gone so far as to trespass on one property, driving up the long stretch of gravel and getting out of the car to check out the old barn. But it seemed intact.

An apartment the Hernandez family had lived in was on the other side of the property. Luke told her how the boys would come out and play in the barn, which was at the time in better repair. She couldn't go up into the loft now without fearing for her safety. She hadn't even gone inside because, again, she'd gotten the sensation that she was being watched.

So she climbed back into her car and followed the gravel road back out to the main highway, none the wiser for her searching. Though she was tempted to head home, something nagged at her. A few moments later, she found herself pulling up to a tiny house indistinct from the others in the row of tiny houses.

It stood on a lifted foundation, clear of the flooding they sometimes experienced. Vinyl siding, a much older version of her own, sagged and gapped in a few places. Near the front door, a smudge marred the color and she recognized it as a trail of cigarette smoke left by someone who stood there talking to her neighbors or just maybe watching the world go by.

Without much hope, Ivy put the car into park on the gravel driveway behind the small beater that took up most of the space. Pulling her coat tighter around herself, she headed up the short walk and climbed the steps and knocked on Mrs. Hernandez' front door.

CHAPTER FORTY

It was one in the morning before Luke finally called her back.

"Luke!" Ivy frantically answered the phone. She was awake, sitting in her living room, the one torch lamp on. She left it lit most nights, not willing to make her house entirely dark and signal to someone whether she was awake or asleep.

The old rifle she bought herself after an assault walking home from her waitressing job years ago sat beside her. It was loaded and ready, though she really didn't think she would need it.

"I'm sorry," Luke said. "We were out on a run."

"I understand. Is everyone okay?" She wasn't angry, just concerned.

Their runs could be anything from a cat in a tree to a domestic dispute to a raging fire. So she always worried, but she didn't tell him that as she listened to him talk about a kitchen fire in which an older man had forgotten he was cooking bacon.

Though her heart broke for the man who'd burned up his own kitchen, she was still focused on what she'd learned. "Do you have a few minutes to talk?"

He seemed to check with the others and again, Ivy was reminded that everyone in town pretty much knew their business. No one had commented on her relationship with Luke other than to say that they knew it existed. But a few had told her they hoped she stayed safe and she was trying to do that now.

"Yes, I can talk as long as we don't get another call."

"Luke, you're going to be so mad at me." *Not a good opening.* "I went and talked to your mother this evening."

"Oh, Lord. How did that go?" He didn't sound angry. Yet.

"It was okay. I asked her all these questions about you boys ..." Ivy let her thoughts trail off.

"And?" Luke prompted. At least he still didn't sound angry.

"She has to be covering for Mario. We thought she was covering for Tiago. And she did, but that was to help cover for Mario." Ivy said.

"What do you mean?"

Ivy shook her head. It was a difficult trail to follow. "The exterminator at the spa couldn't have been Tiago and it probably *was* the arsonist. I'm assuming he wouldn't trust anyone else to lay down the accelerant. So it isn't Tiago. But your mother covered for Tiago for something on the night of one of the fires! And she covered for Mario on another night."

"Okay, I'm following now."

"Honestly, I re-asked her questions that you said you asked. None of it quite added up. I can't put my finger on it, but she's lying about something."

She heard him suck in a breath. It was hard enough on him to think it was one of his brothers. But for Ivy to point a finger at his mother? Her heart broke for him.

"Okay, what did she say?"

"She said that Mario was there at the house with her. On one of the nights when we can clearly place him at a bar with friends. One of the fires we think he set after leaving the bar."

"Which one?"

"The third house. The empty house." She told him.

"Okay." Luke knew which one she was speaking of. "And he doesn't have an alibi for the spa. At least that's what Taggart and Kane said."

"But what about Tiago? What your mother said didn't add up there either. The night that Tiago was supposed to have been with her, she said they were out together. But when I asked, she said she thought she was out with friends that night, until I prompted her about Tiago. Then she said her friends were at the house when Tiago came over. So I asked her for names and she couldn't provide them. Don't you think the police would have found that?"

"I know they questioned her." Luke sighed heavily and Ivy hated putting this on him, but they couldn't work without him, he was the one who knew what was going on in that family.

"Yes, she told me the police questioned her and asked why I was asking the same things. I don't think the police will tell us what they find. We're not officially part of the investigation, except as witnesses." His sigh spoke volumes.

"I think she's just protecting you boys against anything anyone asks. Like, for any date anyone brings up, she'll say her sons were with her."

"Okay," Luke said again as she gave him a moment to process it.

But if his mother was doing that, then almost nothing she said was reliable. So Ivy walked over to the table where she had the pages laid out and shuffled through them again. "If you look at it that way, if you say that Mario is our arsonist and Tiago did one of them for him, *and* if he did it on the night that your mother is covering for him, then Tiago did the old convenience store fire."

Ivy could almost hear Luke thinking as a silence settled over the line. "It works, doesn't it?"

"I guess. What was the accelerant on that one?"

"Paraffin," Ivy answered with a knowing tone in her voice. She'd been doing her homework. "Paraffin is less volatile. Mario could have set it out and left it, established his alibi with your mom. All Tiago had to do was light it."

"That was the one where they found a lighter, not a match," Luke filled in.

"Exactly." A melted yellow Bic had been found at the scene. "And it's out in the middle of nowhere. Tiago doesn't even have to be a decent arsonist. He doesn't have to take a lot of time. He simply shows up, lights the place and leaves."

"But why would he do that for Mario?" Luke asked and she knew he was just asking for himself.

This was the part Ivy hated. "It could be because they're brothers and he feels a loyalty. Look at what you did." She knew Luke felt bad now, simply because his brother was on the line—not just one brother, but two. There was a reason she hadn't gone to the police with this. *Not first.* Luke would want a chance to talk to his siblings and let them turn themselves in. And he would want solid evidence before he did even that much.

"It could be that Mario has something on him," she added, waiting while Luke absorbed that too. "Tiago's got a criminal history, Luke, a long one. There have to be some activities the police didn't catch. And he and Mario seem infinitely malleable. They both must have things that they'd want to keep hidden, which makes it possible to manipulate them."

She spoke for a few more minutes, speaking things that he clearly already knew about his brothers—things that neither of them had wanted to know. Now, it appeared his mother was involved—at the very least she was covering for one or more of her sons.

When silence settled over the phone line, Ivy waited. She could only fill the space so much.

Luke sighed again, the heaviness of it filling Ivy's heart about to breaking. "I guess I just have to be glad that Carlos got out unscathed."

Ivy would simply agree. The youngest brother had moved somewhat out of town. He had stayed close enough to his family to be there but was far enough away not to get caught up in this the way Luke had. The boys had had such a rough childhood. But Luke and Carlos seemed to have come out okay and Ivy wondered if it was wrong to think that two out of four wasn't too bad a number given the situation.

"This isn't going to be easy for Carlos to hear. He's the baby."

Ivy thought about it for a moment. Her family, as far as she knew, had never quite had a *baby of the family* because more babies simply kept coming. But she knew how she felt about Violet and Rose, that they were so much younger than her. Even though she wasn't there, and even though they were much older now, she still felt so protective. She could only imagine Luke feeling the same level of protectiveness toward his own baby brother.

"Do you want me to come home?" Luke asked, his voice soft.

For a moment Ivy shook her head, forgetting that he couldn't see her. "No."

"Do you think you're in danger?"

Yes. But she fought the bark of laughter that tried to erupt. It was wholly inappropriate right now. He was being nice and sweet and protective of her. And she was in no more danger now than she ever was. Lately, though, the dial had been set pretty high.

"I'll be okay," she told him, her head turning to look at the rifle beside her. The words *I love you* almost rolled off her tongue, but she wasn't quite sure what to do with the words or how to handle them. She didn't know if she'd ever said them before.

She'd come from a place where love was supposed to be understood and not stated. In life number two, she loved nothing but pleasure. Here in life number three, she was finding out that she loved Redemption. She loved Jo and her friends. And she thought she was falling in love with Luke.

But she didn't say it.

Not certain and not ready, she said, "I'll see you in the morning before I go to work."

They hung up, their goodbyes hanging like warnings in the air.

CHAPTER FORTY-ONE

"Hernandez."

Luke looked up and listened to his assignment even as he continued to move. He pushed his feet down in the waiting pants, already loaded into the boots, so he donned it all in one economy of motion. Next, he pulled the suspenders up and over his shoulders. Having heard his own name, he only vaguely listened to the Chief's assignment for the other positions.

Climbing into the last of his turnout gear, he headed to the truck and swung up in. Embedded in the back of the seat was his SCBA—the last of the gear he would need to be ready to plunge into the fire as needed.

Once again, Ronan Kelly was driving and he swung up into the front seat with a fluid motion. Kelly was starting the engine even as he closed the door, calling out names and checking positions.

They pulled forward, the big truck running smoother than people would expect, but the bounce at the end of the drive was always enough to lift you from your seat. Luke held on as they hung the sharp right turn toward their destination.

His gaze was aimed out the window, but he wasn't watching the scenery. Just because he was in the back didn't mean he was off the hook. Everyone had eyes on the road, watching for cars on side streets, for people who didn't hear or simply didn't stop.

The comms all buzzed to life with the chief reading off the address. Luke felt the heavy pounding of his heart slide to a stop.

He knew that address.

Dammit. Things had been quiet for a while. He'd started to let his guard down. He and Ivy had a whole week with zero bullshit and no fires and not even any word about Tiago doing something stupid. Luke had let himself revel in it.

He checked the dash—6:34am. Monday's call had come in at 7:15 in the morning and kept them until well after ten, clearing out a space that had not had a fire at all.

A false alarm—one that he'd missed passing by Ivy on her way to work for. This fire would definitely ruin that again. But he pushed his thoughts back to the side roads, watching as one by one the locals pulled to a respectful stop as they honked and plowed on by.

He couldn't think about Ivy. This had always been part of the job: shift ended at eight sharp, unless it didn't. Today, it wouldn't.

He could swing by the library later and say hi to her—if he was upright. But he needed all of his focus right now on the job.

As they pulled to a stop, his heart doing a dull slide, he saw the small house he recognized from his childhood. This time the neighborhood was at the outskirts of town and featured houses relatively far apart on a country road. Still, half of them were boarded up and so was this one.

Jesus, the number of decrepit houses in his history made him begin to understand how poor the family actually had been while he was growing up. It couldn't possibly be normal to have moved so much, and it couldn't possibly be normal to have so many of the places where you had once lived fall into such disrepair and abandonment.

The house was now blue, or it had been blue most recently, and honestly calling it *blue* was a bit of an overstatement. Half of the roof had started to sag in. Interestingly enough, it was the opposite end of the porch that seemed to want to slide off the front of the house. Particle board was nailed over the windows, not even level or plumb. At some point, some asshole had attacked the poor decrepit home with spray paint.

But the murmurs were going through the truck like waves. Everyone saying the same as Luke had seen with his own eyes: no roiling black smoke.

He glanced quickly around the truck but didn't let it stop him from doing the job. Jo, sitting opposite him, was reaching for the door and the two hopped down just as the Chief pulled up right behind them in the red truck.

"Hernandez, Huston, take a lap!"

They nodded and were off. Moving quickly, they looped once around the building at a wide berth, checking out everything they could by visuals alone. Luke used the thermal scanner and checked from every angle. By the time they cleared the fourth corner, the entire team was standing on the lawn looking at the house, arms crossed and shaking their heads much the same way.

Not what they'd expected from the report.

He wanted to call it a prank, go back to the station, and maybe get off by eight a.m. But that simply wasn't allowable. Someone had called in a credible threat and, if they failed to check it out to their fullest ability, the liability would be on them.

Chief divided them up. "The structure may not be sound. We'll have to do checks from the outside. Heat signatures?"

"None," he reported. "Not fire, not human, not warm-blooded mammal inside." But then he added, "I know the place."

Luke's eyes flashed to Sebastian Kane, the other arson investigator.

"Another one?" Chief asked.

"Another place that's part of my history, yes. But part of the chain? I don't know." All he could do was shrug. "It doesn't look like it's on fire at all. So does it count?"

Everyone knew about his history with the arsonist now, but no one had an answer.

The problem was that the Chief was reporting a call like this each morning. Monday had been the first … this was now the fourth. There had been solid reports from dispatch, yet each time the crew arrived to find nothing amiss. The first time they brushed it off. It was illegal to call in fake fires, but people still did it. The second time was annoying, but Luke could tell the Chief was now very concerned about these calls and their regularity.

Still, they had to inspect everything. It took quite some time to check and double check everything before they could pack up, declare it a prank, and head back to the station. B-shift was already there. They'd shined the ladder truck and begun daily chores and were over an hour and a half into their shift as the others poured out of the truck. They packed away their turnout gear and hit the showers.

They'd been running around in heavy equipment the whole time. So even though they hadn't encountered a thousand-degree fire and backdraft they were still sweaty and dirty. Luke waited his turn, dried off and climbed into his casual clothing, before heading out. He thought about going by the library but, given the time, the doors were already open. Ivy would be chatting with people and helping them with their book checkouts and research questions. His presence would simply be an interruption.

He did, however, head to her place. He had the key. They said they wanted people to see his car in her driveway and know that she wasn't alone. But he liked the idea that people would see his car in her driveway and know that he was with her. He wasn't sure if the better end of that deal was that people knew that he had somehow snagged Ivy Dean or if people believed that Ivy Dean loved him.

He didn't get much time to think about it. He went face down into the pillows, the long shift behind him and sleep ahead of him.

He curled up under the blanket in the bed that smelled like Ivy and didn't hear the buzzing of his phone as he fell quickly and deeply asleep.

CHAPTER FORTY-TWO

"Hey, Shannon—" Ivy looked down at her phone, excited, but as she spoke the door chimed and several patrons entered the library and she couldn't ask.

"What?"

"Never mind. Later." The timing sucked. Orlando Tavares had sent her more information. But she couldn't read the attachments on her phone. He'd found something more, something he thought critical, or even plausibly helpful to the case and he'd sent five new documents from various sources to the email.

Ivy set her phone and her excitement aside and checked out two different patrons who were leaving with stacks of books. That made her happy, but as soon as they were down to a single man wandering the stacks, she'd tried again. "Shannon, can you cover the floor for a bit?"

Her assistant readily agreed, and Ivy ducked into the office. It wasn't her office but the communal space for anyone working the library. She couldn't close herself into her own space for this because she'd need to keep an ear out in case Shannon needed her. But she looked over her shoulder, double-checking that no one could see the screen of her tablet. Though there were honestly only three people in the building and she knew where Shannon was, and almost exactly where Mr. Miller was. He would be in thrillers, perusing the new releases carefully, then he would check them all out anyway.

Opening the email, she read quickly through the paragraph that Orlando had written.

Hi Ivy,

Hope all is well. Thank you for keeping us posted regarding the case. We're both sorry it hasn't been solved yet. Still looking through old documents for you though and found these. See five attachments. Not sure how useful they are. Hope they help.

Orlando

Ivy immediately messaged Luke, letting him know that Orlando had sent additional documents. She didn't expect him to reply. He'd messaged about nine thirty that he was on his way back to her place, exhausted.

Knowing she could have an hour or only a few minutes of time, Ivy quickly downloaded each document. Some had several pages and she had to wait as the ancient printer chugged its way through simple black and white prints. Her only consolation was that the beast was too old to retain what it had printed.

As the last page was coming off, Shannon stuck her head in. "Hey, Ivy, we're getting people."

"Thank you! I'll be right there." Ivy jumped up, standing over the printer, motioning for it to spit the last page out as though her encouragement would change its speed. Grabbing the documents, she shoved them down into her bag and headed to the front desk.

When she'd first opened the library, she had a small rush of excited patrons the first few weeks. But eventually, the usage had faded to a handful of patrons a day. One of her goals was to increase library traffic. She was even considering running a small after school program staffed with high school volunteers starting in the fall of next year. But they'd gotten more and more of these rushes the longer she'd stayed.

While she desperately wanted to read her documents, she was excited that people were coming into the library more often. A slow steady increase would do more than enough for her numbers.

This time, she let Shannon check out the patrons and set herself up to answer questions. A student needed information on Marie Antoinette. Ivy set him up with several references. A young woman wanted local Native Heritage wondering if it was her own. Ivy turned her to the city birth records in the back room and showed her where the books were on the local tribes. Another needed recipes for sourdough starters. Ivy helped them all.

It was one thirty before the rush ended, and Ivy bought sandwiches for her and Shannon for lunch. She sent Shannon out to pick them up, allowing her to stay at the desk but get them both fed. At three, Shannon headed home and Ivy stayed to close up at six.

Thursday was an early day and she was looking forward to getting home to Luke, but that was still several hours away. She helped patron after patron. They'd seemed to perfectly space themselves out, so that she wasn't pulled in two directions, but she barely managed a drink from her water bottle ... until about five thirty when it finally slowed and she had the place to herself.

Fifteen minutes later, just as she thought she might be done until closing, the door opened.

A young man walked in and, instead of perusing the stacks, or checking the rotating bookshelf for any new releases, he walked right up to the desk. He was chewing gum as he asked, "Ivy Dean?"

He looked so familiar, but she couldn't quite put her finger on it. Though it seemed odd that he knew her name, she couldn't deny that's who she was. As the librarian it was her job to let everybody know who she was. "Yes."

She watched as his face lit up.

"Carlos Hernandez."

As she reached out and shook his hand, she thought she liked the warm, firm grip. And that smile? That charm? That must have been what she recognized, so like Luke's.

"It's so nice to finally meet you." His grin got a little wider. "Luke talks about you all the time."

"Same," she said, her own smile in place, glad that she could legitimately say that to him and didn't have to tell him *for a while we considered you a suspect.*

"So, Luke messaged me asking if I could make the loop for him this evening."

"The loop?" Ivy asked.

"You know, he drives around and checks all the old haunts."

Ah! She did know.

"I was wondering if you'd come with me. Then we can grab some dinner and take it back to meet up with Luke."

"He's not going?" she asked. This morning he had said he was exhausted.

Carlos shook his head. "That's why he asked me to do it."

Ivy nodded along. She hadn't heard from Luke all day. And that made perfect sense, given that he'd been working for twenty-four straight hours before that. "That sounds like a plan."

"Shall we head out?" He hooked a thumb over his shoulder and tipped his head toward the door.

"I have fifteen more minutes."

But as she said it, he scanned the empty library and tipped his head as if to say *is anyone else really going to come in?*

But Ivy didn't care if anyone else came in. This place was her baby. She shrugged it off as though it wasn't everything to her. "I'm legally obligated to be here fifteen more minutes.

Make yourself at home, though. Grab a book. I'll check it out for you."

Carlos did as she suggested and wandered over to the new release paperback carousel. When the place stayed empty and it felt as if she was just watching him, Ivy headed back into the office. She would hear if the door opened again.

Quickly, she flipped through the papers Lando had sent. The first was a recent arrest for Tiago—for car theft just three weeks ago. She tried to place it in the arson timeline and wondered if it lined up with the burning car that Luke had told her about. The next document was an arrest for someone whose name she didn't recognize. But Mario Hernandez was listed as a witness. The report was for a drug bust by the Redemption PD. Mario had been extensively questioned but eventually released. Next were two much older documents from Redemption Fire Department—Luke's application, listed as "accepted" and behind that Carlos's application, listed as "rejected." The last page was from just that morning. It was a pending warrant, waiting for a judge's approval to search Mario Hernandez' house.

Ivy looked out the open door and past the front desk to spot Carlos across the way. He was now wandering the stacks. Given the aisle he was in, he was looking at fantasy novels. His head tipped as he read the titles, his expression as flat as could be. Probably not his genre.

She looked back down at the last page, again reading through it. The wording was broad so that the police could search for things that weren't specifically listed and could confiscate anything they found that linked him to the string of arsons. It was clear, they believed they would find evidence at Mario's apartment.

Carlos approached the desk again, pointing to his watch. "Five-fifty-eight."

Beyond the windows, the sky was darkening and once again

a light dusting of snow was falling. She conceded to the two minutes. Even if anyone did come in, they wouldn't have enough time to check out books. So she walked through her last check of the stacks and by the time she made it out the front door, locking it behind her, it actually was 6pm.

"My car's over here," Carlos told her and pointed.

Did he expect her to ride with him? She frowned. "How about I follow you?"

He shrugged as if to say *if that's what you want.*

Ivy felt the need to explain herself. "Then I can get my car home without having to come back around here for you to drop me off."

He nodded as though that made perfect sense and she crossed the parking lot and climbed into her car, revving the engine before pulling up behind him. As Carlos exited the library parking lot, Ivy tucked in close behind him not paying much attention to where they were going.

She thought more about Mario, about Luke. Should she call him and let him know that they were issuing a warrant to search his brother's place? If she did tell him, would there be anything Luke could do about it? He was too tired to even go out and do "the loop" tonight, as Carlos had called it.

She decided not to wake Luke from a sleep he needed for something he couldn't prevent. At the next stoplight, she sent a quick message to Jo and then followed it up with a text to Orlando, thanking him for the documents.

She watched as Carlos slowed down as they passed an old apartment building. Next was a convenience store that two of the brothers had worked at. Then Mrs. Hernandez' home. All places that Ivy knew Luke checked on regularly.

Then, Carlos took a turn out onto one of the older roads and they pulled up in front of the old barn. She'd been here before, too. Carlos drove along the gravel drive, surely trespassing, just as Ivy had days before.

Stopping behind him and putting her car into park, Ivy cut the engine as he motioned for her to get out. "We should probably make a circuit. The place is pretty big."

Ivy followed him, gingerly picking her way through the tall grass in her nice heels. As they looped the barn a gentle snow began to fall and she pulled her coat tighter around her. Anything more than just the one loop to check that the back hadn't been soaked in kerosene or gasoline and she'd get good and cold.

Carlos got ahead of her, his sensible shoes and heavier jeans giving him a speed she couldn't match. But she did her job, slowing down and checking for any damage to the place. Anything that looked different since the last time she'd been here, anything that made it look like a target.

As she turned the last corner, she saw Carlos near the cars. He stood, looking up at the barn, chewing his gum, his expression once again stunningly flat. His arms were crossed and he looked almost dead behind the eyes, and in that moment Ivy knew.

CHAPTER FORTY-THREE

I vy stared at Carlos as all the pieces snapped into place.

But it didn't matter if she understood. It only mattered if she could run.

The grass was up to her knees. Her heels were sinking into the dirt. If she kicked them off, she'd be barefoot in the snow on the outskirts of town.

She hated thinking it, but she was confident that Carlos would catch her if she bolted. The dead-eyed stare as they assessed each other told her he wouldn't hesitate to hurt her.

Though she hated it, she had to play meek. She had to hope she was situated to break away later. Her new work pants were stretch material, so she could move if she had to. Her twinset sweater hopefully made Carlos think she was softer and more malleable than she was.

Pasting a scared expression on her face, Ivy blinked hard several times and reached into her coat pocket, feeling for the face of her phone. She checked the case, her fingers finding the home key and activating the screen. Keeping her eyes on Carlos, she had to hope her coat was thick enough that her pocket didn't light up. She tried to act concerned, but as though she hadn't just figured out that Carlos was their arsonist and would be murderer.

He'd applied to the Redemption Fire Department and been rejected … and firefighters were the best arsonists. He and Mario had been taken in as juveniles for filleting open a live squirrel. Sociopaths did that, only Mario hadn't been the one to do it. The report said he was remorseful about killing a creature —easy enough because Ivy was now willing to bet that even at eight, Mario had been forced by his brother into the confession. There was nothing but calculation behind the brown eyes that looked so much like Luke's.

Mario, the drug addict, had his problems but he wasn't a sociopath. In fact, he might have been using drugs to deal with seeing the real Carlos.

Ivy moved her thumb across her phone, to where she thought the letters would be. She could only hope her phone caught her message.

— It's Carlos.

She hit the spot where she hoped the send key was.

"We're leaving your car here," Carlos told her as if it were some reasonable request. But he wasn't asking.

She fought for time and tried to act dumb. She could only hope that her facial expression hadn't completely given her away. She was furious. But she tried to sound confused. "Why?"

"You're riding with me now."

"Oh, I'll just follow you again," she said, waving her hand as if to say it's nothing. She turned to head back to her own car, as if he would allow it. Ivy didn't for one second think he would actually let her climb back into her own car, but she had to try.

As she turned her back on him, he covered the distance surprisingly quickly. One arm clamped around her neck. The other around her waist.

Shit, shit, shit.

She struggled to twist her head and neck so she could

breathe. But he'd clamped his arm into exactly the right place to cut off her air. The arm around her waist was tight—too tight—holding her left arm down to her side and making it useless.

Her body tried again to suck in air. Despite the way she bucked and fought, Carlos didn't let go or even loosen his hold.

If she couldn't breathe, maybe she could at least incriminate him. She reached again for her phone, pulling it out quickly while tucking her chin down in an attempt to bite him and distract him.

She hit the buttons frantically, opening first one app and then another. She struggled to find breath and to work her phone at the same time. She needed the map. She needed it to trace her.

But Carlos finally let go of her neck because he was reaching for the phone. She bucked against him, trying to slam her heel down onto his foot, but he was fast and anticipated her moves far too easily. The arm around her waist continued to grow tighter, pinning her other arm down.

She could fight—which she was clearly not going to win—or she could try something else.

Ivy dropped, going limp. As Carlos fought to hold onto her, she collapsed forward, hiding the phone from him and hitting the button for her map. The screen lit up the night, but she had no hope anyone was nearby to see her struggle.

He got his arm around her and hauled her back upright, hurting her ribs as she tried so hard to stay limp. Relaxing her muscles went against every fight or flight instinct she had.

Though she tried to hold the phone out, Carlos still managed to grab it. Squeezing hard, his fingers covered her grip on the device like a vise until she felt her bones would break.

Tossing her head back suddenly, she hoped to make contact with his nose. But he managed to turn his head to the side and all she got was the back of her head to his jaw.

As he uttered out, "Bitch!" he grabbed even tighter, making

her cry out in pain as her fingers flew open. He managed to snatch the phone and she watched hopelessly as he tossed it into the grass.

Aiming again for surprise, Ivy tried to elbow him in the side with her now free arm, but he caught her hand. Grabbing for her wrist, he clamped her hand between his thumb and forefinger, which shouldn't have been difficult to get out of, but he'd found a pressure point. He pressed until she felt nausea roll through her belly then he twisted until she cried out.

His mouth came in close to her ear, hot breath making her squeeze her eyes shut in disgust as he tightened his hold on her ribs and her arm until he whispered. "Luke is sleeping. I drugged him. There's paraffin all around your house."

He dragged out the last words, knowing it would make her cringe.

"But more importantly, Mario is standing by, and he'll light it as soon as I give the word. So you're going to calmly climb into the passenger seat of my car, and we are going to go for a little ride."

Jesus, he would burn his own brother?

But Carlos held up his phone and showed her a string of texts.

— Are you ready?

— Yeah, man.

Mario had sent back.

Son of a bitch.

"Now," he said, "I'm going to let go and you're not going to try anything."

Though he loosened his grip slightly, he didn't let go of her. He walked her awkwardly toward the car, his feet propelling hers, his front pressed against her back, still holding on. He directed her every move over to the passenger side of his car, where he opened the door and pushed her down into the seat.

With a sarcastic motion for her to get every spare limb

inside, Carlos made it clear he would slam the door on any fingers or feet that weren't accounted for. Ivy reached for the seatbelt, pulling it across her body and buckling herself in as she tried desperately to think of her options. He was in the driver's seat before she could develop any concrete plan.

Pulling forward, he then swung a dramatic arc backward, just missing the corner of her car. It might have been better if he'd hit it, if there was some evidence of damage. Instead, he turned completely around and headed down the gravel drive, leaving her car there as though she had simply wandered off ... at one of the sites Luke regularly checked.

Would Luke find her car here tomorrow?

Would they find her phone in the grass?

This would break Luke's heart. Carlos was the baby, and whatever was wrong with him, he'd hidden it expertly for all these years. Both Luke and Tiago seemed to have no idea. And she was so stupid.

"You figuring me out?" he asked with a sly smile and his eyes glancing her way.

Ivy wanted to say yes, but she couldn't be sure.

On the main road, he picked up speed and Ivy sat demurely with her hands clasped in her lap. She didn't even have her bag. No small pocket knife tucked into the corner pocket. She carried it every day, even though she wouldn't have let a patron bring one into the library. She had no phone, not even a pen with which to reach across the seat and jab into his neck.

But, she thought, she could reach across and grab the steering wheel. Didn't she know that rule? *Never let them take you to a secondary location.*

If they tried you were supposed to crash the car.

She aimed her eyes straight ahead, but her brain checked out all the various landmarks ahead. Ivy was scanning the area for large trees, a telephone pole, something she could aim for from her seat. But the road was relatively devoid of anything but young saplings. The ditches that allowed for runoff along the side of the road hindered a lot of her possibilities ... but ...

One of the driveways up to a farmhouse had a stone bridge that crossed the ditch. If she could dip the car nose down right in front of that she could crash them into the base of the bridge.

That would do it.

"Oh, no, you don't." Carlos seemed to know what she was thinking as he reached over and popped her seatbelt out. She couldn't help it as her eyes flew wide.

"Now, if you crash us, you're going to kill yourself. Think twice before you do that, Ivy." His tone was chiding and sickening. He was going to kill her anyway. Maybe it was better to take her chances with the accident, seatbelt or not.

Reaching frantically for the seatbelt as is reeled itself back up, she grabbed it and tugged, only to be thwarted by the auto-locking mechanism. It took three tries to calm herself down enough to get the stupid seatbelt to unfurl, but as she felt the relief of getting it across herself again and she moved to click it into place, Carlos took the gum he'd been chewing and stuck it down into the slot.

"Sorry," he said, his tone clear that he wasn't.

Now she couldn't buckle herself in. She couldn't run them into the ditch.

"What do you think?" He grinned as he tipped the wheel back and forth on the deserted road, knocking her almost across the center console into him and then changing directions and smacking her against the door. "Better hope the locks hold or that I don't have to hit the brakes."

He was laughing.

She wished to God she had a fucking pen. She'd drive it through his neck, but that would now crash the car.

Carlos had effectively made himself safe from any overture she might make. She was stuck here with him until he at least stopped the car. There were no moves she could play.

She took a deep breath and tried to steady herself. Ivy took stock.

Luke had no idea where she was. He would only worry when he decided that it was far too late for her to not be home. But, like his job, sometimes hers didn't end right on time. So she had no idea how late that would be.

The dash clock glowed in the dark. 6:43

Even if Carlos was lying, Luke wouldn't even begin to wonder if she was late until seven or seven thirty. And that was only if he remembered that tonight was an early closing night and if he was awake.

She didn't know who she'd sent the last text to or even if she'd managed to slide her way around the keyboard enough to actually write "it's Carlos" or to hit "send."

Jo, like Luke, was probably still sleeping off their overly long shift.

As Ivy watched, Carlos pulled up in front of a small house. It had once been blue. The roof sagged in on one side, and ironically, the porch sagged on the other. Putting the car in park, he turned to look at her, his smile almost demonic.

"We're here!"

CHAPTER FORTY-FOUR

Luke woke up groggy, the sky already dark around the edges of the window. He'd missed the entire daylight except for the little he'd caught this morning on his drive home. He rolled over and looked at the clock—7 p.m.—and he blinked.

Grabbing his phone, he shot a quick text to Ivy.

— See you in a little bit.

He could make dinner for her when she got home. But she might have already eaten at the library.

— Have you eaten?

Obviously, she was closing tonight. His brain still wasn't making fully linear thoughts. Maybe he could pick up dinner.

Though Ivy had been lamenting eating too much fast food lately, he didn't have time to put something in the crock pot. While Luke was no chef, he could make a few things. So he rolled himself out of bed and tried to figure out what he might be able to do with what was on hand.

In nothing but his underwear, he rummaged through the fridge and the cabinets, his heart twisting at the sight of three beers sitting in the corner of Ivy's fridge. *They were his.* He bought some of the groceries here, and though they slept at his apartment occasionally, he'd nearly abandoned it. He'd even come here to sleep though she wouldn't be home.

Was that because he wanted the arsonist to see his car in her driveway or because this was where he really wanted to be?

He wouldn't have ever moved in with someone this early in a relationship. Then again, he thought, he'd never had anything that qualified as a relationship before.

Spotting a box of pasta, he set it on the counter and went in search of a jar of sauce. He grabbed shredded mozzarella cheese from the fridge but only moved it to the top shelf, not quite willing to let it sit out. He didn't know when they'd both be back.

There was no time to bake anything unless he sat at home and he wasn't quite willing to do that either. Leaving everything on the counter, he climbed into his clothing and headed out to the car. He'd make the circuit around town tonight a little late, but he still felt compelled to get it done.

He left Ivy's little neighborhood behind, took a few turns, and crawled slowly through the old section of town. He lingered at one house he'd lived at for just over three years, looking like a stalker in his own territory.

The night was dark enough and the slight snowfall thick enough to obscure most everything. One of the houses could already be ringed with accelerant and Mario could be standing in the back, match in hand, ready to go and Luke wouldn't see him.

There had been no reply from the Redemption Police Department about what they'd done with the information that he and Ivy had sent. Luke could only assume that meant they hadn't done anything with it. Or that it hadn't been enough. Not yet.

He kept pushing forward, leaving the neighborhood behind before anyone came out, asked what he was doing, and recognized him. They would try to hug him and then want to update both their entire life stories. He made a clean getaway and stopped at the next light.

Luke knew the dangers of texting and driving, so once he was fully stopped he checked his phone. No messages from Ivy …

Next to him, the scanner crackled to life, kicking his heart into high gear. But it was just an RPD officer writing a ticket, and Luke ignored the rest of it.

He was pulling forward taking a turn heading toward Mario's house when his phone buzzed. He waited for the next light to see that it was Jo.

— You awake yet. Did you see what Ivy sent?

Jo must have also just woken up. They'd agreed when they left the station this morning that they were both going to go face down into a pillow and sleep for approximately three years.

But he had not seen what Ivy sent. Since he couldn't very well park himself in front of his brother's house without raising suspicion, he pulled into a convenience store and picked one of the spots around the side. The area was now dark and he didn't care if he looked suspicious, he wanted to see what Ivy had sent. Maybe it was her responding to his texts.

He noticed the snow began to accumulate on his windshield as he scrolled through everything he could on his phone. Sure enough, there in his emails was a forward from Ivy that had originated with Tavares. It wasn't recent though. Ivy had sent it while he was asleep.

It took Luke a moment to scroll through the short email, but then he had to get each document open and attempt to read the very tiny type on a very tiny screen.

Another message from Jo came through.

— Did you know Carlos applied to RFD?

Luke felt his eyebrows lift. He hadn't seen anything about that in the documents, but he'd only given them a cursory flip through. The only one from the Redemption Fire Department had been his own application, he thought. But he opened it again and read it more carefully.

Everything was the same, but this time he also noticed the scroll bar on the side. His application was only half the document and, scrolling down, he saw that, yes, Carlos had applied and been rejected.

Another text came through. From Jo again.

— Holy shit. The search warrant!

This time, Luke noticed that the texts he was getting from Jo included Ivy. But she wasn't responding, and it appeared she wasn't getting his replies.

He told himself it was a good sign, that the library was doing well. Ivy was busy.

He pulled up the search warrant, the last document attached, and gave it a scan. It was as surprising as everything else and he was pleased that the RPD had done something with the information about Mario.

The police were after his brother. At some point, the signature would come through for this warrant and they would search his place.

Thinking quickly, Luke put the car into gear and peeled out of the gas station fast enough to arouse suspicion. He had to force himself to slow down as he headed toward his brother's house. Even before he was close, he could see the place was ringed with officers and flashing lights. Hanging back, he wondered if his brother spotted his car as Mario came out onto the porch, hands high in the air, expression dejected.

Thank God.

The relief rolled over Luke in waves.

As much as Mario broke his heart, he could relax. It was over. And Ivy would be home soon.

Though he hated to leave his little brother in trouble, there was nothing he could do here. The police department wouldn't appreciate him hanging around, even if he was just watching. So he turned to leave.

He could go home—home to Ivy's place. He could make pasta for dinner when Ivy got home at ...

Wait, he thought. It was Thursday. Didn't she close the library early on Thursdays?

He wasn't far away. He messaged her.

— Ivy, where are you? Just let me know.

As he swung the car the other direction, he pulled into the parking lot. The library was closed and dark. He knew where Ivy usually parked and her car wasn't there.

Doubt creeping in as he pulled close to the front door, Luke checked the hours she had neatly posted there. On Thursdays the Library closed at six.

It was after seven-thirty.

Where was Ivy?

With his chest cracking as fear shoved its way in, he called her.

But the call went immediately to voicemail ... it didn't even ring. Did that mean something was wrong with her phone?

He was sitting in the car, with his foot on the brake, texting Jo, when the scanner crackled to life again.

He didn't need to hear the address twice.

Right now, he didn't even care that his brother was getting arrested for the crime.

Once again, he shoved his foot down onto the gas and drove too fast. Luke headed for the fire.

Aiming his way out of town, he sped toward the old barn.

CHAPTER FORTY-FIVE

Ivy was draped in a chair at the small table, her hands bound in front of her, her head down on the smooth but dusty surface. She blinked slowly. Her brain was fuzzy, her mouth full of cotton.

She remembered trying to fight. She remembered getting out of the car and trying to run. Again Carlos had caught her quickly, his hand clamping over her mouth. She remembered recognizing the sickly sweet smell for what it was: chloroform.

The only thing she could say now was that she had fought valiantly, though, once again, she had lost.

It took longer than people thought to knock someone out with chloroform. It wasn't like in the TV shows or movies and, honestly, that made her more disappointed in herself. She should have had time to get away. She should have landed a good elbow jab or a head smack. She should have been able to get her head away from the chloroform for more than just the one quick time she'd managed it. She'd gulped fresh air but hadn't had time to also scream before he got his hand back over her mouth, his words harsh and angry that she fought him.

In the end, all it had done was make her struggle take longer.

Carlos sat opposite her now, watching as she blinked herself awake, her head slowly coming up off the table.

He must have carried her in and set her here. As she straightened, the chair rocked, startling her. The amusement in Carlos' eyes told her he was most pleased the more upset she was. Whether she was startled, scared, angry, whatever, didn't matter to him, just that she reacted.

She wouldn't give him any more.

She wouldn't even swallow. He could see that. Straightening herself, she didn't speak as he pushed a bottle of water across the table in front of him.

"This is for your mouth—probably feeling a little dry. You'll want to stay hydrated."

There was an undertone to his voice that told her there was no concern for her well-being. It was probably poisoned. It would probably knock her out again.

"Go ahead, drink it," he told her.

With her hands tied, she tried awkwardly to unscrew it, but he didn't offer to help. Her only consolation was that she broke the seal and she tried to discreetly look for an injection site on the lid but didn't find one. Hopefully, the water was clean.

After taking a reasonable sip, Ivy put the cap back on.

"Drink more."

"I'm good." The harsh cadence of her words was enough to make him smile.

Shit. Had she just made herself into a worthy opponent?

She curled her fingers around the bottle, the weight of the water comforting. But he'd managed to give her one of the high-end recyclable bottles that Leo favored for sustainability. It was made of less plastic and crumbled down to almost nothing. Unless she could throw the contents in his face, the water was worthless as a weapon.

"Now that you're awake, you can join my fun."

Ivy hadn't noticed the static of the radio before. But as he pushed the small device across the table between them, the signals in her brain cleared. The noise became a voice and she made out the words of the dispatcher.

It was an old model scanner, tuned to local dispatch. It probably ran on batteries and it might make a good weapon. There seemed to be no electricity in the old place to plug it in. A couple of D batteries might make it reasonably heavy if she could pick it up and wield it.

But Carlos only tapped on top of it, as if motioning her to listen to the words. One of the officers reported he was leaving the scene from writing a ticket.

But almost immediately, dispatch crackled over the line again, reporting a fire.

The address sounded familiar, but Ivy couldn't quite place it.

"That's the barn," Carlos told her, a small grin settling on his lips. Pride.

She tried not to let it show that she read it and was disgusted by it. She wouldn't give him the satisfaction of seeing her emotions. But even as she thought that, she made the stunning realization that her car was still at the barn.

She heard the response from Patrick Kelly, Captain on B-shift and acting chief at night, as he replied that the engines were rolling.

Carlos sat with her, waiting, moving with infinite patience. She tried to show no reaction, but she wasn't confident he hadn't seen when she realized her car at the scene would make them think she was in the barn.

Long silences gaped between dispatch notices. One engine arrived, and the other came for backup. She listened as Captain Kelly—who'd sold Jo her new fridge—called in her license plate number.

This time she was working hard to keep her expression flat as Carlos smiled. "You know they already know it's yours. They're just checking to be sure."

Sure enough, RPD was back in less than twenty seconds, listing her name and her home address under the car's registry. They said they'd send someone to knock on her door.

Luke! she thought. At least that would wake him up.

But Carlos had an uncanny ability to read her. That he saw her recognition of Luke being told she was in the fire, her stomach rolled.

"Now he'll know for sure." He smiled at her. The problem was, it wasn't for sure.

She had wondered what Carlos was doing when he'd left her car at the barn and realized now that her offer to follow him from the library—her concern about getting into a car with a stranger—had played right into his hands. Had her car been left alone at the library parking lot, it would have been far more suspicious.

She should have ridden with him, but that would have meant trusting him. It would have meant not having her own route home—something she'd treasured. Her ability to hop in her car and leave anywhere at a moment's notice was her sole definition of freedom.

Again, the scanner crackled to life, the report coming in that they suspected there was a person inside the barn.

She couldn't help the cringe that showed across her face. B-shift was going to go into a dangerous situation to look for her. And she wasn't even there.

"It's good, isn't it?" He grinned with pride.

No. It's anything but good.

"The beauty of it is—" Carlos elaborated, "By the time they get here, they won't think anyone is inside, because no one was in the barn …"

"They'll think I'm not in here?" She was confused.

"Oh!" Another smile, another point of pride. "Did you not realize this place is next?"

CHAPTER FORTY-SIX

Luke sped up to the barn, bumping his way along the gravel as he raced ahead to where the engines were parked.

They brought the water tanker, thank God. Because there were no hydrants out this way, they would need the water trucked in. Luckily, there was a pond just beyond the barn. Luke watched as B-shift unfurled the hose, ready to connect to the water if the tank got low.

He was out of the car and running before he even realized what he was doing. He'd heard them call in Ivy's car and he'd managed to speed even faster after that.

As one of the firefighters came toward him, Luke looked beyond the man in the turnout gear. He would have recognized his brother but he didn't have the brain space for it. "Ivy is in there!"

But the man physically held him back. His large yellow turnout jacket enveloping Luke and his own standard winter coat. The snow was coming down heavier and Luke stepped back as the man held him away. Looking at him now, Luke recognized Jory Buckland.

Jory's mask hung to the side, because he was dealing with Luke and not the fire. Luke understood.

"We know. We're going in to get her."

But Luke knew they weren't. This was a "surround and drown." The brittle old wood of the barn went up like kindling. The only thing that might have slowed it was the snow. *If* the water seeped into the wood, it might hinder the burn. But they couldn't go in for Ivy until it was safe.

And that would be too late.

B-shift ringed the old building as best they could, wetting everything. The accelerant at the base of the barn continued to burn. Luke watched his fellow firefighters handle it all expertly.

But no one went in to save Ivy.

Had Mario planned this? Had he known that Luke was off shift, that he wouldn't be in his gear and wouldn't be able to go in and search this time?

Saving Ivy from her own house fire had been both Luke's greatest triumph and his biggest source of guilt. Now only the guilt remained.

Ivy was targeted because of him. It was *his brother* coming after them and here he stood, no gear, no ability to help. All he could do was wait and watch.

"Stay here," Jory told him firmly and Luke nodded. He did understand that if he made a move, he would hinder their efforts and slow their ability to get to Ivy. So he stood as if planted and watched, unable to do anything but feel his heart in his throat.

His phone buzzed in his back pocket and—needing something to do—he reached for it. Maybe it was Ivy. Maybe she wasn't inside. In fact, maybe she was outside of the barn. Without answering the phone, he took off, following his train of thought.

The firefighters had to concentrate on the fire. But Luke began walking the perimeter of the scene. He made a wide ring, hoping he could see something, find Ivy having escaped the barn, standing back, and watching.

He ran and scanned the landscape. Luke was a quarter of the way around the barn before he remembered his phone had buzzed. He pulled it out and looked. There was no name, only a number with the text message.

— This is Orlando Tavares. Have you seen Ivy?

Shit. Everyone was beginning to realize that Ivy was missing. Which meant no one had seen her and no on had heard from her. He was messaging back when his phone rang from the same number.

Luke answered. He was opening his mouth to say, *I'm at an old barn that's been lit. Ivy's car is here.* But Tavares beat him to the punch.

"Hey, Luke. Orlando here. Sorry to bother you, but Ivy messaged me an odd message just over an hour ago. I've been messaging her and she hasn't replied. I just called and it went straight to voicemail."

"Me too." Luke hated that he had to answer that way. He was halfway around the barn. One of the firefighters had caught sight of him and again motioned him to stay back. He moved a few feet further back out of respect, but continued on his loop.

"Is Ivy still at work?" Tavares asked, clearly trying to put all the pieces together.

"No. She left at six." Luke was grateful for a simple question he could answer.

"This text came in over thirty minutes after that."

Luke stopped still in his tracks. Ivy had messaged Tavares *after* she left work. Something strange? "What did it say?"

He stood at the edge of the pond, staring blindly at the water that might be the only thing that would save Ivy's life.

"It said, *it's various.* Does that mean anything to you?"

"No." Luke replied quickly. "Why would Ivy have texted that? What time did it come in?"

"Six-thirty-seven." Orlando replied. "She hasn't responded to anything since. It was fifteen minutes age her phone went to voicemail. I called again right before I called you but ... nothing."

"Me too." Luke looked down at his own phone, popping up the keyboard. "What was the phrase she sent? What could she have typed that would have been corrected to that?"

Silently, the two men each thought about that for a moment. Luke traced his own finger over the keyboard but saw nothing.

He tried swiping the word "various" to see what was close. He got "basis," "carrots," and, of course, the word he intended.

"Carrots," he said out loud.

"Carrots?" Orlando asked.

"Sorry. That's what autocorrect suggested. She wouldn't have said *it's carrots* would she?" But even as he asked, Luke felt his heart stop beating, his blood and his muscles came to a standstill, as he looked at the keyboard, and swiped what he now suspected. Sure enough, the name was corrected to "various."

He told Orlando, "It's *Carlos*."

CHAPTER FORTY-SEVEN

L uke was numb by the time the barn fire was out enough for two of the firefighters to safely check the ground floor.

Honestly, it wasn't safe for them, and they did it anyway. They did it because that's what they do. And maybe because it was Ivy.

He watched as they slowly and carefully entered the charred space. It could come down at any time, on them, on Ivy, on his dreams of the future. If he was breathing, he couldn't tell. He stood back on the gravel drive in this spot where he'd stayed since he completed his loop. There was nothing more he could do. Though he'd debated running back to the station, pulling out his turnout gear, and coming back to help, he'd not wanted to leave the scene.

Even though Redemption was small, the time that would have taken was too long ... or so he deemed at the time. Now that time had passed and they still hadn't found Ivy, he wished he'd done it. He wished it was him going in and searching.

Luke watched as two of his fellow FD brothers emerged from the space. He watched as they spoke but couldn't hear as he wasn't connected to the comms. Patrick Kelly had stood next to him the whole time … until now when he moved away specifically so that Luke wouldn't hear the report.

Did it matter though?

The firefighters emerged with no Ivy supported and coughing between them. No person thrown over a shoulder as they raced for safe space. If she was in there, they weren't bringing her out.

Kelly listened closely then came back. Whether it was to report to him, or for emotional support, or to be able to grab him if he decided to do anything stupid like running inside and searching, Luke didn't know.

Captain Kelly only shook his head. *No.*

But quickly, the older man opened his mouth. "She wasn't in there."

"Are they sure?" He had to ask. *How many times had a body been found later?* People hid. They died trying to escape in any number of ways. And sometimes they were hard to find. Ivy would have tried to escape.

"Did they search the loft?" He knew this place, had played here as a kid. Hours spent with his brothers, going up and down the ladder, running in and out of the doors, hiding in the tall grass. He still wanted to believe she'd escaped the burning building and was somehow miraculously safe.

But he looked around the building, too. Aside from some recent markings in the tall grass, where it appeared someone besides Luke had walked a loop closer to the building, it didn't seem anyone had even been here.

That would have been Carlos, he thought. But then he turned again to the Captain. "Was she in the loft?"

"We couldn't get up to it. It's not safe," Captain Kelly told him.

"The ladder?" He'd climbed that rickety, dangerous thing so

many times years ago. It had been insanely dangerous, Luke knew now. But as a kid, it had been fun.

He watched as Kelly asked the two firefighters still walking toward them slowly as the others did their best to finish the job. The building would have to be thoroughly inspected to be sure there were no stray sparks, no burning embers that could ignite and set the building on fire again later.

There was clean up, double checking every piece of wood, and more. Making sure every last thing was taken care of was more than half of the job.

"There was no sign of the ladder. They don't think it was even there when the barn was lit."

Luke nodded. *What more could he do?*

He could break free and dash inside and do his own inspection. But he didn't have his SCBA, so what would he breathe? Though he honestly didn't care if he had air or not, the others would run in to save him. If Ivy was in there, she wasn't still alive and they would find her later.

There was nothing more to do but hope that she'd never been in the fire to start with. He would simply ignore that her car was here and her phone was off and no one could find her and he would hope.

With a soft nod, he turned away from Captain Kelly, pulled out his phone and called her again as if it would ring inside the barn or behind him, and he would suddenly turn around and she would be there.

But again, it went straight to voicemail. Her car didn't light up as though the phone had been left inside it. There was nothing more Luke could do except follow up on the last message Ivy had sent.

They'd been so wrong, thinking it was Mario. The irony was that Ivy had been right from the start. Mario's addiction made him too unpredictable to carry out a plan like this. But Luke was slowly putting the pieces together, memories from his childhood. The rejected RFD application. Carlos's ability to charm their mother, even at a young age.

Had his youngest brother always been a sociopath?

Luke didn't know. He just knew what Ivy had told him: A highly intelligent and charming sociopath could get away with anything, including making people believe that they weren't exactly what they were.

He'd had such hopes that Carlos had broken out of the family cycle of poverty, that he hadn't taken Tiago's path or suffered like Mario did. Instead, it seemed the baby of the family was the worst of them all.

With his first deep breath in, the rage filled him. He calmly turned and thanked Captain Kelly, but then Luke walked away.

He climbed into his car and was halfway to his brother's house in Lincoln when the scanner crackled to life again.

CHAPTER FORTY-EIGHT

Ivy woke again to the sound and feeling of her own coughing.

What had happened?

As she opened her eyes, she felt the sting, and she quickly squeezed them shut again. She inhaled, but it burned, and she shallowed out her breaths, but it didn't help. She was on the floor with her hands still tied and her brain full of crackling static noise.

The last thing she remembered was Carlos coming around behind her. Though once again she'd fought valiantly, once again, he'd won. He put the chloroform soaked rag over her mouth and held her tightly in the chair, one arm wrapped around her, pinning her so she couldn't fight.

She almost laughed now. Despite her new stretch fabric work pants, there had been no movement she could make that would have worked. She was unable to kick him in the head over her own shoulder. He'd held her so that her range of movement was nothing.

Her head rang and her senses were filled with cotton again.

Though, as she squinted her eyes open and looked around, she realized some of it wasn't her.

The wall crackled with flames. She could only see peeks of orange and yellow through the cracks they'd burned into the walls and plywood over the windows. But she could see the smoke they brought.

Ivy now had a reasonable idea of how Carlos worked. There would be an accelerant all around the house—an unbroken ring —so that even if she could find a door or a window and escape, it was unlikely that she would be able to get through without burning herself.

But she wasn't going to die without trying.

Staying low, she moved her still-bound hands in front of her and lifted to her knees. She was more than a little unsteady with her hands tied, but the cord wasn't too tight. Still there wasn't much she could do.

Quickly she reached up to the table and found the bottle of water sitting there. She could do this. Ivy twisted the top and drank a small amount, hoping to clear some of the smoke and chloroform that had made its way down her throat. It didn't work, she couldn't drink into her lungs, but it did feel a little better.

She was still in her coat and the bottle offered a pitifully small amount of water, but she poured it over her head and neck down her front and then her back. She ran it underneath her coat where the wetness would stay and hopefully prevent any burns. She wasn't confident that she hadn't just set herself up to boil alive. She had a feeling she'd find out soon.

Next, she crawled quickly around the space. The home was tiny—a kitchen, a living area, two small bedrooms, and a bathroom. But at each window she checked, she saw what she'd mostly only heard before. The orange and yellow dance of flame.

How long had she been out? She couldn't say. But it did seem that the accelerant was not the only thing burning now. The very act of busting out of a window or door would put her in contact with the fire for too long. But still she considered it.

She wasn't ready to gulp the amount of air it would take to yell and scream. So she stopped to hunker down under the table as though that would help and did her best to listen beyond the flames.

She heard no sirens.

If she was going to live, she would have to save herself. She couldn't say for sure how strong her desire to live was, versus how strong her desire was to thwart that asshole. Then again, if she survived out of spite, she wasn't going to be mad about it.

Crawling around, looking for anything that might help, she didn't expect much. There was no way that this place would have a working extinguisher or a fireproof blanket, or anything that she could wrap around herself to push through the flames. Despite her conviction she wouldn't find anything, Ivy crawled toward the kitchen, the nearest source of water, and lifted up into the denser smoke and tried the faucet handles. It took three tries popping up and grabbing quickly at them to get them to turn. Each time she had to drop back down to get cleaner air. On the third try, she actually managed to get both of the faucet handles to the on position but nothing happened.

Ivy wasn't surprised. She had figured before that the house had the water and power cut off some time ago. With her one idea thwarted, she turned around to crawl back to the living room, thinking if the walls were on fire, she might be safer in the middle. But as she crawled back, her hands touched something.

She'd been keeping her eyes closed as much as possible. Lord knew she didn't need a repeat of having her eyes bandaged. She wasn't sure they would survive a second time. Then again, surviving this—blind or not—was her one and only goal now.

So she opened her eyes to see what her fingers had brushed across.

Sure enough, it was the edge of a door set into the flooring. Could it possibly be …?

Her friend Maggie had an older home in the area that had internal access to the space under the house.

Smoke went up. So Ivy—if she could—would go down.

Making an excited circuit around the floor, she felt for the edges of the door, but there were no exposed hinges. It was designed so no one would trip. The house, though uncared for in recent years, appeared to have been well crafted when it was built.

Her brain raced as her fingers worked, Ivy knew to stay low, keep her breathing down near the floor, and she thought through what she knew about old Nebraska homes.

The door should lift and allow her under the house, but her fingers couldn't find the edge. She traced the entire square and never found a way to lift the door.

She sat back, defeated and let her head fall against the floor. *Now what?*

CHAPTER FORTY-NINE

Frustrated and angry, Ivy felt tears leaking at the edge of her eyes. But, honestly, it was the best feeling she'd had since she'd woken up.

Had she not been crying before? Had she been too frustrated that she managed to keep her eyes closed enough that they hadn't teared on their own?

She wanted to take a deep fortifying breath and tell herself she could do this. But only the second part was an option.

Pulling her wetted shirt up over her face, she breathed through it for whatever filtering it offered. She could still smell and taste the smoke, but she wasn't going to give up.

She peeked through squinted eyelids, moved her hands along the floor again, felt the edge of the door, and this time moved her hand in soft arcs flat against the surface of the floor.

That was when she found it.

A small indentation that had maybe once held a ring that would lift the door. The ring was no longer there, and Ivy was about to swear every word she knew.

But she crawled away as the smoke continued to filter into the room and her vision got hazier. She felt her way over to the cabinets and pulled out the drawers, dropping them in a clatter on the floor. Let someone hear her!

Sure enough, each had a few items in it, left behind like the table and chairs, like the old shelf against the one wall. She grabbed a huge serving spoon, hoping that if need be she could dig with it. Next she grabbed a knife. There were only a few things here, but she would use them to the best of her ability.

Though the missing ring wouldn't help lift the door, it did tell her which side lifted. Ivy shuffled her way back awkwardly, now scooting forward on only her knees, her face low to the floor. Her movements were as fast as they could be, her bound hands each clutching a utensil that she'd found.

When she found the edge again, she jammed the knife down in. She worked until she pried enough of a gap to get her fingers in. Ivy could not recall ever being so excited in her life and she'd had far more than one close call.

With her two hands tied so closely together, the work was even more awkward and, as she lifted the door, it slipped shut, frustrating her further. But now she knew she *could* get it open.

The second time it went smoother. She was ready with one hand on the knife and the other twisted around to jam her fingers into the space as it appeared. She moved her head lower now that the door was open, breathing air from the crawlspace and noticing a difference.

She thought about flipping the door wide but realized it might be better to shut it behind her. Then again, *would they find her?*

She stopped, the door held high, firmly in her hand now revealing almost two feet of space. She should be dropping down into the dark opening she'd created, but again she listened.

No sirens yet.

Surely Carlos would have called this in if no one else did. He wouldn't want them to find the burned-out shell of the building after the fact. He would want them to rush in. In fact, he might be nearby, waiting.

Ivy turned her head one way and then the other as though she would be able to see through the smoke and the walls out beyond to the tall grass and know if he was standing there. If he had a thermal detector, he might be watching her do this. Once again, Carlos could thwart every move she made.

She didn't care. If she died, she would die fighting.

She didn't know what waited below her--crawlspaces were not known for being the cleanest. She told herself rats, bugs, snakes, who knew? But she was ready and grateful that as soon as the door was open, she'd reached down and felt the staircase. Old and wooden, it might not hold her. But it didn't matter. It was the only thing she could do. So she turned around and crawled feet first down into the dark space.

The only light now seemed to be coming from the crackling of the flames around the house. Very little filtered through the heavy smoke and even less shone down into the crawlspace. But there seemed to be something coming from her right, and she had to take that as a good sign.

Smoke was starting to fill the area, though luckily it rose and she was taking advantage of that. If only she had her phone, or a flashlight, or any of the things she didn't have, she told herself … Again, it didn't matter, she would make do.

Heading down the steps, Ivy decided to aim toward the edge of the building or at least close. How much she could tuck herself up against the foundation would depend on how warm it was to the touch. That would be the safest place if anything collapsed around her.

How long could she survive here? Could she escape? She had no idea. But she moved downward, the step breaking under her foot as she put weight on it.

Screaming into nothing, she tumbled backwards. Luckily, it

was the lowest step that had broken and she fell a mere matter of inches. It was still enough to twist her ankle.

Standing gingerly, putting weight on the ankle, and attempting to regain her bearings, Ivy reached up the ladder. It was much higher than she expected it to be.

How far down had she come?

She moved slowly, checking out her new space and quickly bumping into a wall and wood planking at her waist height. Confused, she reminded herself to get low. Just because the air was better here didn't mean it was good.

Reaching out, she felt her way around. Shallow shelves lined a short wall next to her. Of course, she thought, the ladder, the indoor access—It was a root cellar!

A small one, but big enough for her. She wouldn't have to dig down into the earth and create her own hole. She clutched the knife and the spoon in the one hand, the other still feeling its way around as she shuffled on her knees.

Would it be enough?

Again, she had no answer.

She stopped and listened and still heard no sirens.

But this time, she wasn't sure if she could. The crackling of the fire above her had gotten much, much louder.

CHAPTER FIFTY

How long had she been down here?

Ivy didn't know. She'd dropped the spoon and the knife and now hoped she didn't cut herself. Huddling down she breathed through her still wet shirt.

With the little root cellar, she was able to be lower than she'd even hoped. Still, the smoke was swirling in, she could feel it getting denser. Opening her coat, she lifted her sweater, doubling the layer she was breathing through, but exposing her abdomen in the process. With a few awkward but quick movements, she managed to button the coat back closed.

Would it do any good? Was all of this in vain? Had she simply prolonged the time it would take her to die?

Dear God, let her die of smoke inhalation please. She did not want to burn.

She had a brief moment to be grateful that Carlos had not also doused her in whatever accelerant he'd used. She breathed in slow, shallow movements, trying not to inhale any more smoke than she needed to.

When she thought about it, there was probably no way to make it better. The air was full of smoke whether she inhaled it or not. But her body didn't want a deep inhale and right now she did exactly what her body told her.

She sat on her knees, hands in front of her face, still bound and holding the sweater tightly over her mouth and nose. She'd put her forehead into the dirt, trying to stay small and compact and breathe from the lowest point possible. As if that could help her escape the fire.

Above her, something cracked and broke. Ivy flinched.

The root cellar was open. It wasn't covered by anything. As soon as the floor caved, it would cave on her and it sounded like parts of the structure were already collapsing from the fire damage.

She wanted to turn and open her eyes and look up but knew she wouldn't be able to see anything anyway. What little light came from the flames didn't travel very far through the smoke that thickened with each passing moment. So she huddled down and waited for the sirens she still didn't hear.

She wondered if prayer would do her any good. She had long since stopped believing in a God that cared more about sin than love. A God that believed she was chattel and not a person. A God that believed self-appointed men determined right and wrong on Earth—whatever that might be.

But, as she possibly entered the very last moments of her life, she was grateful that she'd found Luke. She was grateful she'd found the town of Redemption. She was grateful for Jo and Maggie and Seline. For the Kellys and their friendship and their dead daughter-in-law's refrigerator that they sold Jo that let her get a coffee table. She was grateful for the librarians who'd sent her on the path that she'd followed diligently. And she prayed to a God that she wasn't sure existed. She prayed to a God that she *wanted* to believe in and she hoped that she had done enough.

CHAPTER FIFTY-ONE

L uke turned the car around. The words on the scanner
changing his resignation to fresh dread. The streets of
Redemption were virtually empty at this time of night. But the
voice from dispatch rattled off another address he recognized.

Skidding his way around corners, he forced himself to pause
for traffic lights and waited for blue lights and sirens to pop up
behind him. But it didn't happen.

Maybe they were all scrambling the way that he was. The
fire department had just barely finished the other fire and this
second one had been too-well timed.

Son of a bitch. He thought he knew his brothers. Mario would
never have been able to pull this off, but Carlos was smart,
calculating, the best salesman on the floor at his car lot. Maybe
there was a better reason for that than just that he was driven to
escape the poverty they'd grown up in, Luke thought now.

He pulled up to the blaze even before the trucks arrived,
though, right behind him the small red pickup that the chief
drove plowed its way in. A second fire in the same night
brought out the big guy.

Pulling into the drive, Luke hung an immediate right,

parking on the grass and making room for the crew that was on its way. The two vehicles parked next to each other and he was out and rushing for the house even as the chief climbed out, a little more cautious in his movements.

With his tablet tucked under his arm, Taggart looked at Luke with a deep and abiding sympathy. "I figured this might be another place you knew."

Luke only nodded as he pulled up short, as close to the flames as he could be, still empty from the loss of Ivy. All he could do now was fight. He felt like a child on the verge of a temper tantrum, about to lash out at anyone and everyone. He tried not to do anything too damaging to the chief.

Logically, he knew the man was only trying to help. So he tried to be helpful. "We lived here for six months after my father left."

The chief pointed up and down the long street. The houses on either side of this one were also boarded up. "Were you the last ones who lived here?"

"I don't know." He'd been a kid, not even ten when his father had left. He didn't remember much of the logistics aside from worrying that his mother wouldn't be able to pay the rent, regardless of which house or apartment he'd lived in. Other than that, his big concern was that he might one day get his own bedroom. It hadn't happened until he was an adult.

"Engine's on its way," the chief said as he reached back into the truck and pulled the massive flashlight out. It was handheld, shaped like a bullhorn, and put out an unbelievable number of lumens. "Want to do the preliminary sweep with me?"

Luke nodded. He had to have something to do, he needed an assignment and rules to follow. He could feel that his body was preternaturally still but inside every cell was abuzz.

Where was Ivy? Where was his brother? Would they find Ivy's body in the barn? Or would they find her somewhere else?

He stopped, reaching out to grab the chief's arm. "What if Ivy's here?"

"Her car's not here," said the chief.

"They didn't find her at the barn." His fingers now dug into the man's arm. He would have stopped but he couldn't. All he could do was be grateful that his chief was wearing a thick coat so Luke probably wasn't hurting him. Luckily, his boss didn't argue further. "Why do you think she'd be here?"

Luke felt everything in him fall. He didn't have a better explanation than the one he gave. "Because my brother is salesman of the year."

Obviously, that didn't land very well and Luke scrambled to explain. The words gushed out of him. "Ivy left work at six when the library closed. She texted Orlando Taveras—maybe the last person who'd texted her—and she sent 'its various' at 6:37 p.m. He called her. I called her. But her phone's been going straight to voicemail since about that same time."

"What's her number?"

Luke watched as he flipped the tablet on, lighting up his face, and tapping in a request.

Jesus, Luke thought, the chief was going to trace the numbers. Thank God. Ivy might not be alive … but she might be. And they could use every bit of information. He could hold on to the hope that he might find her again.

"Alright, keep going," the chief said once he'd hit the last button.

"Look at your keyboard," Luke instructed. "We're pretty sure she was writing *It's Carlos* and it got autocorrected. It sure doesn't match Mario. Or Tiago."

Taggart was frowning at him, but Luke motioned to him. "Try it. Do *Carlos*."

Sure enough, *various* was one of the words that was suggested.

"Son of a bitch." He muttered the words, then looked up. "So why does it matter that he's a salesman of the year?"

"He reads people. He's calculating. Maybe Ivy wasn't in the barn. Maybe he left her car there to throw us off the track."

"I'll be honest," the chief said. "I don't remember your brother as calculating. But he didn't pass the psych test. That's why we couldn't take him."

Luke sucked in a breath. He'd missed so many signs. But he turned back to the only thing he could do now. With the request to track Ivy's cell phone done and the chief having tried the wording on his keyboard, they started to circle the building. The flashlight shone at the base of the small house, illuminating the parts the flames left in shadow. The chief occasionally reached to his shoulder, talking into his comm to the engines that were on their way. He discussed getting backups in from Beatrice if those finishing up at the barn weren't able to leave quickly enough. He set dispatch to calling in firefighters from A and C-shift to help cover the extra work.

"That was fast," Taggert commented, stopping to look at his tablet again. "Ivy's phone last pinged at the barn."

Luke felt his heart stutter and stall. *Was he wrong? Had she died there?*

The Chief smacked a brusque hand against his shoulder. "I'll have the team see if they can find it and bring it back. See what we can learn."

It was the best they could do, but Luke wasn't ready to give up. They made their way around the corner to the back of the house. The light only showing them what the fire already had. The place had been ringed in accelerant and the structure was beginning to collapse.

"My brother is charming but, in a few moments, I've seen him have real rage. He always covered it up so quickly that we thought he'd gotten over it." But after seeing these fires Luke thought his brother's rejection from the fire department may have had a bigger impact than it should have.

Had he been trying to follow Luke?

Jesus, how many times had Carlos tagged after him as a kid, and he'd shaken his younger brother off because he was too little, a pain in the ass? Pieces were clicking into place, but the one piece needed wasn't here: Ivy.

They took the third corner as they heard sirens in the distance. Red lights appeared at the end of the street as the team raced toward the small house and the blaze.

At that moment, he thought he heard a voice.

Help!

Help!

But Taggert didn't even falter. Had Luke merely wished to hear something?

CHAPTER FIFTY-TWO

L uke wasn't confident he'd heard anything.

But the third time he thought he might have heard a voice, the chief also stopped.

His hand coming out, he almost slapped Luke flat in the chest to shut him up.

"Hello!" he yelled to the burning house. "Redemption Fire Department!"

Then, Luke heard it!

"*Help! Help!*"

"Where are you?"

"I'm under the house!" The voice was tinny and rough all at the same time. Luke had never heard anything better. His heart soared. "Luke!?"

The glorious sound of her yelling back to him flipped his body from ice cold to blazing hot. "We're coming."

He was racing back to the truck as he yelled to the chief and watched as the light began to sweep along the foundation of the house. He scrambled in the bed as he watched the fire engine make its way down the long street. They wouldn't get to the house before him.

Every firefighter knew to always put everything back in place. Each item was clean, it was repaired, it was inspected every shift, for exactly this purpose. So Luke put his hands on the Halligan quickly. Even as he grasped it, he felt hope surge as though it were a current that passed through the equipment he held.

He almost laughed with the relief. She was alive. But they'd have to keep her that way.

Racing back, he scanned the house, looking for the best point to break in. He calculated for the fire, the burning wood, and the accelerant that burned hot and fast at the base. But the clatter of cracking wood almost stopped him. Plywood had dropped off one of the front windows. The fire had burned it away enough that it was no longer held in place and it cracked and popped as it clattered to the porch.

He looked up where the flames raged now. Whatever was up in the attic seemed to blaze the hottest. Ivy had been smart to go low.

Closing the distance to where the chief stood, he stepped toward the house, Halligan ready. But, as he reached the heat of the fire, rough hands grabbed him and pulled him back.

"You're too close!" a voice yelled through the face mask.

Luke turned to look at Captain Kelly, this time in full turnout gear. On the other side of him, Patrick's son Ronan also held Luke back from reaching Ivy.

For a moment, he thought about swinging. He had a heavy and deadly weapon in his hands and he was not going to be thwarted. But, as if they could read his mind, Ronan reached out and grabbed the Halligan from his hands. "I've got this. You step back."

They pushed him until he stumbled, more hands grabbing him. Human fingers not thickly covered and gloved like the two firefighters had been. This time the chief held him tightly. "They're here now. Let them do the job."

Luke fought. Ivy was there. Ivy was alive. He'd heard her yelling.

Only now, as the two other firefighters had taken over the job he heard her coughing, and then she went silent.

He watched as the Halligan swung hard into the vent, as the firefighters fought against the foundation, trying to open a hole big enough to pull Ivy through. But it wasn't working. Ivy was no longer yelling.

Another firefighter, heavy in turnout gear, stepped into the fray. And Luke still struggled against the Chief's hold. But the man—for all that he wasn't quite as tall and not quite as thin as Luke—was stronger than he appeared.

The new firefighter wielded a sledge hammer.

"Are we good here?" Luke could hear the question over the Chief's comm, they were standing so close.

"It's our only option," the chief called back, still holding Luke where he'd hauled him away from the fray. He pulled his bullhorn from the truck, one hand still firmly on Luke's arm and he told Luke, "Don't you dare move. You might kill her if you do."

Without waiting for an answer, he lifted the bullhorn to his mouth and his voice boomed. "Ivy you need to step back. Can you get low and cover your head?"

Luke didn't hear anything. But the firefighters up close called back, "We've got her!"

The sledge hammer began to hit the cinderblock as the other end of the house cracked and boomed and caved in on itself.

CHAPTER FIFTY-THREE

Luke sat in the small interrogation room by himself. Being held like this made him feel like he was a criminal. And he was pretty certain he was getting investigated as one.

He looked out the small window embedded into the door, it was his only view other than cinderblock walls. The wire running through the glass didn't obscure the flurry of activity in the hallway. He was confident Mario was being held just a couple cells down.

Had it only been seven hours since he'd watched them execute the warrant at Mario's house?

He'd been so foolish. He'd thought they'd pick up his brother and that would be the end of it.

He thought maybe it had been eight hours or more since then. They'd taken his phone. He couldn't check on Ivy. He couldn't even check the time. But he'd seen the firefighters pull her from under the house. She'd been alive when they'd done it, but she'd been coughing, covered in soot, blinking.

He hadn't even gotten to step forward and hold her. Immediately, the hands on him had changed from belonging to

Chief Taggart to belonging to the Redemption Police Department.

The more he sat here and stewed the more he admitted it looked bad. He'd known he was on the suspect list from the start. His goal had been to prove to Ivy that it wasn't him. Now he had to prove it to the detective on the case. After all, he had shown his face at both the fires tonight, just like an arsonist proud of his handiwork would do.

He sat and stared at the walls for a little while longer and tried to tell himself it would all be okay. How many times had he repeated that in his brain before the door opened again?

He recognized the detective who walked in but, behind him, a blond woman in a pale gray suit followed. He knew her. Why did he know her?

"I'm agent Melissa Watson with the FBI."

Lovely. He just nodded. There was clearly no need to introduce himself. They knew who he was. "What can I help you with?"

"Well, I need to know what you know about the fires tonight."

"No worries," Luke replied calmly. "But first, I need to know how Ivy Dean is."

"I'll tell you after we talk."

"Then we won't talk." His heart pounded. Was he really playing hardball with an FBI agent? Normally, it wasn't anything he would have done. But, right now, he desperately needed to know about Ivy.

"You're not holding the cards here," she said, tilting her head as though he were crazy.

"I believe I am." Unless she already had all the documents from Tavares, he should have a few cards to play … if he could play them right now.

"You're a firefighter who knows how to light fires." She leaned forward, hands clasped, shoulders still squared. It was a wonderfully non-threatening, threatening pose. "You're related to every single one of the arson sites. And it's your girlfriend who's now been inside *three* different burning buildings."

"Exactly," Luke said. "I wouldn't lay a finger on her."

"No, setting her up and saving her just makes you the hero."

She wasn't wrong. That was a motivation for any number of arsonists—it wasn't about the fire at all for them. It was about the glory. He looked her up and down, his heart still flooding. He needed to know about Ivy. And he liked this agent less and less right now. "Lots of FBI agents get off on it, too. They're not immune."

"What have you got?"

"Did you know my younger brother Carlos also applied to the Redemption Fire Department and was rejected?"

She kept her face mostly still, but one small twitch gave her away.

"I have more like that. So tell me, how is Ivy. *Please?*" The last word rolled out on its own. Not much good at negotiating there, was he?

"Ivy is fine. She got checked up by the medics, treated, and released."

"Released to where?" Luke asked, realizing he should be negotiating for his own release now, but he simply didn't have it in him. He needed to know about Ivy.

"Home."

"*Alone?* Tell me you have Carlos in custody!"

"We have Mario and we have Tiago," Agent Watson told him.

Not good enough. "Look, I suspected them, too. But it's not them. You can't send her home if Carlos is still out there."

"She'll be okay," Watson assured him far too easily. She sat back, crossed her arms, her long ponytail swaying with the movement. "RFD has someone stationed in her driveway. They're watching her all night."

Cool, Luke thought sarcastically. *What a great way to get Ivy killed.*

Did they really think Carlos would be thwarted by an officer at her front door? "Is the officer *inside* the house with her?"

"I don't know. I'm going to trust the Redemption Police Department to get the job done."

Luke didn't trust anyone but himself right now. "What do you need from me to let me go?"

Watson shrugged and almost laughed. "Proof that you're not the arsonist."

"Perfect. Contact detective Orlando Tavares—well, *ex* detective Orlando Tavares." He spelled it out as she pulled a small pad of paper and a pen from her pocket.

Interesting. She'd looked as though she'd walked in here with nothing. She wasn't even recording the interview. Her ease slowed the beat of his heart a little because it made him confident they didn't believe he was the arsonist. But the cold chill in his veins was creeping deeper the more he thought about Ivy with the police department sitting in front of her house.

Carlos was still out there. He asked Watson for his phone.

"You can't have your phone," she told him, casually denying his request.

"No. *You* want my phone. I'm going to talk you through the documents that Taveras forwarded today. It will help make your case."

Watson frowned at him, but at least she went to the door, stuck her head out and made the request. He answered a few more of her questions, the tension ratcheting up every second.

He'd hoped Ivy would be in the hospital. She'd be safe in the hospital, right? But in her own home … Carlos had already proved he could get to her there. Luke needed to get there and fast, but Watson was taking her damn sweet time as he talked her through the documents and directed her to the message Tavares had gotten from Ivy.

"Where's the message?" Watson held up his phone facing him.

Luke almost rolled his eyes. "I told you Ivy sent it to Orlando and he called me. So contact him."

He was tapping his fingers on the table and for the first time he realized he wasn't handcuffed. He had silly, stupid thoughts about escaping and running for Ivy's. But even if he could overpower the agent and leave the room he wouldn't make it out of the department. So he forced himself to sit still.

After he gave Decker everything he had, she left him in the room to stew alone. Wondering once more if Ivy was okay.

CHAPTER FIFTY-FOUR

Ivy stood at her kitchen counter, guzzling cranberry juice. It probably wasn't the smartest thing. She didn't want to burn her throat further.

She looked back into the fridge. She had orange juice, but that would be too acidic, and apple juice. Pouring that into her partially drunk glass, she then added water from the filter.

That should do it, she thought, then downed more. The need for so much liquid had to be psychological, didn't it? But she didn't know.

The chief had dropped her here. He'd seen her car at the barn but couldn't get her to it. It still counted as evidence. So she was stuck.

The RFD officer was already outside as they arrived and the officer volunteered to come inside and search the place. Though she valued her privacy—something she'd never had growing up —she was now more than willing to let someone make sure that Carlos wasn't in her home.

When she asked if they had him in custody, the officer only said he didn't know. When she asked for Luke the answer was that he was in custody and so were Mario and Tiago. So, they'd managed to sweep up every Hernandez brother except the one they needed. She told herself that Luke had the evidence. If he'd seen it, he could share it.

She told herself he'd be home soon. But the officer had gone back out to his car, sitting in the driveway, just to the left of her front door. One short set of paver stones away should she need him. She downed the rest of the juice and moved to close the front curtains. She should have been home long before now to shut them. It obstructed the officer's view, but it also obstructed whoever might be watching her, and the feeling was even stronger tonight than usual.

That was no surprise, though.

She told herself that her neighborhood was not as wealthy as Maggie's and Seline's. Her backyard didn't border on to the Greenway, but a small border of a single row of trees ran between the houses accompanied by a fence falling down in places from the roots of those very trees. It was a ridiculous system she intended to fix at least on her own yard.

Her brain ran crazy circles, thinking about everything except the man who kept trying to kill her. If she stood here for a while longer, she'd be able to watch the light change as the sun came up.

What a shitty night. And Luke wasn't even here yet. She decided to wait up until he got here. She wouldn't be able to sleep anyway.

A noise bumped from the back of the house and everything in her went still. It was nothing, she told herself, just the creaking of an old house.

Pausing, she listened, then when she didn't hear anything, she tried to calm down. But, if she didn't check on it, she was no better than the woman in the horror movies.

Could it have been the back door? Maybe.

The living room sat at the front of the house, the kitchen to the side by the garage. The back door was through a short hallway that cut between the bathroom and the bedrooms.

She reminded herself the odd design was part of why the house had been affordable. When she got to the back door, it was not only closed, but still locked. It was nothing, just the settling of the old bones of a house.

She should get a dog. They'd had dogs while she'd been growing up, but it had been clear that they were working dogs. She and her siblings had wanted to have them as pets, but her father and mother insisted they couldn't be treated as such. So maybe she could have a pet that had a job, which was to tell her when she was being ridiculous about noises her house was making.

Ivy went into the kitchen again, her body tired but needing food. She'd burned every fuel reserve between fighting Carlos and the fire. All she'd had was the few sips from that stupid bottle of water. The juice hadn't made her throat feel any better, but her body was starting to. Still, she blinked again, her vision occasionally still going blurry. At least it wasn't as bad as the first time or, she guessed, actually the *second* time. Lesson learned. Hopefully one she wouldn't need ever again.

She thought through her possibilities. The detective was out front. Carlos could light the back of the house on fire without him seeing. But then she could just get out the front door.

What if he'd already put accelerant around the front? But no, she told herself. She'd made the detective walk around the entire house and together they'd checked the flowerbeds and inspected the grass near the foundation. There was no accelerant. Carlos's earlier threats of burning Luke alive had been just that—threats and nothing more.

The police had come and checked the place out while she'd been in the hospital. So had the chief and Sebastian Kane. It had all been just a lie to keep her in line. She was safe in here.

Ivy considered fixing herself a grilled sandwich. The thought of the wonderful crispy edges that she liked, and how it may feel on her throat, was enough to stop that idea. She settled instead for softer foods that would slide down easier.

It was another twenty minutes later, sitting on one of her new stools at the bar, that she heard the noise again.

The creaking of an old house. That's really all it sounded like. But she checked. Lord knew she'd almost died far too often in these last months. She wasn't going to die now of stupidity.

So she went to the back door and again found it locked and closed. But as she turned around, she heard footsteps heading down the hallway toward the back office.

CHAPTER FIFTY-FIVE

I vy crept slowly down her hallway.

He was here, wasn't he?

She pulled her phone from her back pocket, glad the team had found it and returned it. The number for the detective out front was already on speed dial. Hitting the button, she waited, but even as the line rang, she turned the corner.

Holy shit.

Ivy pushed the button, hanging up and shutting down the sound.

Carlos was in here, talking. "Don't talk out your ass, dear. I'm not letting you get away again, you stupid bitch."

Ivy couldn't see him, but it sounded like he was in the office talking to *her*. But she wasn't there.

A voice came in return and Ivy found her suspicion had been right.

She had to be crazy.

There were *two* people in her house.

"Who *are* you?" the mysterious second person asked.

She recognized that voice, and still … It couldn't be. Sliding slowly forward, Ivy saw the back of the blond head, the hair tucked low at the neck, same as always. Her heart both soared and cracked.

Carlos laughed at the seemingly ridiculous question. "Left your phone in the other room? Too bad."

His tone mocked. Freezing in her tracks, Ivy stood with one hand on the fresh paint of the wall, the other still clutching the phone. As she looked down, she saw the hand holding the phone was shaking. Hard.

She needed to call the detective. But she couldn't. Thank God he hadn't picked up. She couldn't bring him in on her sister.

CHAPTER FIFTY-SIX

L uke pulled to a stop behind the police cruiser that sat in Ivy's driveway. But even as he was opening his door, the officer was opening his and stepping out to face off. A frown pulled at his features and his stance was set wide, his hand on the butt of his gun. The officer planted himself directly between Luke and the house.

The young officer wasn't someone he'd interacted with much. "Luke Hernandez, Redemption Fire Department."

He pulled his badge out of his back pocket and held it up. This was one of the few times it was useful to badge someone as a firefighter. Unfortunately, it did nothing.

"I know who you are. I know you're in police custody. Why are you here?"

"No, not in custody. They asked me questions and let me go. I need to get in and see Ivy."

But the officer held up one hand to stop him.

Jesus. He was so close. But Watson had told him before he'd left that they'd not found Carlos yet. With everything he had, he had to believe that Carlos wasn't already here.

"Carlos Hernandez is on his way here." Luke said it with an

authority he felt in his gut. "If he isn't already here."

"She's fine," the young officer said, his hand making a braking signal as if to slow Luke down.

But Luke couldn't. "If I'm not going in, then you need to."

With his brows pulling together as he tried to figure out what to do, the officer said, "I need to call in and check on you."

"Fine. But do it damn quickly," Luke said. "And maybe, while you do that, walk up and knock on her door and make sure she's still okay."

"I just checked on her. She's fine."

Jesus. The kid was green, an overinflated sense of himself in that badge.

"You don't understand my brother," Luke told him even as the guy dialed into the office. "He's a sociopath. He's calculating, and he's charming. If you just checked on her then that's the best time for him to go in."

The officer looked at him a little sideways. So Luke shut up.

With his phone to his ear, the officer said only, "Yes. Yes. Okay." Then he turned to Luke. "You're cleared. But hold on!"

He yelled the last part as Luke began to run toward the house. But the officer dove out and grabbed his arm, tackling him to the ground. His voice growled down while he fought to turn Luke face down into the snow. "You're cleared from the police department. Not from Miss Dean yet."

Oh, sweet Jesus, Luke thought, as if Ivy was going to say no. Then everything in him fell. Now that he thought it through, he had to consider that maybe she would turn him away.

He'd spent this entire evening being thwarted at one step or another.

But maybe he deserved it. He'd brought all of this to her doorstep. She didn't deserve any of it.

He'd been right the first time: He was the reason she was targeted. He'd made it into the fire department. Carlos hadn't. He'd made it out and gotten the good job. One that he liked.

Whether or not Carlos had, he seemed to hold the grudge anyway. More and more little things had filtered back to him ... Him telling Carlos they were better off without their father and Carlos yelling back that he was going to find the man.

Fuck. Maybe he had found Santiago Hernandez Senior. Maybe their father was an arsonist or criminal or a pimp. Luke didn't even know but understanding filtered through and things he'd paid no attention to at the time now fit together.

He turned his head back to the officer who was shaking his head. "She's not answering."

Jesus. Luke told him, "Now! Go in now!"

He grabbed the officer's arm and propelled him forward. "We have to go in and check."

The officer fought back, twisting his wrist and easily breaking the hold Luke had. His tone was condescending. "She might be asleep."

"Get your fucking ass in that house right now!" Luke shoved him forward. The man still had one hand on the butt of his gun, but Luke had ceased to care. If the officer didn't get his feet moving, Luke was going to pass him and maybe take a bullet in the back as he opened the front door.

But as he moved forward, he was tackled again. Face down into the snow, he turned and landed a punch. A hard one. Right under the jaw.

He watched as the officer's eyes rolled and he hit the snow with a hard thud.

Good God, what had he done?

CHAPTER FIFTY-SEVEN

I vy's phone rang in her hand, and the slow cautious steps forward she'd been taking stilled. Her hand shook violently as she reached out and hung up on the caller—the officer out front. But it didn't change anything.

In the room, the other two had heard the phone ring as well. She heard Carlos tell her sister, "Don't even think about it."

"I don't even know who you are." Her sister was so confused. Her voice clear and Ivy so desperately wanted to turn the corner and take a peek. It would be the first time she had seen her sister in well over a decade.

She thought it was Lily. But who knew?

It had been long enough that this could be Peony or Meadow or even Violet. The genetics had run strong in her family, it could be any of them. Her heart broke—if her sister had escaped or been kicked out and found her way all the way to Ivy only to die at Carlos's hand …

No. This had to be Lily. She was the only one who looked exactly like Ivy.

Ivy wasn't going to let her sister die. She was going to fight back.

She began to slowly back her way down the hall. Right now, she had to pray that he didn't just shoot her sister because, as of right now, Carlos didn't know that she existed. Whatever Lily was saying, Carlos was arguing with her as though she were Ivy. Ivy couldn't hear much, but she had to hope he wouldn't figure it out very fast.

Further away now, she picked up her pace, rolling her feet with each step to minimize the noise. She hoped he wouldn't even figure it out if he did hear her. He thought he was holding her at gunpoint.

The big, comfy chair in the living room still had her rifle propped next to it from where she sat up on nights that Luke worked. Though it wasn't normally her habit, lately she'd been keeping a bullet in the chamber.

She'd probably only have one shot and it would break Luke's heart. Gun in hand, she raced as quietly as she could down the hall.

Carlos was the baby. Carlos had been Luke's favorite. Carlos had been the one that he hoped would break the family curse and do the best—even better than he himself had.

With the weight of the gun in her hand, she flipped her phone to silent and shoved it in her back pocket. Creeping the last few steps, she lifted the rifle and pushed herself up close to the open door. She peeked around the corner with a smooth movement.

Crap. Carlos was facing her, Lily was facing away. Carlos clearly had a gun on her sister. Ivy swung into the room, barrel aimed at the man who threatened everything.

For a long, drawn out moment, the three were at a standoff. Lily unarmed and in the middle and Ivy trying to aim at Carlos's head over her sister's shoulders. She knew Carlos had a weapon she couldn't see, and it was clearly trained center mass on Lilly.

As Carlos's eyes widened, she could see him looking back

and forth between the two of them. Ivy would have loved to have taken advantage of his surprise, but she couldn't see his gun. The three of them stood so close, the room was so small, there was almost no way he could miss.

Her sister was here!

Ivy was not going to get her killed. What could she do, though?

It took a moment to weigh her options. And then she said in her slowest, lowest voice, "Hello, Carlos. Hello, Lily."

She still hadn't seen her sister's face. But it was the only explanation for Carlos's thinking this was her. "Lily, I'm going to need you to pray."

Hopefully, it was enough of a clue to her sister, but not to Carlos.

She waited one heartbeat. Two. Then three.

And watched as her sister crumbled to the ground, knees hitting hard, head down, hands clasped in front of her. Ivy knew it was the only advantage she was going to get. She lowered the gun, aiming for his chest.

Killing Carlos would kill Luke.

Ivy took a slow breath, watching as Carlos raised his gun toward her.

"*Lily, run!*"

She watched as her sister scrambled past her, into the hall and she heard the back door slam as her sister disappeared from her life as quickly as she'd come.

But it didn't matter, she lifted the gun and pulled the trigger on everything she'd built.

CHAPTER FIFTY-EIGHT

Carlos' eyes rolled as the blood bloomed on his chest.

But the son of a bitch didn't stop. His hands lifted the gun and fired as Ivy screamed.

She felt the sting of the bullet tearing through her skin and making her whole arm jerk. She dropped the rifle, staggering backward and hitting the wall. But she wasn't far enough away.

The roaring of blood and shock crowded her head.

Had she failed? Had she been so close to killing him and now she was going to die by his hand?

He looked at her oddly. Her hand clasped her upper arm, blood seeping through the clean sweater she'd put on. The asshole was ruining all her new clothes. But she could see he was trying to figure out if she was really Ivy, if killing her would really hurt Luke or if she was just another impostor.

Ivy laughed, low and resigned.

Carlos had won again.

She saw the moment when he decided that it didn't matter if she was the real Ivy or not. He had to kill her to get out of the house.

Her rifle was on the floor. He'd kill her before she even got close to it. So she stared him in the eye, the roaring in her head now a scream that started in her soul and let all her rage out at him.

Ivy's vision was hyper-aware as adrenaline flooded her yet again. She saw the barrel of the gun as it entered her peripheral vision. Carlos saw it, too. But maybe his cool reserve worked against him.

Luke was here.

And she and Luke were full of fury.

She would always believe she saw the bullet leave the barrel of Luke's gun and enter Carlos' chest, dead center, before she laughed one triumphant sound and passed out cold.

CHAPTER FIFTY-NINE

It had been three days, and Luke was still sitting on his couch drinking beer in his sweats at ten a.m. He'd missed A-shift because the chief had put him on leave. Probably it was the appropriate thing to do.

Getting back to work would have been the best thing for him, but not for the people that the Redemption Fire Department treated and saved. As every single firefighter had drilled into their heads, the job wasn't about them.

He took another sip of the beer. His phone rang and he looked at the face. Once again it wasn't Ivy. This time it was his mother. She was on his case to give her precious baby boy a proper burial.

Mario was getting shipped off to rehab and Luke had once again offered to pay for part of it. But there had been no money left for Carlos. Honestly, Luke couldn't give two shits about a proper burial. But he'd answered the phone.

"You have to do this."

"No, I don't. Carlos may have been your baby, but he tried to kill the woman I love *multiple times*."

"That bitch shot him! That bitch shot my baby!"

He noticed she didn't mention that Luke had actually been the one to kill Carlos. But he'd had enough and, for the first time in his life, he hung up on the woman who had done everything she could to give her sons a better future.

The police department had shared information with the family. It didn't matter. They all knew Carlos was dead now, so there wouldn't be a trial or prison time. There wasn't much that could happen, but the details revealed just how much Luke hadn't known.

Carlos had done a stint in juvenile hall after Luke had moved away for school. His mother had never told him. Mario had broken under police interrogation. They'd waited him out, and as soon as he started hurting for his next fix, he'd been willing to tell them anything.

Mario, despite being just a few years older, had been under Carlos' thumb most of his life. That was probably the reason for the drug use. Luke drank more of the beer. He felt like complete shit. He'd protected Carlos at the expense of Mario. Carlos the Sweet Baby. Mario the idiot who kept making bad decisions.

According to Mario, his only involvement in the incident with the squirrel had been in trying to stop his brother. He'd confessed because Carlos had previously mangled one of the neighbor's pets and threatened to turn Mario in for it. His youngest brother had been a calculating little piece of shit from at least the age of eight. And while Luke mourned the brother he'd believed Carlos had been, he also was learning to admit that man had never existed.

His phone buzzed. His mother again. Despite him hanging up on her, she wasn't done. When he didn't answer, she messaged for money for Carlos's funeral.

Carlos could be put into a pine box or even a mass grave, for all Luke cared.

Everyone had stopped by or checked on him ... but not Ivy.

He'd heard nothing from her except for one message two days ago, that simply said, "I am so sorry."

He had messaged back – Can I see you?

But she immediately replied – No. Not right now.

That had been it. He wanted to ask if she was okay, but he'd heard the shot Carlos had gotten on her was just a graze. Just enough to bleed and look bad. So he needed to know why she didn't want to see him, but it was painfully clear. He was the sole reason for everything she'd suffered. Was she setting up to sell the little house even now?

He felt the pressure at the back of his eyes, the tears welling up. He'd done it—he'd taken something beautiful and perfect and once again his family and his history and his shitty upbringing had managed to ruin it.

He messaged Taggart as he took another sip. Might as well find out if anything was left at all.

— Do I still have a job?

If he'd lost the very last thing he had to hold onto, he figured he should know now. At least that reply came back quickly.

— Of course, you do. I just think you should take one more shift off. Make sure everything's square for your family. But we're anxious to have you back.

As he read the last sentence, the dam broke.

Luke leaned forward, his face in his hands. He had one thing left out of everything he'd worked so hard for. Everything he'd been so lucky to get.

He looked up then, his vision blurry, the beer still clutched in one fist.

What did he even have?

He had a shitty apartment on the bad side of town.

He now had no money in savings. Every damn time he managed to put something away, his mother needed her plumbing fixed or Mario needed rehab or Carlos had needed a loan to get a better car, so he could bump up to the sales job.

Jesus, Luke thought now, he'd *funded* that little piece of shit. And this was how Carlos had repaid him.

But he had the job. Firefighting was in his blood now, it was who he was. It was all he had left.

He finished the beer, sat on the couch, and stared at the wall, trying to count the hours until he could go back to his shift.

He made his decisions. He would cover Mario and he might help their mother if something broke at the house. But he wasn't doing anything for Carlos, no matter how much she demanded. She needed to see the truth about her youngest child. Luke refused to think about how much she might have played a hand in how Carlos had turned out. She'd given everything and they'd still had nothing. She had somehow managed to be both the best mother and the absolute worst.

He didn't know how much later it was, but the sky had brightened as the day passed into noon. It was hard to tell time with the sky always cloudy and the snow always falling. So far none of it had managed to pile up.

He'd held off on having another beer. After all, it was barely midday and he was talking himself into what he was about to do.

After showering, he threw on jeans and a thermal T. He considered a nice shirt and tie, but Ivy would have wondered what he was doing in one anyway. He took deep breaths as he drove to her house, parked in the driveway, and checked the place for damage or "for sale" signs.

The garage door was down, the house intact and each time he'd driven by he told himself that was a good thing. But was she home? Was she watching him as he walked up to the front door and knocked?

He held his breath until she answered, his heart soaring as he took in her long khaki skirt that reached almost to her ankles. The pink sweater twinset was buttoned only at the top and her hair was pulled back into a bun at her lower neck. She looked like she did when he'd first met her and just the sight of her made him smile.

But Ivy looked him up and down as though he were a stranger, checking his hands as if he should have brought flowers. "Why are you here?"

He should have brought her flowers.

"I'm so sorry about what my brother put you through. I hope you know that if I could change it, I would." She opened her mouth to say something, but he held her off. He needed to say everything. "The time we spent together was the best time of my life. I've never been as happy as I was with you. And I'm sure you can't say the same, but—" She opened her mouth again and again he plowed ahead, far too scared to stop. "Is there any chance for us?"

She blinked at him, unspeaking. She shook her head at him, confused at the idea that he would even darken her doorstep and he blurted the words he should have said well before now, "Ivy, I love you."

This time she did speak, her voice quiet. "You don't love me."

He felt then everything that shattered inside him.

"Luke?" she asked "Luke?"

But he couldn't hear her as he turned away and trotted down the steps. His head roared and the pressure squeezed his eyes and his ribs, but he tried to look normal. He tried to not break into a run as the pieces of him cracked and crumbled and fell to the ground.

It was all more than he could handle.

He held his hand up, waving goodbye to her behind him without looking back. He shook his head. The pressure mounting as he sprinted to his car, climbed in, and sped away.

CHAPTER SIXTY

I vy came out of the shower, towel in hand, drying her hair. "What was that?"

She looked to Lily. Her sister had come back the next day, knocking softly on the back door once the commotion had died down. Now she looked concerned. "It was Luke, your Luke."

"What?" Ivy's heart tightened. She missed him so much but she hadn't yet figured out what to do with her sister.

She'd called off work, grateful for yet another very valid excuse to miss—a gunshot wound to her arm would do it. She'd done everything she could to help. They'd ordered Lily's birth certificate from the hospital. Ivy and Lily had been the last ones born there. Their mother had all the other children at home. Lily had no social security number, Ivy knew, she'd had to file for her own at sixteen.

The sisters had talked for hours. Lily was married, she was Lily Baker now. And she desperately needed a divorce from a man who would sign no such papers.

Just as Ivy had suspected the moment she'd seen her sister, Lily was bringing trouble. No one left easily.

Lily told her how she'd been caught sneaking out of the commune—a commune Ivy hadn't known existed. Since she'd been kicked out, and in part because of that incident, several of the families had bought land together, built homes and a church and taken themselves further out of society.

There weren't walls, Lily said, but there were definitely borders. "I got on a bus and made my way to a women's shelter and then I made the mistake of going back for my things."

That had been six months ago. Six months they'd held Lily until she managed to escape again.

But Luke had just come here. Lily, wearing some of Ivy's clothes—that of course fit her—looked at her sister.

"You need to do something about him," her sister chided.

Ivy almost smiled. She damn well did. "I don't know why you answered the door."

Lily was supposed to stay hidden. "I thought he might be delivering my birth certificate, and that I'd have to sign for it. Anyway. He told me that he loved me. Meaning he loves *you*."

Ivy stopped, her heart clenching. Lily would be okay, Luke could be trusted.

She had to go find him.

She would have run out the door right then. But she was wearing only a towel and she had this stupid bandage to change. "What? What did you say?"

"I told him he didn't love me. I tried to explain that I wasn't you."

"You can't tell anyone!" Ivy spouted it off, just as she had for the last few days, but Lily was finally looking like her old self. Like the sister who'd snuck out to a club with her at sixteen. The one she shared all her secrets with. The one who called Ivy on her shit and who she looked up to for all of Life Number One.

"I know what you've told me about him. And I know you're not a liar. And I saw the way he looked. You can trust him, Ivy."

284

That was all she needed. If her sister had met the man for all of thirty seconds and made that deduction, then she would trust herself and trust Lily.

Ivy ran down the hall. She'd never gotten dressed so quickly. She could only pray that Luke went back to his apartment as she threw on jeans, sneakers, and a sweater she pulled from the drawer. She grabbed her coat, shoved her arms through it, and stopped only to hug her sister tightly before heading out the door.

She barely caught that Lily glanced up and down at the outfit. While she thought of herself as having been free a lot longer it only now occurred to her that also meant she'd been captive a lot shorter.

What Lily's future held, she didn't know. A hard lesson. The other one she'd learned was that, if she wanted something, she had to fight for it. She had saved her money. She had gone to school. She fought for every penny of financial aid. And she'd scrabbled her way through every A she'd earned. She'd lobbied hard to get the job here in Redemption and, as she looked back, she'd won all of it. She was going to win this, too.

She made it to Luke's apartment, knocking, realizing only then that she had left her keys in the ignition and the car door open behind her. She didn't care.

She knocked again, but no one came.

"Luke? Luke!" she called through the door but then she turned and looked around the parking lot. His car wasn't here.

Where was he?

But the town wasn't that big, she told herself. So she climbed back into the car—still running—and she drove. The snow began falling again. The weather had predicted the first good pile up, plausibly several feet overnight. The sky was darkening despite the early afternoon, and she wouldn't be able to stay out much longer.

As she passed the park, she saw him. Or at least she thought it was him.

Ivy no longer cared if she tapped a random stranger on the shoulder and bothered them if she found Luke in the end.

But, sure enough, there he was. Sitting on the park bench, his butt planted in the snow that had already fallen, his eyes staring out over the pond.

Sitting beside him, she took in the strong profile, the straight nose, the blank stare.

"Luke," she said his name softly.

He looked up finally, hope in his eyes for a moment before his expression shuttered. "Ivy."

It wasn't a question. It wasn't an invitation. But she made it one anyway.

Moving closer, she shoved her hands down into her pockets and spoke from a place of fear and hope. "I have a lot to tell you."

"There's nothing you can tell me except what you already told me." But then he turned to her, regret and acceptance in his eyes. "You may think that I don't love you. But I do and there's nothing you can do about it."

She grinned, tears pressing at the corners of her eyes. It was too cold outside to cry and she did it anyway. He was shaking his head at her, his hand lifting, probably to wipe away her tears. But then he shoved it back in his pocket.

"I didn't say that to you," she tried to explain.

"I was there. It wasn't that long ago."

"No," she almost laughed. "You were there, but I wasn't. That was Lily."

She waited as his realization slowly dawned on him. "Lily. Your Lily?"

She nodded. Who else could it possibly be? Who else would share her face? She'd never imagined that she pulled a twin switch as an adult. "I should have told you more when I talked about her. But I told you it was hardest of all being betrayed by Lily."

"Because she's your twin," he said.

Ivy nodded, looking out over the pond now herself. "We were always together, always alike in everything. Sometimes they even treated us like the same person." She watched as he shook his head. "Whatever you said, you said to Lily, and Lily was right: you don't love her. At least I hope you don't."

There was so much to untangle, so much to do for her sister. So much to deal with, because no matter how much she helped, and no matter how much Lily needed, Lily had still betrayed her in the worst way. Though Ivy thought she had left all the hurt of it behind, seeing Lily's —her own face—staring at her had brought it all flooding back.

"I'm a mess," she told Luke. "I can't tell anyone about her. We have to get her birth certificate and social security number. She has to file for divorce. I don't know if her husband is on the way here to find her." Her hands were out of her pockets now, gesturing wildly in front of her as Luke grabbed them to steady her.

But his expression had changed. His eyes had softened.

"If you can keep a secret, I'd love to have you come back. Move in with me—well, right now with me and Lily." She watched as he smiled.

"I love you."

The sound of those three words spoken with conviction bloomed inside of her, heat against the cold of the day, strength against everything to come.

"Good, because I fell in love with you some time ago."

They sat on the bench and, despite everything that was still wrong, everything she still needed, she felt hope.

She'd have to explain more about Lily and her family. They needed to have hard discussions about Carlos and everything he'd done. But she could do that if Luke was with her. She had everything she needed.

Luke's hands moved from hers up to where they gently cupped her face. Though the cold and the snow swirled around them, Luke kissed her.

And Ivy felt Life Number Four begin.

CHAPTER SIXTY-ONE

"I'm heading home," Ronan pulled out his money and tossed it onto the table for Tierney.

"You sober enough?" Luke looked up from where he sat, his arm draped around Ivy's shoulders.

The two of them seemed much more relaxed without an arsonist out for their blood. Hell, the whole town was sleeping better now. He grinned, stood up straight and tipped his head. "I'm good."

He was Irish. He hated to embrace a stereotype but a man named Ronan Kelly had to be able to hold his liquor, didn't he? And he didn't need to get a DUI.

It had taken another several minutes to say goodnight to everyone.

"Night, Ronan," Tierney called from behind him.

He turned to say it back, but she'd already gone back to polishing the bar as though it offended her. What was up with her lately?

He should ask. She was Siorse's sister after all and looking out for her was the right thing to do. But he didn't have it in him right now. Everyone else got to sleep in the next morning, but he had errands to run bright and early.

His dad wanted him to check on the house and fix a few things before he and Ma got back from their cruise in a few more days. Though if that was just because his Pop was trying to keep him busy with the anniversary coming up, Ronan didn't know. His pop did that every year, and every year it half worked and half didn't. Every year Ronan wished he didn't hold his liquor so well and that he could get rip roaring drunk.

But it was still several weeks away. Maybe his dad just actually needed something done around the house that he didn't want to ask his Ma for. Ronan didn't like to admit they were getting old, and neither did they.

Getting into the car, he started the engine as he once again pondered his dad's future. There were always more firefighters than chiefs. Taggert had been promoted to the position long before Patrick Kelly had even passed his tests to apply. But Taggart was good in the job and he wasn't going anywhere. His pop was still on the line a lot, and though the man was a damn good firefighter, Ronan was beginning to wonder how long he had before he tapped out … or before the boys had to force him to.

He aimed toward the newer section of town, in a small area slowly getting populated with suburb type neighborhoods. Ronan hadn't been able to bring himself to move out after Siorse and Paddy … after them. And tonight, heading home felt bittersweet for some reason.

He pulled up under the damn light.

He must have seen it coming and that was the reason for the sudden hit of nostalgia. But he hated this intersection. The wistful thinking turned into too-rapid breathing and the wholly unnecessary flood of adrenaline at nothing. Absolutely nothing.

The last thing he needed was a damn panic attack.

Redemption was too small to have much traffic and that

meant he was sitting at the first spot under the light. That was the place that still got to him.

He'd grown beyond avoiding this spot. He was able to pass under a green light without hyperventilating or sit and wait calmly if he was a few cars back. He didn't even think of her then. But when he was first—especially when he saw another car coming up behind him—the old feeling hit again.

Anger, resignation, and despair swamped him.

But Ronan told himself that it was just memory, not prophecy. What had happened to Siorse and Paddy wouldn't happen to him. Some days he told himself it should and then he could join them.

But the street was empty behind him. Despite his hyperventilating at pulling up to the light, today would not be the day he got slammed.

It was over five years ago that his young wife and son had been plowed into from behind while sitting right where he was now. For a long time, the black marks had stayed on the road, telling the fatal story again every time he passed. He almost thought the city might have finally paved it over as a kindness to his family and Siorse's.

The two of them should have survived that hit. It shouldn't have killed them. But the car had been pushed into oncoming traffic and they'd been hit again from the side. The small compact car hadn't stood a chance getting t-boned by a huge pickup.

Paddy had died instantly.

Siorse had died in the hospital the next day. A-shift had been called to the scene of the accident and Ronan had been held back, screaming, as his team members pried his dead child from the wreckage.

It happened to all of them—not usually as bad a scene as his was—but it happened. In a small town, the accidents were people you knew. You heard the address over dispatch and it was your parents' house, your sister's apartment building, your best friend's car on fire. That day had been his turn.

But he couldn't just leave town and leave it all behind. His family was still here. This was where he'd grown up. He'd been in no shape in the early days to be away from that, and as he'd gotten better and grown past it, he'd been able to handle staying.

Looking up at the light, he watched the other direction as it changed to yellow. There was still no one coming up behind him, and that helped him slow his breathing a bit. As the light turned green, he let out his breath and pulled forward, the panic finally fading.

He didn't even see the huge SUV that completely missed the red light. He only felt the impact as it smashed into the side of his car and flipped him like a rag doll.

Thank you for reading! I love romances with real love and believable characters, and I hope you found all that in these pages. I want to fall in love right along with the characters, and I do, while I'm writing it.

About Savannah

I started writing when I was eight--I hand wrote an 80-page novella that I believed to be (adult) romantic suspense. I'm proud to say, I've gotten a lot better since then. I've grown up to be a nerd at heart! I love neuroscience and people watching, and if you look, you'll find some of that in each Savannah Kade book. Most days you'll find me in my office, looking out my window at a handful of the neighbor's cows, or watching my dogs or my cat roam the backyard.

Follow me, find me, ask me questions! I would love to hear from you.
www.SavannahKade.com
Savannah@SavannahKade.com